EROTIC TEASERS

EROTIC TEASERS

EDITED BY
RACHEL KRAMER BUSSEL

Published in the United States by Cleis Press, an imprint of Start Midnight, LLC, 101 Hudson St, Suite 3705, Jersey City, NJ 07302.

Printed in the United States.
Cover design: Allyson Fields
Cover photograph: iStock
Text design: Frank Wiedemann
First Edition.
10 9 8 7 6 5 4 3 2 1

Trade paper ISBN: 978-1-62778-264-7
E-book ISBN: 978-1-62778-265-4

Contents

INTRODUCTION: SUCH A TEASE

L ike the stories and characters in this book, I'm going to tease you with my introduction. I don't want to give away too many of the sexy secrets in these pages, because they're the kind of sensual bliss you have to immerse yourself in to truly capture their erotic essence.

I'll keep it short because these sexy stories speak for themselves and I imagine you're eager to dive into them. Unless, that is, you love the thrill of denying yourself, as many of the men and women you'll read about here do.

Whether they're playing with a pair of vibrating panties at a work party, as the narrator in Eliza David's opening story does, or engaging in orgasm denial, as happens with Nora and Nico in the closing story, "Coming and Going," by Tiffany Reisz, these characters relish being made to wait. Of course, they've partnered with lovers who they know will reward them with plenty of sexual excitement along the way.

The teasing that happens here occurs in all sorts of inventive ways, from the use of technology in "Ava

Receives a Text," by Ella Dawson, to the title activity in "Guessing Game," by T.C. Mill, and far beyond.

What ties these stories together is that while all the characters want to get off, whether with kink or fetish or by other means, they aren't in a hurry...or else they relish the agony of being teased and taunted. They would rather go on a wild and sometimes wicked erotic journey than take the express route. From edging to bondage to exhibitionism and voyeurism, these sexy couplings show how arousing it can be to hold off on the big finish.

I hope you find these stories as hot as I did, whether you tease yourself by savoring them slowly, one at a time, read them with a lover, or greedily devour them.

Rachel Kramer Bussel
Atlantic City, New Jersey

PINK PANTIES

Eliza David

I stepped out of the steamy shower, sighing as I dried myself. These annual fundraising dinners for the firm got more pedantic year after year. Nonetheless, the Silvas must be in attendance, which was Ramon's annual insistence. *It just looks good, honey,* my husband had explained this morning before he left for the courthouse. I understood as much. It was a look, an aesthetic. Ramon and I stood out among the sea of white lawyers and their dutiful wives. He was convinced that the added perk of us being an interracial couple is what led to his hiring six years ago. Diversity was a buzzword you could find on Franklin, Dowd and Associates' website on multiple pages. Thus, Ramon and I—his black wife—were welcome with open arms and private parties. The latter, I suppose, was my payoff for the many nights Ramon spent nestled in his office while I waited over a cold dinner for him.

Balance.

Nonetheless, I'd spent the day dreading this event.

It was just another indicator of how predictable our marriage had become after ten years.

When I'd met Ramon in a dive bar after finals during my senior year at DePaul a decade prior, I thought he was way out of my league. He had resembled a young Marlon Brando, a strapping body with a thick head of dark hair and a devilish smile. Ramon was the Package, a gorgeous and debonair law student who had wowed me with his intellect and titillated me with his sensuality. It's no wonder we ended up in bed together in my cramped Lake Shore apartment just hours later. Just the memory of my nubile brown body twisted with his tanned muscles made me wish for time to go back to the beginning of our marriage. We were wedded six months after our fateful meeting, which was meant to be a one-night stand but blossomed into love. During our first year of matrimony, the sex was daily; during the weekend, almost hourly. Ramon embodied all of the elements of the stereotypical Latin lover, taking his time with every avenue of my body. The motions were never rushed and the satisfaction lingered for days.

Then life moved fast. After I finished school, I had fully intended to become a social worker. I wanted to give back to the West Side of Chicago, the raw but impoverished community that had raised me. That hope was dashed once I'd discovered I was pregnant. Ramon thought it best I stay home and raise Justin while he began his career as a paralegal under the firm's founding lawyer, Warren Franklin, Esquire. While he fought cases about petty theft and small-time extortion, I earned my homeschool teaching license online. When Ramon vied for partner status, I joined a charity group headed by Berta Franklin, Warren's wife. I hated every minute of it but it helped Ramon with his professional goals while mine were put on the back burner. A decade later, old man Warren was dead, Ramon was a late-night working partner, and me? I was an unfulfilled mother whose only recourse from my stay-at-home existence was raising money to save dolphins and bumblebees.

I was slathered in shea butter lotion and twisting my dark brown braids into an upsweep when Ramon came in, his tie undone. Without pause, I reached for the tails of the tie with a smug smile.

"This is your sixth gala and you still haven't mastered tying a bow tie," I said with a laugh.

He chuckled in return. "Well, think of it as an incentive for this," he said, waving a flat, square black box at me. I tightened the bow and tilted my head at the box.

"And what is that?"

"Just a little something to make the night more exciting for you. For *us*," he said before I took the box from him. I lifted the top and, nestled between two sheets of thin black tissue paper, was a pair of hot-pink panties. The color looked cheap (which my husband knew I'd like), but the intricately woven pattern within the French lace told a more expensive tale. I raised an eyebrow as I lifted the thong out of the box.

"You haven't bought me lingerie in a long time," I said before giving him a playful side-eye. "Spill it. What'd you do?"

Ramon laughed before pulling me into his arms. "Now you know damned well you are the only woman in my life," he said, stealing a peck from my lips. "I just know how mad boring these dinners are and I wanted you to feel sexy tonight."

"Hmmm," I said, returning the kiss with a touch more tongue. "Well, I thank you for the gesture. Are you sure these are appropriate for a night out with Chicago's legal elite?"

Ramon eased his hand under my silk robe and squeezed my bare ass. "Mmmm, it's more than appropriate, *mami*," he growled against my pout before we indulged in another drugging kiss. He let me go and paced himself out of our master bathroom backward, his eyes dragging over my naked body peeking out of my robe. "Now you get dressed. Mrs. Flax is downstairs to sit with Justin and the car'll arrive in fifteen." He turned on the heels of his black Italian loafers and walked out, leaving me in a bit of shock. While Ramon hadn't lost his mojo in the sack, long nights at the firm lately had kept me from experiencing his lovemaking for weeks. Now he was surprising me with expensive pink panties?

I tossed the empty box on the black marble-topped sink and slipped my legs into the lace garment. They were a perfect fit except for what felt like a small strip of added fabric that swept the length of my intimate folds. I assumed they just needed to be broken in for the night and continued on with my prep.

"Honey, car's here," Ramon yelled from downstairs as I slipped my feet into my Manolo Blahnik stilettos. Fifteen minutes had gone by faster than I had expected. I grabbed my silver satin clutch and dashed down the steps, the skirt of my knee-length emerald-green dress rustling against the backs of my thighs. I kissed the top of Justin's curly head, nodded to Mrs. Flax, and threaded my arm through Ramon's before we headed out the door.

Downtown Chicago's Chandler Hotel was a sea of black tuxes and shimmery gowns when we arrived. I nodded and waved, per the wifely protocol for corporate fundraisers. The organizers selected a legal fund to donate to every year. This year, it was for the Chicago Technology Foundation. I wasn't sure why a nonprofit STEM organization would ever need legal assistance, but it gave the firm's good ol' boys a reason to drink heavily and dance to old Sinatra covers all night long.

Ramon pulled out my chair at our assigned table. I felt his warm breath on my neck as I sat down. "You like your new present?"

I drew a blank before he sat beside me and I realized that he was talking about the panties. "Oh, yes," I said, shifting my hips in the seat. "I'm not sure they fit, though."

Ramon's brow scrunched. "What? You're a perfect size four. Besides, you live on the treadmill. Wish I had time to work out as much as you do," he said, giving his small paunch a rub.

I blinked at him, feeling that familiar surge of annoyance rise in me. It was innocent-sounding comments like that that made me feel as if Ramon didn't value what I did every day while he was at work defending his clients. While I did manage to fit in a daily workout, that wasn't the totality of my day. I prepared third-grade lesson plans for Justin, cooked three square meals every day and—until recently—fucked my husband almost every night. I kept the house sparkling clean and managed the finances. I made sure the house was running on all cylinders while Ramon was working sixty-hour weeks. And, on top of all of that, I was still the same size I'd been ten years before when Ramon met me at that dive bar. Given all of that, I thought I deserved a run whenever I felt like it. Ramon's condescension about my one daily moment of peace was not needed.

"I do a lot more than work out, Ramon," I said through clenched teeth, hoping the guests sitting on either side of us didn't hear.

"Hey, relax. I just—"

"Don't tell me to relax!" I said, my tone just loud enough to solicit a head tilt from the gray-haired gentleman to Ramon's left. I bit the inside of my cheek in an effort to keep myself calm as Ramon took my hand.

"Listen, I know how hard you work for us. I was just trying to give you a compliment."

I tilted my head, my attitude dissipating thanks to his touch. "Well, don't think that a pair of panties that don't fit are going to get you out of the doghouse, sir."

A sly smile slid across Ramon's ruggedly handsome face as he let go of my hand and reached for his cell. "I wouldn't bet on that, baby," he said as the waiter approached to take our dinner selection.

I shook my head at my husband and met the eyes of the waiter.

"Ma'am, will you be dining on chicken or fish?"

"I'll have the—"

I felt a jolt against my pussy that startled me. I looked down at myself and back at the waiter. "Sorry, um, I'll have the fish, pl—"

Another shot. This one hit right on my clit, which was already slightly aroused from the initial sting. I felt a drop of wetness escape my softness before I clenched. "Fish, please," I answered, keeping it short and sweet. My breath was slightly jagged, unaware of what was happening with my seat. I turned to Ramon, whose eyes must've been on me the entire time I struggled to talk with the waiter.

"I'll have what the lady's having," he answered to the waiter, his gaze never breaking from mine. When the waiter moved on to the next guest, Ramon twirled his phone in his hand and placed it on the table. It wasn't until he swiped his finger across the screen and I felt a longer vibration that I realized what he was doing.

My hips shivered under the sensation, this time lasting ten of the longest seconds of my life. Once it stopped, my shoulders dropped and I licked my lips. "What...what are you doing?" I breathed out.

Ramon leaned into me, his hand easing around the exposed back of my dress. "I'll ask again: you like your new present?" He gave my neck two light kisses, which felt extra arousing thanks to the jolts that had consumed my body.

"You'll be under my control for the remainder of this party," he started, his firm voice making me pool with wetness. "You won't see me, but you'll know I'm not far away."

He swiped the phone and my body jerked. A soft moan escaped my lips.

"Ramon . . . stop," I begged softly.

He took my earlobe into his warm mouth, suckling

it for a moment before he replied, "You really want me to stop, *mami?*"

"No . . . " I said, letting my eyes close for a second before darting my gaze around the table. Not one of the other six people was paying any attention to us. Stuffed in their self-important tuxes, ties, and gowns, they were none the wiser as my husband's hand traveled up my inner thigh. This was the wrong place for this sexual experiment, but my body needed the mystery and the sensation. I turned to him, my clit swollen and my body sizzling.

"Don't stop."

My breath caught as the tips of his fingers grazed the dampened fabric. I watched the knuckles of his free hand move across the phone, a warning of the sensation to follow. The vibration started again, softer this time, as the pressure of his fingers moved the small motor woven inside of the panties. My lips parted as the jolt shifted to the underside of my clit, sending the current straight to my G-spot.

"Mmmmm," I groaned, slightly moving my hips until the vibration suddenly disappeared. I turned to Ramon, his bearded face aglow with a sinister smile. It was clear the smug bastard was loving every minute of my torture. And, quiet as I kept myself, so was I.

"Why'd you stop?" I asked in a whine, half mad. I felt his hand slip away as he turned his body from me.

"There are rules," Ramon started, taking a sip of the water from the crystal goblet to his right. He spun the cell phone in a circle on the table. It was a habit of his that annoyed me in ordinary circumstances. But now, the move was a power play. I dragged my gaze from the phone back to his lips.

"What are the rules?" I asked, an excited tremble in my voice.

He turned to me, his face a visage of pleasure and power. "Rule number one: the panties stay on until I take them off. The vibrator contains a body warmth detector, so I'll get a notification on my cell if you take them off and stuff them in your purse."

There wasn't a chance in hell I was taking them off but I entertained the man in any case. "Got it. Next?"

"Rule number two: you are not allowed to stimulate yourself in any way. No touching, bouncing, rubbing. Your only source of stimulation will be the pink panties."

I nodded, the band starting a rendition of Sinatra's "My Way" in the background. "Anything else?"

"Rule number three: I reserve the right to operate the vibrator at any given time tonight. If we see each other during the gala, you are to lock eyes with me while the vibration occurs."

The banquet hall we were in was fairly small. It excited me to think of the enhanced probability of seeing Ramon as he controlled me from across the room. "Duly noted. Continue," I purred.

"One last rule," Ramon said, halting the spin of the phone. He pointed the device at me. "Rule number four, *mami*: you cannot orgasm."

Now that I didn't like. "How will you know whether or not I came?" I mused, closing the space between our chairs.

Ramon lowered his mouth to my ear. "Because I've been fucking you for over a decade. I know exactly what you look like when and after you come. I know the sweet smell of your pussy that emanates from you and takes over my senses. All dead giveaways," he growled in my ear, causing me to clench below. I was soaking wet, certain I was leaking through the dress.

"We'll start after dinner. Do we have a deal?" he asked me as the waiter arrived at the table with our platters. What I assumed was my dish was placed in front of me but I hadn't glanced at it. Ramon had my undivided attention.

"Yes," I said, turning to my meal of overcooked halibut with a side of asparagus and mashed potatoes. The food was bland, as expected, but my clit throbbing with anticipation of Ramon's little game made me get through dinner quicker than expected. This was the most sexually exciting thing we'd done in years, and my dripping wet pussy was ready to continue what Ramon had started.

An hour after dinner ended, my pussy was on fire in the most delightful way. Walking was exacerbating the sensation, with or without the electric shock. Though I hadn't caught Ramon's gaze, he'd clearly spotted me and brought it to my attention with spontaneous jolts to my clit. I was in mid-conversation with Berta Franklin, the widow of the firm's founding lawyer, when Ramon decided that would be a fine time to play with the panties.

"I want to thank you again for your service at last weekend's Save the Sea Turtles event," Berta said, giving my arm a soft squeeze. "My Warren, God rest his soul, always had an affinity for marine animals."

My body jerked, the vibration drawing a lazy smile from me. Ramon knew exactly what he was doing.

Asshole. "Of...of course, Berta. Anything for the foundation!" I said a little too perkily. Another electric pulse passed through me, edging me closer to the orgasm I was ordered to avoid. If I didn't get Ramon's dick inside me soon, I was going to come. This little game of his needed to end in the sex I deserved after enduring his carnal torment. I began backing away, my pussy clenching with each footstep. "Berta, I hate to be rude, but if you'll excuse me while I go to the ladies, I'll—"

"Of course, but let me first tell you about the group's next initiative: chimpanzees!"

Another jolt made my legs shake beneath me. I grabbed the top of a chair for support. "Sounds...sounds great, Berta. Sign me up!" I spun on my heel and turned to walk out of the banquet hall, my knees knocking together. I knew I must have looked like a child rushing to the restroom at the last minute, but the ache! My head spun around, searching for the man who was no doubt laughing at my sexually frustrated expense.

I stepped out of the banquet hall, my voice shaky with every "Excuse me," and "Pardon me," I tossed over my shoulder as I weaved through the partygoers. The next jolt, which shot right on the swollen tip of my clit, made me reach for the wall for support. I looked around, hoping no one would notice my near collapse. Still no sign of Ramon—*where was he?*

I turned a corner down an empty corridor lined with darkened conference rooms. My steps were more deliberate now, for every motion of my hips brought me near the brink of climax. My skin felt electric from the inside. The fabric of the dress across my thighs, the jewelry adorning my neck and wrists, my quivering mouth—my entire body was on fire, and my frustration grew the longer I went without seeing the man who was the cause of it.

"Hey *mami*," I heard him say behind me. I started to turn but paused, remembering rule number three. I leaned my sensitive body against the wall.

"I know what you're trying to do. I'm not looking at you."

"Smart girl," he replied, his sexy, smug voice edging closer to me. "I must say, I enjoyed watching you tonight. Seeing your body squirm with each swipe of my cell. Watching you attempt conversation while I had complete control of your body's sensations. Shit turned me on."

I straightened my posture against the wall when I felt his arms circle around my waist. I reached behind his neck, stroking the back of his hair. "Please let me come," I begged, my voice husky with yearning. "I need it."

I felt his beard brush against the nape of my neck as he walked me backward. "Not yet," he whispered against my skin, sticky with heat. We entered a dim storage room tucked between conference centers. Ramon was sandwiched between the wall and my aching body. The dank smell and dust particles were the only witnesses to our escape. The glow of his phone display was the only light I noticed before I felt that familiar buzz between my thighs. Moans escaped my lips as my ass rocked against his hardness. I reached for the hem of my dress and raised it up, grinding the vibrating thong against his cock. If I was going to feel this electric tease, so was he.

He groaned in my ear, giving me confirmation that

he was struggling right along with me. I lowered my torso until I touched my toes, the vibration bringing me closer to the brink. When he slapped my ass, I shuddered in delight.

"Don't you dare come," he demanded, his voice rough with desire. I smiled as I snaked my body upward and turned to face him. I reached into his trousers and gripped his cock, swirling the precome on the tip. He moaned into my braids, reaching around to clutch my ass. Ramon pulled me into him and took my mouth in a searing kiss.

"I'm close," I cried, trying to stave off the climax. Ramon placed the cell on a shelf and lifted my chin, the illuminated screen making his brown eyes visible in the darkness.

"Get on your knees so *papi* can feed you," he growled. I dropped to my knees and hunted for his cock, unzipping his pants as fast as I could. Once his cock was freed and bobbing at my lips, I paused. Two could play this game.

I licked the moistened tip, igniting a whimper from Ramon. He sank his hands into my braids and pulled my head closer before I grabbed his cock and stroked it. I looked up at him and shook my head. He took the challenge and reached a finger to his phone, swiping upward. The vibration between my thighs quickened, as did my stroking of his cock, which grew harder within my grasp.

"Let's come together," Ramon reasoned, as he eased my head closer to his cock.

I lowered the tip to my lips with a smirk. "Good. We both win," I said, before I placed him in my hot mouth.

I took him to the hilt, as always, enjoying his taste and musky smell. I felt the jolt vary in speed—fast, then low, and fast again—urging my orgasm on. Ramon fucked my mouth faster as I squeezed my thighs tighter together, savoring the throbbing pulse of the panties. When I felt the warmth of his come fill my mouth, I felt my own peak rising. I moaned against his cock, allowing myself a deserved release after over an hour of endless stimulation.

I rose to my feet to face him. Ramon reached underneath my dress and slipped the still-vibrating thong down my legs. I stepped out of the garment, my pussy dripping with sweet relief. He raised the balled-up fabric to his nose and inhaled, his gaze locked on mine.

Ramon tossed the panties onto the shelf. "Let's go home so I can fuck you properly," he said, easing his arms around my waist.

I stroked his beard. "But what about the gala and your colleagues?"

"We both know I've spent too much time with them, which has been a sacrifice for us," he replied in a sorrowful tone. "And, for that, I'm sorry."

I nodded. "Thank you."

"Besides, I'd rather party with you," he continued, taking me into a deep kiss. The buzz of the pink panties was the last thing I heard before we left them behind in the closet.

GUESSING GAME

T.C. Mill

G uess."

Sometimes it's easy. Blindfolded, Roland can still tell the difference between his lovers: then Amy's peach fuzz and sticky lip balm against his thighs, now Mike's close-trimmed beard and long eyelashes brushing his stomach. When his hips strain, trying to follow the heat of the mouth drawing away, he recognizes her crystalline sigh, his self-satisfied chuckle close to the skin.

"Michael," he whispers.

"Got it." A hand clasps his bound hand briefly, something between a congratulatory high-five and an affectionate check-in. He squeezes the strong fingers back before they slip from his.

Roland's arms are stretched wide—not so far it's painful, but enough that he can never forget it. His legs, though unbound, are not exactly free. Someone straddles his calf. Amy, or Michael balancing most of his weight on his knees.

A touch traces down his ribs.

"Guess." The third voice over his head takes on a singsong tone.

He twists as the touch reverses course, climbing toward his nipples. It circles one without making contact with the hard point. He can picture the curlicue being looped across his upper body. Amy, he thinks, usually prefers lightning-strike zigzags.

"Mike again?" he asks.

The hand keeps stroking, moving over skin sensitized by the feather she (or he?) had stroked across him earlier. They've been using that feather trick for months now and Roland still doesn't know what it looks like: long or short? White as a dove's, a wisp bent in Amy's iron-firm hold? Or black as an archangel's, with the same beautiful charcoal sweep as Michael's brows?

"Amy?"

"Which is your final answer?" she asks.

Roland shakes his head, the blindfold pulling in his long hair without in any way slackening. "I'm not sure."

"Guess anyway," Mike suggests.

He shakes his head again, more in confusion than refusal. It's not a bad confusion, but he's starting to lose the urge to think. That touch, the way he's tied, have soothed him into a floaty, disembodied feeling. He almost forgets he's there. Except where they prod him, question him, reminding. He relies on them to map him out, and they feel more real than he is.

"Guess."

The word in that cheerful singsong is no hint. It comes from the speaker sitting above his head, between his outstretched arms. Marisol.

She's watching—and speaking, mostly just that one

word. That's been her role these first few times she's joined them. Spectator and referee, an essential part of their game but not a player herself, still deciding how or who she would touch.

The hand stroking Roland's chest adds fingernails. Trimmed, but used with precision. "Amy," he says, certain now. "Final answer."

"You're correct." Marisol's breath sounds a little shorter, and he wonders what she sees that he can't.

The flat of a palm glides up and down the length of his cock. Roland startles, not so much at the abruptness of the touch (they've been touching everywhere around his erection for what feels like hours now) as at the way it causes all of him to flow downward. His blood and very consciousness rush in a hot flood rising under that hand, which could belong to either of them.

The pad of a finger slips lower between his legs and begins to circle his hole. Warm and slick, it eases in as he falls open with a sharp inhalation. Just a little farther... Michael, he thinks, most likely, but it could also be Amy knowing he would expect this to be Michael's touch.

A little farther, and the stroke of that finger sets off fireworks.

Then it's gone.

Roland could whimper. He doesn't.

A hand closes on his cock again, this time with a short, firm slide. And another, longer, not enough but clearly recognizing what he needs. Definitely Mike's.

The next finger up his ass is Amy's—smaller but faster, her approach so honed it nearly comes off as indifferent. This time he doesn't get the choice whether to whimper.

And then it's gone, too.

"Hang in there." Mike's warm, deep voice, Mike's hand patting his thigh before running along the curve of skin in a way that's the opposite of soothing.

"Next," Amy says, "tell us *what* we're touching you with."

"Okay."

It's fuzzy. Not soft, though. Round, he realizes as she rolls it up and down his leg, then over his hip.

"Tennis ball." Probably the one Amy rolls between her shoulders and the back of her chair in a self-directed massage after a long day hunched over jewelry. She knows which kinks to work out and does so impatiently. Meanwhile, when Mike comes home from a day of supervising reno, he stretches out shirtless on the couch for Roland to go over him. Roland doesn't submit through service, but it's no chore at all to see and feel Mike relaxing, the ropes of lean muscle unwinding under his smooth skin, deep brown with tattoos of vibrant green leaves and a red-gold sun, the ink dancing as he gorgeously melts from Roland's touch. Anyway, caring for someone is different from submission. Sometimes he wishes Amy would let him take care of her, too. Every so often, she does.

A batting *pop* sounds over his head—Amy tossing the ball, Marisol catching it. There's a rhythm as they work together, humming in the air, though Roland can only imagine what's going on above the blindfold. Or guess.

He'd met Marisol while dancing downtown. It was a summer weekend event put on by a cluster of local businesses, bars and gift shops hoping to draw more people to them every Friday night. On some weeks, Roland sang outside the combination used-books-and-antiques store, but that evening he'd joined the group of singles, kids, and what seemed to be a sorority from the local college dancing in the middle of the street. A woman in a T-shirt affiliating her with the band onstage modeled simple choreography for them to follow. It owed something to the Electric Slide and something to square dancing. Marisol was next to him, and they exchanged glances during one of the turns, but it wasn't until the unsteady newbie on the other side of her knocked her into Roland that they got to know each other. He caught her, she thanked him, and turned it into a new move, and they shouted introductions over the beat.

"Guess this one," Marisol says now.

He recognizes smooth silicone as it runs along his abdomen, then the buzz.

"Amy's vibe." He pushes himself to be more specific before the toy moves down far enough to annihilate all coherent thought. "The, um...think it's the pink one that kind of curves?" One of her favorites, and he shivers at the memory of how it looks between her legs, as hot pink as the blush that spreads from her thighs while her grip on his wrist shows him how to use it. Or wields him, really, uses him like an extension of the toy.

Though it's Mike, laughing a little, who seems to be wielding it now. Still, this feels too easy. It's an excuse, of course, to touch him with an unknown arsenal. Amy likes to have reasons for what she does, controlling proceedings within some larger design. Mike loves any chance to open the toolbox. And Marisol, he knows, enjoys each new discovery.

The fun of that downtown event was how you found
something different around every street corner. Balloon
animals for the kids and face painting for all ages.
Nonprofits handing out information and collecting
spare change and introducing passersby to rescued
animals. Marisol waved away an invitation to sit for a
live-portrait painter. "I want to keep walking," she said,
already tilting her head to see down another side street.
In front of one stage, an acrobat hung from a wooden
pyramid by thick silk scarves. Roland watched her
swing weightless, overtaken by a familiar feeling that
was part admiration, part envy. Beside him, Marisol
watched, too.

"Guess?"

"Feather," he says, twitching and ticklish as it
brushes his cheek below the blindfold.

"No."

"No?" He turns his face, trying to follow it. Now
the soft, light touch moves over his chin and throat—
there it's too much, almost sharp—and down his chest.
Trailing...

"Ribbon!" he says, recognizing at last the silky
feeling.

"Not bad," Mike says. "He's what, now, six for
ten?"

"Am I supposed to be keeping score?" Marisol asks.

They'd passed the jewelry shop where Amy worked
part-time and the place where Roland gave guitar
lessons. He'd pointed out the latter, not the former,
not sure yet how to mention Amy or if he even should.
She was at home that night, beading a birthday gift—a
necklace of shell and silver beads—for Mike, who

was visiting his sister to welcome his first niece and goddaughter into the world. Roland had bought two cards and a book from Mike's wish list before he joined the dancing. When they strolled by the shop, Marisol looked in the window and pointed out the same book, but he was even less sure how much to say about his boyfriend. He and Marisol were having fun getting to know each other, not necessarily as anything more than friends, but even that could be jeopardized if he did the calculus wrong—said too much, so that she decided he was weird, perverted, gross.

The next object prickles. A quick, pin-sharp skittering along his outstretched arm. Roland's shoulders tighten, and when he shivers, jarring the toy, metal chimes. "*This* thing!"

Mike and Amy's voices overlap:

"Yeah."

"You've got to be more specific."

He turns his head, the pins skipping along his collarbone. "Like . . . I have to name what it is?"

"Yeah, what is it?" Marisol sounds genuinely curious.

"It's the pizza cutter from hell," Roland tells her. "The pinwheel of pain and...pins."

"Warmer," Mike says as the wheel rolls down Roland's chest.

"It's a reflex wheel."

Amy says, "Mmmm," noncommittally.

He tries to remember the name attached to it as the wheel rolls back up and sends tension through his entire torso. Gutenberg? No, but it had also sounded literary. Like...Edith? "Wartenberg pinwheel!"

"I'll remember it as the pinwheel from hell," Marisol says, but she doesn't sound intimidated in the least.

That night, exploring and dancing through downtown, they had passed a stage where a young woman led an all-ages sing-along on acoustic guitar and turned the corner to be confronted by two signs. The people holding them were young, well dressed, and wouldn't have seemed out of place if not for the wary defiance with which they looked at everyone around them. And for the signs themselves. One said, in thick marker, MARRIAGE = 1 MAN, 1 WOMAN. The other was much more vulgar.

Part of him indulged in the fantasy of giving them the confrontation they were expecting, even welcoming. Another part was sickly unsurprised; this town still liked to think of itself as cozy and wholesome and old-fashioned, prioritizing the last two more than the first. But he glanced at Marisol to see her biting her lip and shoving her dark brown hair out of her face.

"Let's go?" he asked softly.

"Yeah." As they strode down another street, she took a deep breath. "I, uh, took that kind of personally."

"I—" Roland started, but when she continued speaking he didn't interrupt. Her words were like steam rising when a lid was taken off after far too long.

"I mean, it feels personal. I'm not sure if it is. Which is weird, right? Not that I don't enjoy your company," she added. "I like hanging out with guys. But women, too..."

Roland nodded. "Would you like to get a drink?"

"Sure." Marisol smiled, but five minutes later she was frowning into her beer. "It's just a guessing game,

I guess." A grimace at the echo. "But how did I get to be twenty-seven without knowing if I'm lesbian or straight?"

"There are other options," Roland said.

She looked at him across the table. "Yeah. And it's even more of a guessing game how people will react if you bring that up."

"Well." He tipped his glass toward her. "My boyfriend, my girlfriend, and I all fall on the continuum."

Her eyes widened. Then her mouth did, showing teeth in a grin. "You have both?"

"They have me." Maybe it was the beer, maybe it was the brightness of her smile and what it did to his heart jumping in his chest, but Roland decided to go all in. He pushed back his shirtsleeves and raised his wrists to show her. "These were both made by Amy, but this one she gave me"—a chain of silver links, fine but not delicate, beautiful yet a bit brutal—"and this one she gave our boyfriend, Michael, to give me." Mike's was a curved metal cuff, clean and straightforward, but more elegant the more you looked at it.

Marisol leaned forward to look at both of them. She was silent for so long that Roland's mouth became dry, uncertain what she would say when the time came. At last, she breathed out a sigh. "That's really romantic."

"Thank you." He turned his arm to meet her fingers, letting her stroke Michael's cuff, then Amy's links.

"Just a shame," she murmured. "You're taken twice over."

"Not necessarily. If you'd..." He had to swallow, because his mouth was still dry, and his heart was a drum line overtaking any melody.

She sat back, tracing designs in spilled foam. "Would you be okay with going slow?"

"Of course. It's great just to know someone else who's not—" He nodded toward the windows facing the street with the sign-holders and made a face.

"Well, I'm definitely not like that. Even if I am straight. Which I may be." She made her own face, more thoughtful. "Probably not. If there's...an inverse of bisexual, where you like everyone, but aren't sure you *like*-like them—asexual, I guess."

"Sure. Or demisexual, when you sometimes grow to *like*-like them."

Nodding, she said slowly, "Maybe that's me."

Roland shrugged, spreading his arms a little as he did so that his bracelets gleamed in the low lights. "Human sexuality is limitlessly..."

"Weird?" Eyes on the bracelets, Marisol didn't ask judgmentally.

"And wonderful."

She met his glass with her bottle, the chime of the toast ringing out. "Here's to that. I just don't want you to think I'm . . . a tease."

"I can introduce you to Amy and Mike. If you want." Even as he said it he realized this wasn't exactly the definition of going slow, but Marisol's face lit up again, after the way her smile had faded with her last word. And Roland couldn't hold back a grin as he said, "They know a thing or two about being a tease."

Something cool and slick wraps around his cock. It almost seems wet, too liquid to also feel so tight, unbearably good. His mind, eventually, returns to him as another coil rolls against his skin and he recognizes the sensation of dozens of small round glass beads.

"Are you going to use those in something?" he asks.

"A personal project," Amy answers in a dry tone, but over Roland's head Marisol snickers. As she turns, probably to get something from the bedside table, the brush of her bare calves against his shoulders and arms startles him. She'd sat there unmoving for so long that their skin had seemed to merge, its own kind of intimacy. And he realizes—it feels like the bottom of him has dropped out—that all along the toys they've used to play with him have passed through her hands.

Whatever she gives Mike now is silent—he assumes it's to Mike, assumes they're taking turns. And because of that, he finds it easier to guess the object that dimples his skin, a stiff, cool point. But, transfixed on that point, he doesn't speak right away. He feels the other end of it—stamping its mark in his skin, so firmly he can visualize it: a pale ring with a cross-shaped, reddened dimple at the center.

And then the shaft rolls over him in coiled stripes. "A screw," he says.

Close to his ear, Mike murmurs, "You guessing, asking, or offering?"

Roland moans as much as laughs.

As his mouth is open, one of his three teases slips something into it. A mint, the flavor startling and bright. The flavor's so strong it makes his tongue feel cold.

So does the tongue that licks along his cock. He's sure this is Mike but can't feel his close-shaved beard— hands are holding his thighs, spreading them wide, and he's sure from the way the nails dig in that they're

Amy's. The mouth tormenting him draws back for just a breath. It runs across his skin. Then the soft slickness of moistened lips and cool tongue again, and the hard mint itself sliding against his shaft. Roland gasps, startled and overwhelmed, and as the tongue tip pries against his slit he winds up swallowing his own mint.

Amy kisses him anyway.

When she and Mike pull back, Roland is only aware of dizzy, desperate loss. So he misses most of the murmured conversation over his head. Amy sums it up with, "One more change of rules. Now, you get to guess *where* we're going to touch you."

That's unfair, blatantly unfair. It's unfair in a way Amy usually isn't—however she tortures Roland, she prefers to give him his wounds to the front. She follows rules and doesn't ask the impossible.

His heartbeat kicks up a notch. Some of it is nervousness, but it's also anticipation and thrill, and some of the thrill is for her sake. For her to be so straightforwardly unreasonable is a good sign. It shows how she's grown in confidence and self-esteem as much as selfishness. She had been shaken after losing Patrick—the loss that had unraveled, for a time, the family she and Mike built together. Roland hadn't met them until two years after the car accident, and still she blamed herself for the death of their lover, for being behind the wheel. Only slowly has she been able to forgive herself, and from there allow herself pleasure again. Just now, to remember that she can give pleasure even in her very unfairness, selfishness, and cruelty.

It's thanks to Mike, often tender and gentle but enjoying a rigged game as much as any of them, and to

Marisol, the appreciative audience encouraging her to show off.

Roland doesn't want to take too much credit, but maybe it's thanks to him, too.

"Belly button," he says now, smiling to hear her laugh at the silly suggestion. Maybe she'll even take it.

She doesn't. Fingernails spiral over his calves, tracing down to the ankle. His toes curl. He's not as ticklish on the soles of his feet as Mike—a discovery made during one of their less relaxing massage sessions—but he's not exactly looking forward to this.

Then Amy's hand lifts. Mike's (he thinks) runs along Roland's shoulder. Another fingertip traces his nipple, then meets a thumb to pinch it. He cries out in surprise.

They stop touching him, but Roland can only pant, beyond articulating any further guesses.

After a moment, Mike tells him, "Marisol's pointing."

Oh no.

"Good idea," Amy tells her.

Oh yes.

A stroke up and down his cock—gliding, the touch smooth and cool against his arousal, lubricated. With a thoughtful hum from Mike and approving sigh from Amy, Roland's thighs are pushed apart. The slick fingers move farther between them.

"There," Marisol says. Her voice is warm with pride like Amy's earlier, at the almost innocent pleasure of issuing arbitrary commands she knows will be fulfilled without question.

She's still discovering her role, feeling it out along with everything else. She seems to enjoy this exploration most of all, without any pressure, knowing there's no

wrong place to land. "I know I'm not vanilla," she'd said
after the first time they played together. "Not anymore,
at least." Whether watching, handing over toys, or
giving instructions—in turns voyeur, submissive, and
sadist—she syncs with them whatever she chooses to
be. There's room for each.

Their roles go beyond submissive or dominant.
Michael and Amy, they rebuild and repair. With needles
and levels, blueprints and beads, pliers and hammers
and, yes, screws. They construct things, too, beautiful
new things that had never been there before. Roland's
also a creator, but of more immaterial pieces. A song,
the memory of a night, a relationship, a household in the
house that Mike rebuilt—each time with the instrument
of his own body. Breathless now, shivering under unpre-
dictable and multiplying touches, he's awestruck to find
himself at the center, to know that this is happening *to*
him and *because* of him.

Marisol is an investigator and experimenter.
Curious, courageous, with contagious delight when
something goes well, yet an ability to set boundaries
and call something off if it doesn't. It's good to have her
keeping watch. To have her *watch*. His new and favorite
audience.

"Where?" she murmurs, tantalizing now. "Guess
where."

Roland's beyond guessing. He can only feel—his
chest, hips, and shoulders stroked by one hand, then two,
then four. Then, startlingly, five. Or else he's just lost
count. Someone carefully smooths fingertips over the arc
of his throat, a gentleness in the touch that approaches
reverence. Another plays with his hair where it falls over

the blindfold. Then hands tweak his nipples, fondle his ass. He can't predict where or how or by whom.

Flat against the line of his cock, pushing it against his belly—the sole of someone's foot. Amy, he knows: he can picture her standing, probably braced by Mike. She rubs against him, lets her toes flex. She puts a little more of her weight down, and he whimpers as her footprint stamps his flesh, not crushing but as if she intends to leave a mark.

"How is that?" Marisol's voice, and maybe her fingertips dancing along his shoulders, pressing away tension.

"Easy now," Mike murmurs, shifting at the end of the bed.

"I'm okay," Roland says, knowing too that nothing they put him through is going to be easy. Every inch of him has come alive, waiting to be touched or bursting at their touch.

The foot lifts. Silky panties settle on his thigh, warm with a touch of slickness seeping through them. He feels more of it as Amy rocks. The hand pinching his nipple on the other side of his body, that might be hers or Mike's or Marisol's. He hears the shuffle of Amy pulling her blouse over her head, and Marisol's breath goes short. He tries to remember if Amy had looked like she'd been wearing a bra.

She isn't now. He feels her breasts, soft with diamond tips, trailing across his chest.

Fingers made frictionless with more lube ease inside him, start to stretch. Roland relaxes into it until they seek out and find his prostate, and with just a few strokes he becomes desperate again.

Amy laughs, riding him as he writhes. She's straddling

his left leg, but Roland spreads his right out of the way, hiking his hips to meet that hand. "Please. *Please.*"

Finally, Mike slides home. Roland presses his right calf to his back, urging him on, wrapping around him as much as possible as Mike delivers the gentle, steady thrusts he needs. While Roland meets them, trying almost despite himself to pick up the pace, Amy crawls forward, freeing his thighs and settling on his chest.

Then Marisol is moving, climbing over his head. She knocks the blindfold askew as she does, so he catches a glimpse of her kissing Amy. Without breaking the kiss, Amy turns, sandwiching Marisol between herself and Mike. Marisol's head falls back, tipping to let Mike brush his lips over her shoulder while Amy's mouth moves to the low top of her cami.

Roland makes a meaningless sound, or one too full of meaning—surprised and glad and curious.

Amy glances over her shoulder and meets his eyes. With a smile, she moves her hips back and brings her groin down on his mouth, blocking out his sight again. He sighs and licks the wet silk of her panties, fabric sweetened by her juices. She wiggles until the tip of his tongue can feel the hard tip of her clit through the thin barrier.

He can hear the slick, shuffling sounds of kissing, caressing, fingering, and fucking. Where Mike doesn't reach, Amy's warmth spreads through him. And Marisol, he feels her legs tighten around his chest as the others do something. She gasps, then laughs, not in humor but delight. Her hand falls to Roland's side, seeming to brace herself against some incredible sensation. For the first time he wishes his arms weren't tied; he'd like to touch her in return.

Mike begins stroking his cock as his thrusts turn harder—close to coming, he wants Roland to join him. Always a romantic that way, Roland thinks with the giddiness these last overwhelming moments fill him with. He flicks his tongue across Amy's cunt and feels her familiar trembling, but then she shudders and cries out, a flood of sweetness baptizing his worshipful lips, and he's awestruck but he's not responsible for that. Something Marisol's doing. If only he could see. Next time he's going to beg to see. They might even let him.

With that thought, he spills over Mike's fist.

Amy grinds down, making him breathless, then lifts up as she comes. She moves off his mouth to curl beside him, balanced on the edge of the bed. Smiling down at Roland, she pets his hair, pulling the blindfold free.

Marisol kisses her, then bends and kisses Roland. It's hard and sloppy—half, he thinks, to get the taste of Amy from him, but then her tongue is tracing his lips with shy tenderness, and he realizes this is for his sake, too. He returns it as Amy's fingertips rub his scalp. It doesn't last long, but next Marisol turns to Mike, a kiss noisy with audible joy. His arm wraps around her waist, and Amy strokes her shoulders. Roland can only watch them.

Marisol reaches behind herself, out of their triple embrace, to find his bound hand and squeeze it. Simple as the gesture is, something about it overpowers him even more than everything that's gone before. Wordless, unthinking—but not for an instant having to guess what it means—he squeezes back.

FIX ME!

Josie Jordan

The doorbell rang. I scooped baby Abigail into my arms and went to answer it.

"Hello," said the man on my doorstep. "I'm Reece from Immaculate Kitchens."

I gulped. He was tall and well built with a shock of dark hair. And so damn gorgeous I could hardly bring myself to look at him. "I'm Chloe," I said. "Um... Come on in."

He heaved an enormous toolbox inside. "Mike's just coming," he said.

Around the corner came the older guy who'd done the quotation, with an equally enormous toolbox.

"I've cleared the cupboards," I told them. "Let me know if you need anything."

Mike opened his toolbox. "I sure will."

My husband, Brett, and I had found mold in our kitchen cabinets last month. With a new baby around, we didn't want to take chances. The whole kitchen would have to be ripped out and a new one put in.

Fortunately our insurance covered it, but I was dreading being without a kitchen all week.

I felt Reece's eyes on me. "Want a coffee?" I asked.

"I'd love one," he said. "Black, two sugars."

"Same here," Mike said.

I'd set the kettle up in the laundry. My daughter fussed and grizzled in my arms as I waited for the water to boil.

Reece glanced over. "What's her name?"

"Abigail," I said.

"She's beautiful. How old is she?"

"Nearly one." Still clutching Abigail, I tried to open the coffee jar one-handed.

"Want a hand?" Reece asked.

"Thanks," I said, expecting him to reach for the jar. Instead he wiped his hands on his jeans and took Abigail. I waited for her little face to crumple, but she beamed.

Reece smiled back at her. His eyes were the same shade as the coffee in the jar. "She's a cutie," he said. "My sister has a baby girl, eighteen months old now."

When I handed him his coffee, his warm hand met mine and I nearly dropped the mug. His fingers were broad and tanned; tattoos of dragons curled around his strong biceps.

"Right," he said eventually. "Better do some work."

He handed Abigail back and picked up a crowbar. The muscles in his arms rippled as he pried out a cabinet. With all the noise, there was no point trying to settle Abigail. Reece bent over, revealing an inch of smooth, tanned ass. I might once have sat back and enjoyed the view, but the sight of him only reminded me how damaged I was.

When I'd fallen pregnant, my sex drive went through the roof. I used to greet Brett at the front door and we mostly didn't even make it as far as the bed, ending up on the hall carpet instead with our legs in a tangle. When my baby bump grew bigger, I used to lie face-down on the mattress with my pillow under my breasts and have him take me from behind. My orgasms were so powerful they almost hurt.

But the trauma of the birth changed everything. We hadn't had sex since. That part of me had simply shut down and died. And each time Brett tried and failed to start something, I think another part of him died as well.

"I'm going back to the factory for the rest of the cabinets," Mike said just then, and off he went.

I saw Reece looking my way. "Want another coffee?" I asked.

"I'd love one," he said. "Want me to hold Abigail again?"

"Okay." I passed her to him.

Abigail gazed up at him. He tickled her toes and she chortled.

"You're great with her," I said.

"I babysit for my sister sometimes. She's a single mum."

Reece must have been in his early twenties—ten years younger than me—yet he seemed older and more serious than other guys his age. I felt his dark eyes on me as he sipped his coffee, and it wasn't unpleasant. Did my husband even look at me like that anymore? I didn't know, because I didn't look at *him*. I was too scared of starting something I couldn't finish.

I thought back to the last time Brett tried to initiate something. It must have been three or four months ago. I'd shrunk away from him. "Sorry," I'd said.

He held me in his arms and I wept, because I loved him, I really did, but I was in a deep, dark place where he couldn't reach me.

"I don't want to lose you," he'd said.

"What are we going to do?"

"Counseling. Time. Whatever it takes. You've been through a lot."

But we couldn't afford counseling, and time didn't change anything. Instead, month by month, I felt him slipping farther away.

"Is your husband at work?" Reece asked.

"Yeah, he works long hours," I said.

There was a sparkle in his eyes that hinted at possibilities. Possibilities he was clearly open to. *Whatever it takes,* Brett had said. A hot guy in my kitchen wasn't one of the options he'd come up with, but maybe this was what it took—having a sexy guy see me as desirable. So I did my best to force my guilt aside and enjoy his admiring gaze.

"It must be hard being without a kitchen," he said.

"Tell me about it," I said. "Tonight's going to be takeaway. Chinese, probably."

Mike and Reece worked all afternoon, and poor Abigail skipped all her naps. I didn't even try to settle her. It was just too noisy.

"Right," Mike said later. "I'm done for the day."

"I'll just finish the sink," Reece said. "See you in the morning, Mike."

I let Mike out.

Reece glanced my way. "I fancy takeaway tonight. Want me to pick some up, save you going out?"

"Oh," I said, "yeah, that would be great."

He returned laden with bags. I hesitated. Did he plan to eat here? His food would get cold if he drove home. "I've got plates somewhere," I said.

"Don't worry," he said. "I'll eat out of the box."

With a little stab of guilt, I sat next to him on the sofa. Brett wouldn't be back for ages. He and I never ate dinner together anymore.

"Is Abigail asleep?" Reece asked.

"Yeah, fingers crossed," I said.

We glanced shyly at each other. This felt strangely like a date. "Does your sister live near you?" I asked.

"Yeah, she moved closer when she split with her partner."

"Why did they split?"

"He couldn't handle sharing her with the baby."

"It's hard on a relationship having kids. For us, it was the birth that did it. It broke me." *Shut up,* I told myself. *He doesn't want to know.*

But he was nodding in sympathy. "At least you're still together."

"By a thread," I said.

Tuesday afternoon after Mike had gone, I watched Reece drill holes into a cupboard door, the wood braced against his thigh, and found myself imagining his cock. Strange. I hadn't had that kind of thought since the birth.

He looked my way, with a tiny smile, as though he knew I'd been watching him. "Want me to get takeaway again?" he asked.

I felt a funny flutter in my stomach. "Okay."

Abigail had refused to settle, so I rocked her as we ate.

I glanced down at myself, suddenly aware of the baggy T-shirt and sweatpants I lived in these days. "Look at the state of me," I said. "Stains all over my top and I haven't washed my hair for days. Abigail wakes the minute I get in the shower."

"Look at me, then," Reece said. He had wood chippings in his hair and his clothes were filthy.

I laughed. "Okay, you win."

Abigail was grizzling. I stroked her hair, hoping to lull her to sleep.

"Look, I'm happy to hold her while you take a shower," he said.

"Oh, I'm sure you've got better stuff to do than sit around here."

"Seriously, I don't mind."

The thought of a shower was too tempting. I handed Abigail over. Her wide blue eyes gazed up at him. She seemed quite content to lie there in his big, strong arms and I didn't blame her. He stroked her forehead with his fingertip and soon her eyelids grew heavy.

"You must have a magic touch," I said.

"I've always been good with my hands."

I reached for her. "I'll try her in her cot," I said.

I held my breath as I laid her down, but she remained fast asleep.

"You're incredible," I said once I'd crept from the nursery. "You can put in a new kitchen, settle a crying baby… What more could a woman want? You must get horny housewives jumping you all the time."

Reece grinned. "It's happened. My girlfriend doesn't

mind. She kind of gets off on it, actually. One time she had me invite a customer back to our place."

"Really?" Our eyes met and I flushed.

"You go shower," he said. "I'll shout you if she wakes."

With the hot water blasting down on me, I pictured Reece, his girlfriend, and his customer in bed together. *Stop it,* I told myself. Abigail could wake any moment.

I finished my shower, threw on my robe and rushed out, but she was still sleeping. I caught the way Reece was looking at the robe.

"Sorry," he said, although he didn't look it.

"Nobody looks at me that way anymore," I said. "Not even my husband."

"That's a shame."

"It's not his fault. I've shut myself off since the birth."

"Still love him?"

I swallowed. The conversation was getting pretty intimate. "Yeah. But I can't bear him near me." I hadn't told any of my friends that. "I'm broken," I said.

His dark eyes did a slow sweep of my body. "You don't look broken to me."

"Believe me, I am." Although I didn't feel it when he was looking at me like that.

Unbelievably, he reached out to touch my face. I froze. In the silence, I could hear our breathing. He traced along my jaw. I thought about what I was doing. Brett wouldn't like it. He wouldn't even want to know about it. But if this was the price...

Reece's fingers trailed down my throat to where my robe met my bare chest. His eyes searched mine. "You can tell me to stop."

I didn't.

His fingers inched inside my robe until they cupped my breast. I had to clutch the fridge to stay upright. The rough calluses on his fingertips only added to the sensation. He was breathing hard now. I closed my eyes, willing him to continue. I could feel life seeping back to a forgotten part of me.

He withdrew his hand. "You're beautiful," he said. "And definitely not broken. See you tomorrow."

On Wednesday morning, Reece gave me a secret smile when I let him in. That night, as we ate dinner together again, I realized I'd spent more time in his company this week than with my husband.

"I was thinking about your problem," he said.

"My . . . oh." I flushed, realizing what he was talking about.

"And like I said, I'm pretty good at fixing things."

I stared at him. *So fix me,* I thought. *Please fix me.*

"What time's your husband home?"

"About six."

He touched my hand.

Hit by a wave of guilt, I pulled away. "I'm married," I said.

"I get that," he said. "I'm not proposing to fuck you. Unless you want me to. Fingers only. Let me prove to you that you're not broken."

Were we seriously having this conversation?

"What's in it for you?" I asked.

"It would be no great hardship, believe me." He shifted closer until his hips met mine.

Feeling something sharp in his jeans pocket, I reached in and pulled out one of his business cards. *Immaculate Kitchens. We provide a full service.*

It broke the moment. I giggled. "Satisfaction guaranteed?"

He smiled too. "We aim to please."

"I hope you don't offer this to all your customers," I said.

"I don't. Don't tell anyone or they might get jealous. So, do you want the full service?"

I found myself considering his offer. If it saved my marriage, would it really be so wrong?

"Trust me," he said. "I'm pretty damn good with my hands."

Did I trust him? I realized I did. Besides, I wanted what he was offering so damn badly I wasn't able to refuse. Before I knew it, I was nodding.

"Let's get it straight," he said. "I'm not going to fuck you, or even kiss you. It's hands only."

"Okay," I said weakly.

He led me to the bedroom. "Lie on the bed. Want to take that robe off, or can I?"

My throat was so dry I could hardly get words out. "You can."

He untied my belt and peeled it back.

I lay there, completely exposed. "Shit, I'm shaking," I said.

"Relax," he said. "I'll be gentle."

He began with my breasts, cupping them and stroking them until my nipples hardened to tight points. His warm palm swept down my stomach. I felt a finger, his forefinger, I thought, gently exploring me. I couldn't believe this was happening, but my body was responding—big-time.

"You're so wet," he said.

So slowly that it killed me, he slid his finger up and down my clit. It was hard to believe such a big, strong guy could be so gentle. Watching my face, he painted circles round and round the most sensitive point on my body. My pleasure spiraled upward with each one. Then he switched to a rapid side-to-side movement, taking me to a whole new level. I gripped the mattress.

"Inside?" he whispered.

Excitement seared my stomach. I was too turned on to worry it might hurt. "Yeah."

His middle finger pressed into me. I sucked in my breath. "Deeper," I managed to say.

He sank his finger in all the way.

I lifted my hips to his hand. "Fuck me with your finger."

He smiled. "Patience." His finger withdrew and returned to painting circles.

Pleasure raced down my legs and arms. He increased the pressure and after every circle began pushing his finger deep.

"So...good..." I gasped, bucking for more.

A sweet but long-forgotten feeling was stirring in me. The finger pushed in again and I soared upward. I was so close already...

The finger retreated.

I groaned. "Don't stop."

But he stood up and adjusted his cock inside his jeans. "I'm off."

"Are you serious?" I said. "You can't leave me like this."

"Nothing's broken," he said. "We've established that. I think your husband should be the one who finishes the job, don't you?"

Thursday morning.

Reece waited until Mike was out of earshot. "So. Did you . . . ?"

The heat rushed to my cheeks. "No," I said. "Abigail woke. Otherwise we might have."

"Only might?" he pressed.

I shrugged. "I don't know."

He frowned and continued his work. This was their last day. The kitchen was almost finished.

Late afternoon, Mike shut his toolbox. "Right, that's it for me," he said. "I'll leave Reecey boy here to finish and we'll mail you the invoice."

Mike slammed the door behind him. There was an immediate wail from the baby monitor. I sighed and went to get Abigail. Cradling her in my arms, I perched on my glossy new kitchen counter and watched Reece position the final few tiles. His dark jeans hugged his ass to perfection.

He washed his hands. "Give her here, then."

I watched him rock Abigail to sleep.

When she was safely tucked up in the nursery, he turned to me, his eyes glinting. "Want to continue what we started yesterday?"

I didn't even have to think about it. "Yes."

He led me to the bedroom. "Look, I'm not going to fuck you," he said. "I promised you that. But have you got anything I can use to...?"

My pulse sped up a notch. I opened a drawer and pulled out my vibrator. I'd only taken it out once since the birth. Abigail had woken before I had time to use it.

"Take off your clothes," he said.

He nudged my legs apart. I sucked in a breath at the feel of the hard plastic tip. I was wet already. He twisted it gently against me as though it were a screwdriver. My body blocked it for a second, then accepted it. The cool plastic slid on in.

I forced myself to take deep breaths as he eased it deeper.

Halfway in, he paused. "How does it feel?"

"Amazing." I bucked my hips, desperate for more.

He switched it on.

I gasped.

His rough palm clamped over my mouth. "Shh! You'll wake Abigail."

This was insane. I was lying here naked under a strange man, with his hand over my mouth and a vibrator stuffed deep. My husband was far from my mind just then. All my focus was on this sexy young guy and what he was doing to me.

I squeezed my eyes shut and forced myself to lie still. The vibrator buzzed deep inside me. He teased my clit with his finger and I felt like I was going to explode on the spot. And if he sucked my tits at the same time, I would detonate.

He must have read my mind because I felt his warm breath on my breast. Through my eyelashes I saw his lips descending. They wrapped around my nipple and I felt a delicious, almost painful tug as he latched on. He slid the vibrator out and sank it back in deep. It felt incredible. Another few thrusts and I was teetering on the brink, ready to shatter.

But before I got there, he slid the vibrator out.

"No!" I said. "Don't stop!"

"Nothing broken?" His finger rested on my clit, maintaining the lightest pressure.

"I guess not. Now, please . . . " I lifted my hips, desperate for release.

He shook his head. "I want you to want it so bad."

"You can't do this to me." I slid my hand down the back of his jeans and dug my fingernails into his asscheek. He groaned and pressed himself against me, his erection crushed against my thigh. I unzipped his fly, took his cock in the palm of my hand, and wrapped my fingers around its sticky solid warmth.

He groaned again and pulled away. "This wasn't what we agreed on."

"I know," I said. "But you're killing me."

"Don't worry. It's killing me too." He tucked his cock back into his pants and peeled himself off the bed.

"What are you doing?"

"Leaving you to your husband."

Deep down, I knew he was right. This was as far as we could go. He backed out of the room.

"Where are you going?" I said.

"Home. If I don't explode in my pants on the drive, I'm going to sink this thing into my girlfriend."

I drew in a shuddery breath, picturing it.

"While I fuck her, I'm going to imagine what you're doing here with your husband. Don't let me down, will you?"

"I won't."

He gave me a long look and turned to go.

I slumped back on the bed. My clit throbbed like never before. I checked the time. Nearly half an hour until Brett might return. Too long. I pressed my finger to my clit and the pain eased. The softest pressure was all it needed. Soon I was right back on the verge of coming.

No, I told myself. *Wait.* Brett had to be the one to do it. I needed to be like this, crazy for him, otherwise I would lose my nerve and back out. It was agony, but I forced myself to wait. Every few minutes, I stroked myself back up into a frenzy.

At last, I heard the sound of the front door. "Hi!" I called.

"Where are you?" Brett's voice.

"In here."

The eyes on me now were blue and familiar and open wide in concern. "Are you okay?" he said.

"I'm fine."

"What are you doing?"

"Waiting for you." I drew back the covers. "Come here."

He lingered in the doorway. "I don't want to put any pressure..."

"Shut up and get a condom," I said.

He handed me one. Wasting no time, I tore it open. Meanwhile he peeled his shirt off and stepped out of his pants and underpants. He was hard already. I pushed his shoulders down to the bed and rolled the rubber down the length of him.

Desperate to have his warm flesh inside me, I lowered my body over his and sat down hard.

He gave a stunned laugh. "What happened to you?"

"Don't ask."

I rode him, looking down at his face. Imagining, just for a second, a very different set of features beneath me. Dark eyes, a shock of dark hair. Hands that could fix anything . . .

I flung back my head and rode him harder. My

husband gripped my waist, supporting my weight as I rose and dropped.

"I missed you so much," I whispered.

"I missed you too, baby."

I reached down to touch myself, sliding my finger back and forth over my insanely swollen clit as his cock impaled me from beneath.

It didn't take much before I was right back on the brink again. The friction between our bodies was enough so I removed my finger and gripped Brett's buttocks instead. "I'm nearly there."

His gaze held mine. "Come for me, Chloe."

I sped up my movements. He was panting short fast breaths and shunting his hips up to meet mine and giving me exactly what I craved. For a few delicious seconds, I teetered there. That was it! The next time our bodies crashed together, I tipped over the edge. Stuffed full of cock, my inner muscles clamped up in powerful waves.

Brett gasped and lifted me one more time, before bringing me back down hard. I felt the pulses of his climax as his cock went off deep inside me. I collapsed onto his chest.

We lay there in each other's arms until our breathing slowed.

"So the kitchen's all fixed," he said.

"And so am I." I clung to him, braced for the questions that would follow.

But he simply gripped me a little tighter.

A REAL ONE

Leandra Vane

Nine different tubes of pink lipstick were scattered over my bathroom counter. As I scrutinized each one, I was not thinking about which shade would give my pout the most demure look or which tone would complement my outfit the best. To my eyes, each one looked like a deviously delicious punishment.

Pomegranate—demanding stripes from a leather strap. Mauve—hot, punishing bruises. Bubblegum—definitely a paddle. Sunset light pink—the perfect hand spanking. A jolt of pleasure shot up my spine and down to my toes. I picked up the tube to look at the name of the color. Number 11. Bare Blush. *How fitting.*

I tried to keep calm against my thudding heart rate as I popped open the tube and applied the shade to my lips.

I didn't usually get so turned on by my lipstick. But I hadn't been properly spanked for weeks and just the thought of it was enough to send licks of imaginary pleasure down the backs of my thighs. I let out a deep breath. I had been promised release. Soon. Tonight. I just had to hold on for a couple more hours.

My doorbell rang, and I scooped up the lipsticks and tossed them back into the basket above the sink before rushing to answer the door. I was still only wearing my underwear, but I recognized the knock of my play partner before a kink party—timid but full of anticipation.

Sure enough, I found Beth on my stoop as I answered the door.

Beth had dark hair and the biggest brown eyes I had ever seen. She had spent her twenties being mistaken for a teenager and now at thirty-three she could almost pass for twenty-one. We had a lot in common. We both were often taken for being younger and more innocent then we really were. We both had a soft spot in our hearts for baroque-era Italian painters. And we both shared Zach—a Dom with a strict hand and creative mind.

"Joanne!" she greeted me. "Sorry I'm early. You look nice. I brought a cherry cobbler." She held up a covered dish.

"It's okay. Thanks. And uh. Great."

She stood in her nervousness, holding the door open wide as I stood in my underwear. I reached out and pulled her inside.

An embarrassed blush tinted her cheeks as I closed the door.

"Oh . . . sorry. I . . . wasn't thinking."

I leaned in to peck her lips, softly enough not to ruin our makeup. Her rosy-red lipstick matched her short polished nails, and I held back an aggravated sigh. She was driving me mad and she didn't even know it.

"It's fine, relax," I said. "I'm almost ready. Do you want to sit down? Won't be long."

"I'll be fine waiting here, as long as you need. Don't rush for me." Beth smiled and held up the cobbler pan like a perky 1950s waitress. Indeed, the cut of her dress was vintage: a well-fitted navy-blue with pinpoint red dots printed over it that gave her the feminine charm of pulp-era comic books.

"Just let me throw on a dress and we'll go," I said.

I rushed into my bedroom and glared into my closet. I was not nearly as fashionable as Beth. My wardrobe consisted entirely of two-dollar bag sales at the corner thrift shop. But I found what I had in mind: a loose-fitting Bohemian-style dress with bell sleeves. I chose the dress because the material was thin. Not only was the summer night going to be humid, but I was taking a preemptive measure in case Zach decided to torture me by making me keep my dress on for most of my scene. Tingles spread over my skin at the thought of being so crafty against my Dominant.

My attitude wasn't entirely my own fault—he was being difficult on purpose. More than once over the last two weeks I had cornered Zach in isolated corners during quiet times of the day and begged for an emergency scene. A maintenance spanking. A pity punishment. I didn't even need to get off, I told him, just give me something, anything, to think about.

The answer was no every time. With an even tone and stern gaze, he told me I had to wait for the party.

Tonight's party.

I brushed out some wrinkles in the skirt before I instinctively reached for my toy bag next to my dresser.

I stopped myself. Zach had told both Beth and me not to bring anything of our own. Zach was going to supply our scenes himself.

I gave a huff and went to gather my purse and the potato salad I had made for the potluck.

With our culinary offerings safely buckled in the backseat, I drove Beth in my car as she rode passenger with her hand resting gently on my knee. Such gestures had become more common between us, and it was getting hard to remember not to let our touches linger in such ways when we saw each other at work.

I had been working at the Wallace Sullivan Museum of Art for seven years as a registrar. My job was fairly straightforward: I made sure stuff made it onto the walls in time for gallery openings, and if anything in the permanent collection had to be moved it didn't get broken. The directors of the museum weren't so fond of my rough attitude, uncensored opinions on Postmodernism, or my insistence that thrift shop corduroy pants were suitable formal wear. But they liked that they had someone on staff who could both get dirt under their fingernails during installations and knew the difference between Expressionism and Impressionism. I could also work fairly well with artists and give a good tour of the numerous galleries in a pinch.

Beth had joined the staff at the museum as a grant writer and office manager about two years ago. And I immediately spotted the way her gaze devoured the kinky aspects of paintings because it was the same way my eyes roamed over any depiction of power exchange. I didn't know if she really wanted to try the things her eyes hungered for until one month when an erotic photographer landed a showing in one of the smaller galleries. The theme was masochism and I caught Beth touching herself in the gallery early before work one morning. I talked her down from her embarrassment over a cup of coffee on the back steps of the museum and took a leap of faith in revealing my own erotic inclinations. We started talking and after a couple of months I invited her to her first play party to meet my Dominant. The sadist in me loved seeing her dark lips tighten in a little O of surprise when she realized my Dom was also the operations and maintenance manager at the Wallace Sullivan Museum of Art.

Fortunately, our working relationships were not compromised. Besides some interesting after-hours trysts between installations and a lot of inside jokes at the annual Christmas party, we went about our daily routines as though we were as vanilla as the cupcakes served at the assistant director's birthday party. As the year wore on, the three of us became very good friends.

Of course, I wasn't thinking about any of that as I forced myself to drive the speed limit with Beth's hand on my knee. I was thinking about the Bare Blush on my lips and looking forward to relief. Beth broke the silence that had stretched between us.

"I asked for a real one."

I glanced over to her. "A real what?"

"A real punishment. A real scene." She gave a shy smile. "You know."

"Your scenes are real," I encouraged.

"I know. I'm not in competition with anyone. I'm just . . . ready to take it to the next level."

Beth may have had kinky thoughts, but her scenes never edged beyond anything more intense than light sensation play. She and Zach negotiated scenes between them carefully, but most of the time Zach would barely get the scene set up and Beth would call the safeword. Zach was always very comforting and encouraging about her limits and would massage her muscles into an arousal that could withstand a mini flogger or a couple of well-placed ice cubes. Beth wanted kinky experiences. But even after a year of playing, she only lived vicariously as she watched the role-play punishment scenes between Zach and myself.

I reached down and held her hand. She smiled, genuinely, and relaxed a little in her seat.

The play party was a small, private one at our friends Kevin and Tasha's house. They lived just outside the city limits along a gravel road. As we approached I could see several vehicles parked around the front of the house. I knew Beth liked the smaller group and more private atmosphere. I personally liked the energy and sound system of our local dungeon. But just yesterday I had been begging for a spanking in the museum's mop closet, so I wasn't about to be picky.

Of course in our nerves and eagerness we arrived before Zach. The house was cool and welcoming, filled with the mouthwatering scent of the grill from the open patio doors. Some people had gathered in the kitchen and Beth went in to chat off some nervous energy. But I avoided that room. A kitchen full of kinky people with ready access to spatulas and wooden spoons was not a risk I was willing to chance. I quickly took refuge in the living room.

I was soon enveloped in hugs and comfortably intimate touches to the small of my back, and I played it cool the whole while.

Yes, work is going fine. Yes, it's been a hot summer. No, I'm not picturing myself bent over every knee and piece of furniture in this damn house.

I almost blew my cover when I saw Zach appear under the arch that separated the dining room from the living room. Just seeing him made my knees weaken and my hands tremble. But as he said his hellos, I managed to remain standing tall in my thigh-high lace ups.

Tonight was special, but my body always went momentarily weak when I saw Zach. He possessed the look of a Dom without even trying. Dark eyes, dark hair, and broad shoulders with a gym-maintained physique under his black T-shirt and easy jeans. A natural scowl weighed on his features when he was concentrating, and he was usually quiet. This made everyone at work think he was a stereotypical moody maintenance guy, best to be avoided. That's why everyone always came to me first when a lightbulb needed changing. But I knew when you got to know Zach, he spoke with a gentle voice and often flashed a smile like no one else's.

I never wanted for attention from Zach, and neither did Beth. He kissed us both, and when it was time for dinner he pulled out our chairs at the table, then poured us coffee after our hosts had served cheesecake for dessert.

Dinner thankfully went fast. Everyone there had better things to do after cheesecake than sit around and talk about the weather.

We had been to play parties at Kevin and Tasha's

home before, so I wasn't surprised when Zach led us to the front sitting room. Other couples played in the dungeon set up in the basement or the guest bedrooms, but Zach liked the openness of the living room. The furniture had been moved to provide more space, but Zach took us to a corner where a single bar stool stood.

I hoped Zach might ask us who wanted to scene with him first, but my wish was not granted.

"Well, Beth, we negotiated tying you up, but I have nothing to tie you up to. Perhaps Joanne would oblige?"

I bit my tongue. I'd pushed too hard this week, and now he was plucking at my tension by doing Beth's scene first. I let out a slow, hot breath and found my center. I knew something like this was coming and I was prepared to endure the wait. Zach might like to play, but he always made the outcome worth the torment. He was a master of deliverance.

"Sure," I answered with a polite lilt in my voice. At least helping with Beth's scene would give me something to pass the time. "Or should I say, yes, Sir?"

There was that smile. "You should," he answered. "Sit."

I perched myself on the seat, the heels of my boots wedged into the rod between the legs of the stool.

"Cross your arms, so that your fingertips are lined to your collarbones," Zach instructed.

I obeyed his request.

"Now you may wait until I call upon you again."

I closed my eyes. Behind me I heard Zach begin to prepare Beth for the scene, giving her a massage and stripping her clothing away. I strained my ears to hear their whispers as the rest of the partygoers had ramped up the festivities. Laughter and squeals and the pops of impact toys began to pepper the room. There had only been a few at first, but now the sounds were ricocheting through the house. I set my jaw and clenched my eyes tight and focused on my partners as they conversed behind me.

Zach didn't usually resort to bondage—he demanded obedience from his words and bare hands. Thus I was not surprised when he enlisted the help of a rope-rigger named Alana to do the work. My knowledge of rope wasn't the sharpest. I was too much of a slut for paddles and floggers. The rope Alana had was not very thick, but it was soft, and purple, a playful color that in that moment did not amuse me.

Alana started by composing a chest harness around my torso and arms before moving on to tie Beth to me. Beth's arms wrapped around my chest as she stood up behind me. I had left my arms crossed, and Alana secured Beth's hands between mine. If I wiggled my fingers I could almost touch my thumbs to Beth's pinkies.

Alana flashed me a smirk before she left, and something about it made my stomach drop. I almost called her back to check a knot, just to postpone the scene a moment longer, but I held in my sudden dread.

Zach slid into my line of vision and stood before me in total Top Mode. My mouth went dry and my brain buzzed. I didn't understand. This was Beth's scene. Why was I feeling the anticipation?

Zach parted his lips but said nothing. A beat of two seconds passed and he leaned in close.

"I'm going to be very clear and say this once. This is

the only scene I'm doing tonight. So make sure you get what you need. Both of you."

He turned from me before even my gaze could offer a response and rage welled up hot in my core.

I ground my teeth together hard and my nostrils flared with a hot, frustrated breath. I swallowed the whine that threatened to break from my throat only because I had the decency to not ruin Beth's scene. Especially when she was so close to getting what she had been working to get for months. Zach knew I wouldn't mess it up for her. He knew and he was using it against me.

I pricked the tips of each one of my fingernails into the rope instead of cussing out my Dom. Feisty word-play and even outright yelling were common in our dynamic. But not with Beth.

I screwed my eyes closed. *Hush, Joanne, hush*, I soothed myself internally. *Keep it together, keep it quiet.*

My lips remained silent, but my mind was not willing to be so polite.

Fuck me—fuck this—fuck him—fuck everything.

How *dare* he dangle everything I needed inches from my desperate grasp? Did he get off watching me grapple with the impossible?

Oh yeah? Well. Fuck the impossible.

My mental anguish stilled. The thought was a spark of fire in a vast and deep darkness.

Fuck the impossible.

If he won't give it to you . . .

. . . take it.

Zach was going to put his hands on Beth. He was going to punish her because she had asked for it. She wanted a real one. She was going to get it.

She was going to get it and I wanted to be there. I had to be there.

I took in some deep breaths that slowed my hateful heartbeat enough for me to focus. I settled into the scene just as Zach was tuning in to Beth's anticipation.

I gave my attention to the way Beth's body felt so close to mine. She was naked and I could feel her heat and soft curves through the thin material of my dress. I matched my breathing to hers and our bodies seemed to meld together. Her arousal served as a cooling balm to my flare of anger.

When I glanced down I saw that her red-painted fingertips were reaching for mine. I tried to move my wrists and reach my own struggling fingers toward her but in the confines of the rope our touch was separated by a chasm of almost an inch on each side. I pressed my back into her just enough to let her know I was there for her.

In the next moment a swift, sudden clap exploded in my ears as Zach's hand met with Beth's soft, awaiting flesh. A sharp pleasure that felt like a hook behind my navel made me jump. I felt Beth rise to the tips of her toes.

"Oh," she gasped. "Oh."

I blinked hard and my mind swam between my temples. Zach hadn't hit her that hard. It was her reaction that made it so intense.

I heard a rustle of Beth's hair and an inaudible whisper in her ear.

"Green," she responded, breathy but certain.

Zach answered with a proud glow in his words, "That's a good girl."

A shudder shot between my legs. I almost didn't hear Zach as he asked, "How do those ropes feel, Jo?"

I felt dizzy but it wasn't from the ropes. "Fine, Sir."

"Perfect. Let us continue."

After several aching breaths of time, a second impact rang out.

Beth squeezed her arms around my chest and her body crumpled in on itself. Zach allowed her a moment to straighten her legs and stand tall again.

He spanked her again, once, twice, three times in quick succession. Her breathing hitched into a faster pace.

My own muscles contracted and released. I could feel the tension as Beth's body warmed up, exposed and bare, waiting for what Zach was going to give her next.

She let out a whimper, and I imagined Zach was putting his hands on her, sliding his palm over the surfacing pink blush on her ass.

A warmth crept over my hips.

A rhythm of open-palmed impacts ticked off like a metronome, three swats in the span of a second for one . . . two . . . three . . . four . . .

Beth let out a moan and I realized I was holding my breath. I let it out slowly and the repetition carried on for six . . . seven . . . eight seconds.

"No," she moaned, low. "Yes," she gasped. "No, yes, no . . . ohhh."

She squirmed up against me on tiptoes once again. Her breathing was wild now; the warmth in my hips had ignited into a licking flame. A white-hot wetness erupted in my pussy.

The spanking stopped and Beth sobbed in the sudden

silence. He wasn't touching her but she still writhed and panted, her fingers flexing open and closed around the rope. I was biting my tongue no longer from frustration, but to hold back my mounting pleasure.

"Beth. Would you like some more?"

"I . . . Yes. Green. Yes. Please."

Another whimper escaped her lips and my legs locked involuntarily. If I hadn't been sitting on the stool I would have been a puddle on Tasha and Kevin's living room rug.

Pacing us for three or four breaths, Zach waited. And then he delivered.

Slap. Slap. Slap. Three even strokes to one side of her ass then, *slap, slap, slap.* Three more to the other.

"Oh..." Beth's voice in my ear was divine, her hot breath sacred.

A fuller sound popped behind me as Zach's hand collided with Beth's backside. Slow at first, but then faster and faster.

One, two, three, four. One, two, three, four. One, two, three... My mind lost count and my head fell back onto Beth's shoulder. She was moaning recklessly now, her fingertips splayed, her whole body hardening then releasing, processing the tension, rocking and writhing, breaking through to that place she had only visited in the dark corners of her imagination.

"Yes, no, yes, please. Oh. Oh." She breathed in, a high note edging around the intake of air and then she moaned out, "Nooo . . . No. Oh, yes. Yes. Fuck!"

That was it. Orgasm exploded through my body and all I was aware of for several hot, blissful moments was the heavy throb of my heartbeat and the burst of color behind my eyelids—the ultimate painting of my erotic imagination, each stroke of pigment placed right where it needed to be.

When I surfaced again, I noticed the hot slickness against my cheek, a mixture of Beth's sweat and tears. Her whole body had gone limp, and I had to brace my shoulders to remain balanced on the stool. As Zach whispered praises into her ear, the ecstasy soaked through my skin and into my bones. I knew I would be riding on the warm, satisfying buzz of release for the rest of the night.

In order to properly pull us both from subspace, Zach had to release our bonds. I felt the popping of knots, and the tension that had held us together fell loose with a few tugs here and there.

When I was free to move, I slid from the stool and turned around to hold Beth close to me like we were slow dancing. Her eyes were closed but there was a hint of a smile gracing her lips.

"I got a real one," she slurred out, her words heavy like honey after her release. "I'm sorry you didn't."

"Oh, no, no," I said, brushing her damp bangs from her eyes. "I certainly did."

She nudged her body into mine as I planted a slow kiss to the side of her face.

The salty taste of her sweat mingled with the waxy tone of my lipstick, and when I pulled back I saw the shade of pink left by my lips had blended perfectly to the blush on her cheek.

DESDEMONA ON THE FRINGE

Kendel Davi

Malik's body was carved from the most exquisite walnut. As he stepped toward me, I extended my trembling hands and swept my fingers across his firm landscape. My breath ricocheted off his stomach. A salacious moan escaped my lips, soft enough where only he could hear it, and I turned my gaze toward his strong yet caring face. A peek of white teeth radiated from the depths of his coarse raven beard before he opened his mouth and said, "Tonight, I'm honored you've allowed yourself to be my queen."

Malik's approach was gentle but mine was desperate, and he kissed me to calm me down. I pushed open his tender lips with mine. His sweet breath rushed into my willing mouth. I knew I had to say something as my hands fumbled with his belt buckle, but the words were locked in my psyche. My once damp lips were suddenly dry with anxiety. I tossed my head back and shouted, "Line!"

My voice ripped through the cavernous theater. A

dense silence followed, which was punctuated by Vivian huffing, "The heavens shall sing our praises as I claim you as my king."

Embarrassment clutched my soul and attempted to rip itself out of my body. I had played this role less than a month ago, so why were the words escaping me now? Maybe it was the change in location. Maybe it was the pressure of doing this Best of the Fringe Festival? Deep down I knew this lack of focus had everything to do with me playing Desdemona to Malik's Othello.

The guy who previously played this role was pedestrian at best. He was a C-list movie star who ended up being a box-office draw for the production. His presence put us in front of the committee who ran this festival. He booked an acting job that was a conflict with this show, and Malik swooped in and took his place. The differences between the two were blatantly apparent.

Malik could easily pass for a Moorish military leader. His body had been sculpted from lifting heavy stage equipment. He towered over me by at least half a foot. His eyes were gentle yet intense at the same time. His broad shoulders and rich chestnut skin made him a perfect fit for Othello. Me playing a Venetian beauty, on the other hand, was a stretch. My agent told me I had a face and body that were perfect for sitcoms. I could've viewed that statement as an insult, but these cherub cheeks, buxom frame, and light tawny skin allowed me to work more often than not. It was Vivian's trust in my talent that had put me in a role I doubted anyone else would cast me in.

It didn't help that Malik and I had unfinished business between us. When he first joined this company several years ago, I'd locked my eyes on him. As luck would have it, I was involved with a jackass at the time, but as that relationship fell apart, Malik and I started to heat up. After a few drunken nights of heavy petting that left my denim jeans soaked, he landed a tech job that took him away for a year. Now he was back, we were both completely single, but the pressure of this show had us both stressed out.

"Let's take ten," Vivian sighed.

Vivian was the director. This adaptation of *Othello* was her vision. In the original text we never witness Desdemona and Othello consummate their marriage. Vivian felt the passion of this interracial relationship needed to be on full display, where there was no denying their love for each other. This scene had been carefully choreographed to get that point across.

Vivian dropped her notebook on the wooden folding table and approached me. The stomp of her boots against the hard stage floor sent chills through me. I'd witnessed her eviscerate actors who weren't prepared, but I'd never been on that side of her wrath nor did I ever want to be. I had my apology ready, but as soon as I opened my mouth, Vivian held up her hand.

"What's going on, Lara? This scene was so hot last week I had to cross my legs to get through it."

She stood there waiting. The orange stage lights gave her olive skin a goddess-like glow and I swallowed hard, not sure I had the answer to her question.

"Maybe if you two fucked each other it just might help," Vivian mumbled.

"It wouldn't hurt," I quickly replied. That thought wasn't meant to leave my lips. I quickly giggled and took a step backward as I covered my honesty with an intellectual response. "But that would take away from the honesty of this being the moment where they consummate their marriage, right?"

I stared into Vivian's hazel Egyptian eyes, looking for cracks in her stern gaze, but there were none. Her intensity was unnerving, and I cracked a smile to break the tension.

"That's what I love about you, Lara. You sure know how to smooth things over, don't you? The stress is getting to everybody tonight. Let's mark through the rest of the play to save our energy for tomorrow night."

A pained expression graced Malik's face as Vivian approached him. I couldn't hear what they said to each other, but by the way her hand gently stroked his back, I knew he needed the comfort.

"Let's break early. See everyone back here in a little over an hour," Vivian shouted and headed back to her table.

Malik walked toward me, yanking at the fake beard.

"I'm glad she's letting me get rid of this. It's irritating as hell." The skin on his face stretched as he pulled on the beard. "And the smell alone. It's gotta be giving you a headache too."

His frustration was apparent, and I placed my hand softly on his shoulder.

"Let's take care of that in the dressing room, okay?"

Malik breathed at a meditative pace as I carefully applied spirit gum remover to the fake beard as I straddled him in the chair.

"Remember the last play we did together? That one-act where the writer thought he was the next David

Mamet?" he asked with his eyes closed. The timber of his voice carried a sage-like serenity even in this hushed tone. "It was nothing but pages of the words *fuck* and *cunt* with no plot."

The details were a little sketchy in my mind. I played a prison nurse and Malik was a drug lord. The scenes were so poorly written we played in the unwritten elements and turned them into seduction scenes on opening night. The director hated it but the reviews said our scenes were the saving grace in an extremely flawed show. Malik also played the judge. He wore a beat-up gray beard that I helped remove every night for his other scenes. Maybe that's where this memory came from.

"You were brilliant in that. We just clicked on all levels. When Vivian cast you in this, I jumped at the chance to act with you again. I really haven't done too much acting recently. I make most of my money doing lights. I keep looking at those stagehands thinking that's where I need to be and not here. I've been rusty the past few rehearsals and I wanted to apologize for that."

He couldn't be serious. I'd never seen him so focused in my life. The idea that he might be struggling with the role never entered my mind. I'd been too busy watching him, not realizing how much farther we could go. Then again, I wasn't carrying the weight of this production on my shoulders by playing the title character.

"I had no idea you felt that way. Just think of how far you've come in less than a month."

"I can be better. We both know that and so does Vivian."

I pulled the last of his fake beard away from his face. Clean shaven, he looked just like he did when we first met. He opened his eyes, sat up, and placed his hands on my thighs. I lowered my hips so we were close enough that if I pursed my lips we would have kissed. His vulnerability radiated through me, and I broke up the intensity by pulling a loose strand of hair from the beard that was still stuck to his face.

"You know, Vivian said it might help if we just fucked."

Malik released an exasperated sigh and reclined back in the chair.

"The way she's been riding my ass every night she probably thought in some strange way it would help."

"Well, do you think it would, you know, help?"

His eyes danced at the thought of Vivian's suggestion. For the first time since he stepped into this role, I felt his openness, his vulnerability and his strength. I leaned in closer, wondering if I should make the first move, but Malik grabbed me by the back of my neck and pulled me into him. He caught me off guard but not for long. I slid my hand over and seized his cock. It had been over a year since I held him in my hands. This time I wasn't tipsy and I gasped as my fingers clamped around his girth.

"Oh fuck, Lara," he groaned and tilted his hips, forcing his hardness into the palm of my hand. With his mouth open in delight, I sealed our reunion with a kiss. He tugged at my gown, slipping his hands between the layers of soft material, and pulled down my sports bra. His sturdy fingers teased my taut nipples, turning my blood to lava. When I pulled open the gown to gain some relief, Malik engulfed one of my nipples with his warm mouth. He flicked his tongue on the sensitive tip as I blindly searched for his zipper. I was about to take him right here, but a figure in my peripheral vision forced me to snap my head toward the dressing room door.

"Now that's what I need to see more of onstage."

I had no idea how long Vivian had been watching, but the smirk on her face let me know she'd seen enough. I jumped out of Malik's lap and wrapped my gown around my exposed breasts. Vivian walked over to me.

"This Desdemona isn't some woeful chick awaiting her fate. She stands in defiance of her father for the love of a man. Not just any man, but a North African warrior. This is the night she claims her reward in the face of all that racist bullshit, and the audience needs to feel that. Sometimes it feels like you two are scared to touch each other, but I can see now that's not the problem."

I drooped my head like a schoolgirl who'd just gotten scolded.

"I'll give you two some time alone."

Vivian looked at me, and then shot a glare at Malik as she exited. The room dropped to a dead silence. I looked at Malik, who appeared broken. He gazed back at me with guilty eyes. I felt I should say something, but a balloon of embarrassment choked the words from coming out. I grabbed my purse, stormed out of our dressing room, and headed to the alley behind the theater.

I leaned against the cold metal fire door, smacking on a stick of gum, wishing it were a cigarette. The gum wasn't doing the trick. My eyes drifted over to a nearby liquor store. Just a few puffs would clear my head, but as I approached the glass door I caught my reflection. I hadn't taken off my stage makeup, and what I saw in front of me was the purest essence of royalty. Though slightly exaggerated for the stage, the strength of my appearance shocked me. This wasn't the role of girl next door or the lead's best friend that I'm usually cast in. This was a woman who deserved to reign with her handsome lord by her side, and I had yet to fully realize that. Desdemona will always be a classic Shakespearean tragic heroine, but until her demise, my Desdemona will live her life to the fullest. I headed back to the theater. We still had to finish this tech rehearsal tonight but tomorrow, when those curtains opened, I knew exactly what I had to do.

I kept my chatter down to a minimum in our dressing room, mainly due to preshow jitters, but Malik was a nervous tsunami of unfocused energy. During the rest of last night's technical run, we'd raised the bar to where any signs of worry had been erased from Vivian's mind. The scene in which he murdered me had gone so well everyone thought Malik had actually hurt me. I thought about waiting for Malik after the run but Vivian had some notes for him. Instead I went back to my hotel room alone and prepared myself to be taken by my husband onstage for the first time.

I performed my vocal warm-ups in our dressing room as I undressed, which brought Malik's gaze to my reflection. Normally I would've changed in the bathroom but I needed him to see what I was wearing. The sheer black bra and panties left nothing to the imagination. My hard nipples peeked over the top of the bra; the low cut of the cups was designed to create more cleavage.

His eyes soon locked on my pussy. I gently stroked my fingers against the cloth, allowing my wetness to absorb into the material so he could see the *V* I'd trimmed last night to entice him. I hooked my thumb into the elastic band, pulled forward, and let it slap back against my skin.

"How would you feel if I wore this tonight?"

He kept his eyes glued to my pussy as he stated, "If it makes you feel comfortable. Why not?"

"I guess you're right. The only person who gets to see this is you."

His hands fell into his lap in a failed attempt to cover his obvious hard-on. I slipped on my gown, making sure my eyes never left his, and watched as he attempted to tame his cock with the palm of his hand.

"Well, I'm off to get my wig done."

I sashayed over to his chair, stepped in front of him, placed my hands on his thighs, and gave him a soft kiss on the lips. I hovered momentarily, walking my fingers over the hand that pushed down his erection and giving him a squeeze. I smiled, daring him to react to my touch as my index finger slipped under his palm and found the bulge of his cockhead.

"Have a wonderful show, my Othello."

I giggled as I headed toward the door. Malik followed me with his eyes. The muscles in his forearm flexed as he continued to press down on his erection. I opened the door, blew him a kiss, and let the door to our dressing room slam behind me.

I was surprisingly calm as I waited in the wings. Malik had been on fire so far, lifting the intensity of his performance to a place I'd never seen before. There were points where I watched him in awe rather than preparing. As the lights faded, I took a moment to collect myself, and when my cue line was spoken, I waltzed onto the stage. The stage lights allowed me to feel intimate despite being in front of three hundred people.

"Othello!"

I raced behind him and embraced him in a coquettish way, just as directed. I traveled my hands down his body as I spoke my lines. I accented each line I spoke with the snap of a button from his shirt, exposing more of his bronze flesh to the audience. Then I nibbled on his ear, something I never did in rehearsal, and when my fingertips discovered his nipples, I pinched them.

"Oh fuck," he mumbled.

From the sound of his voice I knew that was coming from Malik and not Othello, so I pinched even harder. He threw his hands back, clawed my thighs, and I released his nipples with a snap of my fingers. He threw his body forward, grabbing the back of the chair in front of him. I heard the wood of the chair creak as he gripped it, trying to maintain some semblance of control. I followed the blocking and stepped backward to the bed. He let go of the chair and approached me with desperation, but an open hand slap to his bare chest stopped him. I took one more step back and awaited his line.

"Tonight I'm honored you've allowed yourself to be my queen."

"And the heavens will sing our praises as I claim you as my king."

I opened the mesh that surrounded the bed, grabbed him by the belt buckle, and pulled him inside. Even though there were hundreds of people watching us, as soon as the lights changed they would see nothing but our shadows. When the front lights dimmed, he yanked open my gown and saw the surprise I'd been waiting to give to him. This scene needed to be performed in my most natural state. I'd taken off my lingerie after my wig was finished. With his mouth agape, seemingly still in shock at my nakedness, I grabbed his hand and placed it on my bare pussy.

"Slip your fingers inside of me, my warrior prince," I whispered.

He hesitated but we didn't have time. I had less than two minutes to improvise in between the blocking of this scene to get what I needed. Malik was still in shock so I held his hand steady and lowered myself onto his strong stiff fingers. The girth of his digits had me stuffed. The fact that a packed audience was witnessing this turned me on even more. I used the base of his wrist as a fulcrum until I found the perfect angle to force his fingers to brush against my spot. I writhed my hips as my pent-up energy flowed onto his sturdy hand. I held off the urge to come, gliding my fingers under his and coating them with my juices before placing those glistening digits into his open mouth. The lights faded to an evening blue, leaving us completely in silhouette. The sound of his lips smacking on my fingers teased my ears.

"I can't believe you're doing this," he moaned as he weaved his tongue between my sticky fingers, savoring every drop.

I had to be conscious of how much time we had. The next part required a simulated blow job. As the lights transitioned to a darker blue I knew I had to hurry. He slipped his fingers deeper inside me. I bit my bottom lip to muffle my squeals of pleasure before carefully pulling his fingers from my pussy. I got on my knees and tore away at his belt buckle. Malik eagerly unzipped his pants. All he had to do was stand and watch, but the taste of my pussy seemed to lift him beyond the planned choreography.

He yanked down his pants. Only a thin layer of cotton, already soaked with a glisten of precome, separated my lips from the outline of his beautifully designed cock. I pulled his underwear down to his thighs. Even in this dim light his cock looked glorious.

Malik draped his shirt off his shoulders, obstructing the shadow of my face from the audience. I wrapped my fingers around his girth and ran the tip of my tongue along his glans, savoring his taste and allowing the motions of my head to give him the illusion that I would eventually take him into my mouth.

I raised my eyes to see the hunger in his. His stomach muscles flexed out of control as sweat trickled down his body. I wanted him to get to the point where the needs of Malik and Othello became one. At the rolling of my tongue around the head, he attempted to thrust his cock deeper into my mouth, but I pulled away just in time.

I grabbed his shirt and led him back to the bed just as we were directed. This is where Malik was supposed to climb on top of me, but he had no intention of following that plan. Instead he tossed me on the bed and before I could lift my head, he planted his mouth on my needy cunt. His tongue invaded my slickened sex. An elated howl exploded from my mouth, filling the immense theater just as the music swelled. I clawed at the cheap cotton sheets as I wrapped my legs around his head, mashing his mouth flush to my pussy. I gripped the back of Malik's head, forcing his tongue to go deeper into me. It would be so easy to get lost in the magnificence of his educated tongue but the lights mixed from blue to a royal purple, which signaled the next transition we needed to make.

I hooked my fingers through his coarse hair and snapped his head up. We were reaching the apex of this scene. If he lingered any longer I wouldn't get what I needed—and what Malik deserved as my warrior husband—before the lights faded to black.

He trailed his tongue up my body. His speed let me know he was also aware of our limited time as he sealed his journey up my flesh with a kiss. I tasted myself in his mouth, which lifted my desire. The lack of the fake beard allowed me to feel the full intensity of his lips. Our hands were frantic, exploring each other's bodies in possession-filled lust until the head of his cock landed at the opening of my eager pussy. I felt the head of his cock at the precipice of entering me. As his stomach contracted, I placed my hand on his chest and gently whispered in his ear, "Not yet."

I pulled him down onto the bed next to me and with all the strength I could muster, climbed on top of him. Somehow our actions had now come back to the original choreography. I reached between my legs and grabbed his cock. The anticipation on his face sparked as I lifted my hips, but instead of placing his cock inside me, I laid it flat and lowered my pussy on his unyielding shaft.

A groan of desperation freed itself from Malik's body as I glided my sex along the length of his hardness. Each sleek pass elevated my need to have him in me. I threw my head to the sky as pants of desire were flung from my mouth. Soon the sound of my own sticky wetness matched the thunderous drums of the score. The urge to feel him inside me erupted to the point of fervent need. I lifted my hips, aimed his cock to where I needed him to be, and slowly dropped my hips, allowing him to fill me up.

The sturdy head of his cock brushed past my most sensitive spot. I dug my fingernails into his chest and freed myself of any constraints as I fucked him in front of a full and attentive audience. The brilliance of Vivian's direction was always clear to me. In silhouette, the audience didn't see a North African man and a Venetian woman, or even a black man and a white woman. What they saw was two people making love to celebrate their passion for each other. However, this moment completely belonged to me. Tonight, the zealous lust that I'd carried for Malik took over and I claimed him as my own.

The music crescendoed to a volume where anything I screamed wouldn't be heard as I rode the upsurge of my building orgasm. A few more valiant thrusts from his mighty cock were guaranteed to make me come, but the music and lights faded, leaving us in a sweaty cocoon of darkness as I grasped at how close I was to a resounding orgasm. We heard the stagehands rapidly approaching to move the set for the next scene. I grabbed his cock, glided him out of my pussy, and gave him a gentle kiss on the cheek. I gathered my costume around my naked body and headed to the wings on weak legs, knowing we had an entire show to complete.

The standing ovation the play received fueled my excitement as we stood in costume, greeting the audience. Malik stood at the opposite end of the lobby, but his eyes would occasionally drift toward me. My insides were still fluttering. I attempted to focus on the two elderly women in front of me who kept saying that they had never seen Desdemona played with this much strength. They had just asked me to autograph their programs, something I rarely get asked to do, when I felt a presence standing behind me.

"That was perfect," Vivian stated. I turned around to see her smiling face and before I could respond she embraced me. "Well, somebody was having a lot of fun out there tonight. Now let's see if you two can recreate that for tomorrow's matinee."

She let go of me and took a step back. I forced a smile, snapping my eyes over to Malik for a second. He caught my gaze and flashed me a smile before returning to the audience members standing in front of him. Vivian headed over to Malik. The smile on her face let me know she was happy about his performance as well. The idea of having him tomorrow onstage was exciting but tonight, after the cast party, I planned to allow Malik to have me for as long as he needed, with no time restraints.

AVA RECEIVES
A TEXT

Ella Dawson

I want you to use me, Julian texted me at 9:31 p.m. on Tuesday. *I want you to do whatever you want to me.*

I sat up straighter at my dining room table. A promotion strategy document was open on my laptop, half-finished and several hours overdue for my boss's approval. I'd assumed Julian was off doing something similarly rote and depressing with his evening. Maybe that was how he made slogging away at the firm tolerable: working on Excel reports with the occasional light sexting break. Funny, I'd always imagined him as more of the listening-to-politics-podcasts kind of guy.

I read his last two texts again but they didn't change. It was such an innocuous message to throw me off in the grand scheme of dirty texts: *I want you to do whatever you want to me.* What did I want to do to this man?

Most men were all about what they were going to do to you and how much you were going to like it. It wasn't entirely their fault: even I was used to thinking about what I wanted someone to do to me. That would have been an easier question to answer: I wanted Julian to push me against the brick wall outside of my apartment, shove my skirt up my hips, and fuck me hard, praying no one would notice us in the shadows beyond the streetlights. What did I want to do to him? I drew a blank.

I like that, I responded, bluffing. I was very aware that I was writing marketing copy in my pajamas at my IKEA dining table while my roommate practiced audition songs in her bedroom. Julian was handing control to me across hundreds of digital miles, a power transfer from DC to Brooklyn, and I had no idea what I liked. Some sexually empowered woman I was turning out to be.

The little typing bubble popped up, and I eyed it on my iMessage app window, resting absurdly next to the color-coded Google spreadsheet. *Tell me what to do.*

Oh great, now creative thought was required of me.

Don't move, I texted him. That seemed like a good place to start. I could imagine it, too: Julian sitting in bed clutching his cell phone, the early stirrings of an erection straining at his boxer briefs. I hadn't seen his apartment yet but I already suspected it was gorgeous, a small but beautiful one-bedroom in a historic Georgetown brownstone. Just him all alone in that square footage, idly playing with his dick as he waited for me to reply.

Or maybe he was at some bar with colleagues, sneaking glances at his phone while they discussed the markets. I had no way of knowing and it sent a shiver through my forearms, nerves tightening with thrill. It was easy to picture that, too: him standing in some cluster of finance bros dressed up in light summer suits and loosened ties. They'd have no idea what he was thinking, what he wanted me to do to him. Those preppy motherfuckers with their yields and dividends and all that terminology I couldn't remember from my Econ 101 course taken eight million years ago.

OK I won't, he responded.

I felt a queer trickle of power pinging up the nerves in my spine. He was waiting for me to offer further instruction. Nothing came to mind after a decade of hoping and preening and delicately inquiring about some unresponsive idiot's whereabouts via text message. It felt like some feminist failure to admit it, even to myself, but I wasn't used to being in charge. I knew what I wanted, but I didn't know what I wanted to take.

Fuck, he texted me next, and I could hear it in his voice, that breathless spurt of narration he always shared, even outside of a sexual context. Julian was a talker, extroverted and loud at cafeteria dinners and dormitory wine-and-cheese nights. It never bothered me back at school because he greeted the world with such enthusiasm and openness, the polar opposite of New York cynicism. I heard the text as if it were a helpless announcement, his throat dry. I still remembered hearing it in person despite the layers of postgrad life coated over the memory. He said it right into my ear like a plea.

Shut the fuck up, I typed, hitting SEND before my confidence failed me.

Before I had the time to doubt myself, he said, *OK sorry.* And then he waited.

Julian and I met during our sophomore year at

Liberal University. He lived down the hall in a double room with a lacrosse bro named Peter whom I hated instinctually. Unlike his looming roommate, Julian got along with everyone, full of wide grins and a kindness that I couldn't help but trust. I assumed a guy like that had a girlfriend and I wasn't wrong, there was some girl back home in Virginia who sent him elaborate care packages every few weeks. When they eventually broke up, there was another girl with the same affinity for arts and crafts. Julian retained the sweetness that most men had beaten out of them in high school.

We didn't become real friends until our senior year, when he was finally just Julian and I understood that good things were usually temporary. I had a night of him all to myself, eight giddy hours on his regulation double bed. It was the rare one-night stand that didn't leave me depleted the next morning. I walked home across campus to my apartment feeling warm and whole. And then he moved to DC and I settled down in Brooklyn, wrapped in a new, bullshit Pinterest board of a relationship that spread its depletion out over time. And now I was single again and Julian was texting me and I had an Amtrak ticket to DC in my email inbox.

Julian was still waiting for instruction. I fished for ideas.

Where are you? I asked—curiosity was getting to me.

At home.

That was a bit of a letdown. I liked the idea of him in public attempting to hide what he was up to. He had such a transparent face; how much he wanted me would be all over him.

At home all alone thinking about me?
Yes.

It was darkly funny: in three simple letters, Julian offered more clarity and validation than anything my ex had said in a year and a half of dating. The idea of him sitting by himself on what I'm sure was some expensive—also known as "not purchased at IKEA"—sofa, attention glued to his phone, eager and desperate for whatever I was about to say... I could work with that.

You're not allowed to touch yourself, I said. *I don't think you deserve to.* Nervous giggles flared up my throat and I bit my knuckle, glancing at my roommate's door. It would be generous and inaccurate to call me a naturally authoritative person.

Oh god, he replied.

I picked up my laptop and ducked into my room, closing the door behind me. When religious deities were invoked, it was time to get a room.

Do you understand me? I asked once I settled down on my bed. That same giddy anxiety bubbled within me—I imagined putting it in a box, wrapping it up tight, and shoving it under the bed.

Yes I do thank you.

Holy fuck, now he was thanking me. Nice guy Julian from down the hall was thanking me for telling him he wasn't allowed to touch himself. This was surreal.

Good.

I searched my brain for something else to say. My regrettable binge of the *Fifty Shades* series all those summers ago had taught me nothing useful: the only scene I retained was some grotesque incident in a bathroom involving a tampon. I was in foreign territory.

But maybe I was thinking about this the wrong way . . . Julian hadn't asked me to recreate some mass-produced fantasy from the grocery-store book selection. He'd asked me to do whatever I wanted. And what I wanted, what I always wanted, was to know exactly where I stood. I wanted to be texted back, immediately, and with the correct response. I wanted to be respected—no, I wanted to be worshipped. I wanted my ego dipped in honey and licked clean by someone who adored me.

You won't get anything if you don't beg.

I bit at my thumbnail as I watched my text deliver, wondering if I'd pushed his boundaries. Dynamics like this required sober, honest discussion, not digital fumbling in the dark. I knew that much from cobbled-together sex education and smirk-riddled conversations over brunch at the dining hall. Scaring him off wouldn't be great when my Amtrak ticket was nonrefundable.

Yesss I want to beg for it, he texted back.

Jackpot.

My skin burned and it had little to do with embarrassment anymore. I sank down into the mattress, all of a sudden way too hot under my sweatpants and stolen Henley tee. I toed out of my socks as I read his new text, just one word: *Please.*

Another memory resurfaced across the expanse of other fucks and confessions: listening to Julian lose control as he climaxed, his hand furled around the cheap headboard. The memory of the nonsense that came pouring out of his mouth when he finished followed me for months after that, interrupting other flings that paled in comparison to his vocal fireworks.

"Please please yes Ava yes oh god you feel so fucking good please I'm close so close I'm gonna come oh please oh please—"

I will beg for it, Julian wrote in the present. This was part of a pattern: if I took too long to respond, he would just keep going without me. It was impatient, bratty behavior that I had no desire to correct. *I will beg to touch you, I want to touch you so bad.*

How much?

So much Ava I think about it all the time.

My eyebrows rose. *It?*

You I think about you all the time.

I pushed my sweatpants over my hips and abandoned them to the mess of clothing at the foot of my bed. I felt a little high, my attention narrowed to a dangerous point. He thought about me all the time, and the images that conjured lit me up like a bottle rocket: Julian sitting at his desk at some boutique firm, wetting his lips when he got distracted. Julian tugging at his cock as he stood in the shower in the morning, water beading across his wide shoulders. Julian waiting for me right now, desperate to touch himself, desperate for my next word.

It was the desperation that got me wet, showing through in how fast he answered every message, in how he must have written and deleted and rewritten that initial text so many times, the one that started this all off. If Julian's turn-on was giving up control, mine was teasing and taunting, secure in the knowledge he wasn't going anywhere. The cockier I was, the harder he got. The more demanding I was, the more he wanted me.

I thought about him, too, all the time—not only

these last few weeks but across the years, with memories sneaking up on me as my ex cooked lasagna and gaslit me out of my confidence. A handful of hours with the gorgeous guy down the hall, destined to be someone else's special someone, a girl nicer and blander and skilled with an Instagram filter. I'd thought about how he kissed down my stomach, nose nudging between my thighs. He got off on that, on how I squirmed and wrapped my fingers through his dark hair. He insisted on getting me off, wide eyes watching my face shatter and collapse as I came hard and drunk, mewling my desire and release. I thought about him all the fucking time and never thought I'd get him back, too kind and simple for my jagged edges. I'd read us both wrong.

But I didn't tell him that.

That's what I thought, I replied. It required a few edits to get all the grammar correct, as one of my hands had found its way south. I was wetter than I expected, my fingers coming away thickly coated. *Maybe if you impress me I'll let you taste me.*

Please please that's all I want.

Please was quickly becoming my favorite word.

I bet that's what you want, you desperate little whore. I stared at my message for a few terrified seconds before pressing SEND. In for a penny, in for a slur.

Any doubts I had that I'd gone too far were immediately assuaged. *Oh fuck Ava.*

Two of my fingers sank into my tight and soaking cunt. I bit my lip to smother a groan, frustrated that I was in a tiny shit-box of an apartment in New York, hundreds of miles from the man I wanted, who was desperate desperate *desperate* for me to use him. I wanted to ride him. I wanted to shove my hand over his mouth and grind down on him until I was someone else, strong and hard and benevolently vicious. I could hear his overwhelmed, smothered cries, his lips wet under my palm. I wanted to pull up and feel every inch of his dick as it slid out of me and then hover there, feel my weight on my thighs as he whimpered. I would tease the head of his cock, circle around it but refuse to sink down onto him. I'd wait, pull my hand away and wait until he begged. *Please please please Ava I need you I need you I need you.* And then I would take what I wanted.

I'd taken too long to text him again. *I'm so hard please,* he begged.

No. The word felt like that first sip of white wine at the end of a long day. *I get to touch you. You aren't allowed to touch yourself.*

Fuck okay.

Do I need to tie your wrists down so that you'll behave yourself?

I won't touch myself I promise.

I noted his lack of enthusiasm where bondage was concerned and sucked a string of juice from my fingers. I wasn't in any rush to get off. Soon I'd have three days for him to drag every possible orgasm from my body. This little game of cat and mouse was much more fun than easy relief.

If you do anything I tell you not to, I'll make you watch while I play with myself.

No—and then a few seconds later—*I want it please.*

I know you do, baby, but I want you to wait.

Can I keep watching? This conversation had become increasingly meta but I had no fucking complaints.

Yes. I'll be mad if you look away. That weird, mirthless giggle escaped my mouth again and I grinned through it.

Fuck how could I?

I'd make quite a sight, sprawled back on his sofa with my thighs splayed open. My arousal would trickle down my thighs and onto the upholstery. There'd be no gooey smile on Julian's face now, his jaw hanging slack and desperate, *desperate* to touch me and to touch himself.

You aren't allowed to touch anything without my permission.

I want to touch myself so bad but I haven't I swear.

Good boy. The condescension tasted so goddamn good. *You've been so good for me. Do you want to come?*

Oh yes please.

You've been so well behaved for me tonight.

Fuck fuck fuck fuck . . .

It was temping to draw it out even farther. It would be so easy to exact vengeance on this sweet kid for every disrespectful slight other men had subjected me to. But this wasn't about being mean, it was about play. It was about making Julian feel good by denying him what he wanted.

He was probably weeping with precome by now, his knuckles white. I could see his knotted brow, his pink tongue darting out to wet chapped lips. My little slut, eager to be used and commanded and fucked. *Ava please,* he wrote, and I fucked myself with my fingers, wondering if I would ever say or hear that word again without feeling wet and sinful. *Please I want to be good for you.*

The man wanted to be good for me. Me: Ava Greenspan, marketing associate and ex-girlfriend galore. The *hot mess text me back don't leave me* Queen of Bushwick, hissing as I hit that spot inside of me that made my eyes shutter closed. I bit my lip and tasted blood. I let myself go. He could wait, wait for me to shudder and snap and cry out and break. He'd still be there when I was done. He wasn't going anywhere.

For a while, the only word on my mind was *please*, not desire but exultation.

Such a good boy, I said after sucking my fingers clean. The words didn't come as easily now that the haze of desire was lifting, but I clung to the film of authority while I sent my instructions. *I want you to come for me, Julian.*

Yes thank you finally . . .

Shut the fuck up and listen to me. He didn't respond and that was probably less out of obedience and more because his hands were occupied. *I want you to imagine my hands tight in your hair, yanking your head back as I fuck you hard and fast. I'm dripping wet and hot and tight around you. I want you to come for me and I want you to thank me for it when you finish, you pathetic fucking whore. You're mine. Do you understand that? You're mine now.*

And then I waited. It didn't take long. *Oh my fucking god Ava.*

I let the smirk I'd been fighting all night take over my face and tucked myself under the covers. *Good boy,* I said again.

Thank you.

We were quiet for a while after that. I reached for

a Kleenex from the tissue box on my bedside table and wiped myself off, too lazy to get up and take a shower. I was always wide-awake after having sex but getting myself off always made me sleepy, bones loose and heavy in my body. My unsteady fingers found the lamp and switched it off. I was just closing my eyes when my iPhone came back to life.

Thank you so much, Ava.

I snorted. It seemed correct grammar and punctuation had returned.

For what? I asked.

For being someone I can trust. He didn't elaborate right away but I knew he would eventually. And he did. *I've never gone there with someone before and I appreciate that you won't judge me for it.*

Is this something you've never explored?

There was another long silence, thick with what I knew was coming. Gentle, earnest Julian lying spent on the sofa, moonlight streaming in through the floor-to-ceiling windows, his cock flaccid against his thigh. I hadn't seen him in two years but I knew every inch of his face. I couldn't wait to see it contort and tighten, teeth bared, voice hoarse. He'd never stop talking even when I told him to. And I didn't want him to. That was what I wanted: to hear him beg and gasp and scream. I wanted to tease him until he admitted he couldn't take it anymore. I wanted him to want every single inch of me.

Not yet, but I want to with you. I know that I can with you.

That woke me up more than anything else. I'd been the one stretching out my hand so many times before. I knew how petrifying it was to offer all your weaknesses and wants to someone and just hope, just pray, that they wouldn't fuck you over. It had been a long time since someone extended that level of trust to me. This wasn't a free-for-all, a vacation from my self-esteem at the mercy of some asshole I'd never see again. This was Julian, and I liked him. And he respected me.

Thank you for trusting me, I said, and for the first time all night I didn't think I'd expressed what I wanted to. But it would have to do.

I'll see you on Friday at 8? I made reservations at 8:30 somewhere you'll like.

It was a night of two firsts: I'd called a man a "desperate little whore," and someone had made dinner reservations for me.

Yup, I'll see you then. After I hit SEND, I put my iPhone in airplane mode and shoved it under a pillow. I was in danger; I could feel it creeping up around my ankles like ivy. Miles and miles away, I was sure Julian felt the same way.

Oh well. It seemed I had some shopping to do. I needed a dress appropriate for what I felt sure was a very nice restaurant, the kind of place a young financier would take his woman, and something to wear underneath to make him quiver. Or maybe I wouldn't wear anything underneath at all. I couldn't wait to hear him say *please*.

ONCE UPON
A TIME IN THE
NEAR FUTURE

Georgina Cott

I doubt if I'll ever get used to traveling in a private jet. My husband, Jed, isn't quite wealthy enough yet to own this one outright—but he does have a one-third share.

I'm flying at thirty thousand feet, apparently, but emotionally it's still Sunday.

For everyone else on board, i.e., the staff, this is Monday and I'm flying to the only clinic in the world where the Skinink treatment is available.

Skinink, so the brochures say, enables the ultimate sexual experience, without surgery, without medication, without mechanical intervention, without doubt. The ultimate.

I imagine Jed has spent big to make this preliminary meeting happen for me.

There are brochures to read and a video to watch before landing.

I ought to be excited and I am, but more from memories of last night and this morning.

Whenever I'm going to travel without Jed he buys me a small gift. This time it was very small, a pair of black cotton panties. He got down on his knees and held them out for me to step into. Then, with his hands on my butt, he kissed me with a persistent intensity that took my breath away.

I can still feel that kiss now.

I try to get back to the brochure. Skinink, it is claimed, enables the ultimate prolonged sexual tease leading to a seismic orgasm, which, it is suggested, is repeatable via countless variations. Even the time span of the orgasm can be selected—also the texture and color.

My thoughts skip out of the brochure and back to last night when Jed whispers the word "Skinink" in my ear and then, and only then, lets me come. The word colors, fizzes, and laces its way all through my orgasm and distracts. I crash-land early, short of the anticipated splendor, thinking he must have pulled some deal to get me in on it.

He wouldn't use Skinink as a baseless tease, so I think he must know something. It could even be my birthday treat.

His kisses, hard and inappropriate given my heightened sensitivity, stop my rush of questions. This is unlike him. Rough foreplay is one thing. I'm fine with that, but this isn't foreplay. I've already come. This is supposed to be afterglow time, with Jed taking his pleasure through the long slow descent out of fantasy and back to the real world.

But the pace picks up further as Jed presses a hand over my mouth while the other reaches for the bedside drawer and the gag tape.

He tapes my mouth shut, one-two-three-four strips of tape plastered on.

Passion deepens the blue of his eyes, revealing glimpses of a scary determination. And then I realize— this is a new tease. He's planted this Skinink word in my head then gagged me to prevent questions. So now he'll tie me up and leave me to wonder.

He gets off the bed and hauls ropes and tapes from the play-box.

I relax a little now that I think I know what he's going to do, and lie still, naked, watching. I'm not even tied up yet but wouldn't feel any more vulnerable if I were spread-eagled.

Retreating wisps from the ragged orgasm wave good-bye as high-speed feelings race off into uncertainty. I'm wondering when and how he's going to take his pleasure. His dick looks more than ready.

There is no sign of retreat in his eyes as he flicks the duvet off the bed.

We stare at each other as he binds my wrists together then pulls them above my head, securing them to the headboard without grace or consideration.

He kisses the tape tighter on my lips with a savage outburst of unbridled passion then blindfolds me with a scarf.

Darkness. I'm nervous again.

He ropes and ties my left ankle to the bedpost.

I'm okay with being spread wide, helpless, but a question mark attaches to the "Okay?" when he says, "I'm going to shave you."

My right leg instinctively moves across to protect myself but he grabs the ankle ropes and tugs it toward the bedpost.

We have a safe code. Even when gagged, blindfolded, and helpless, if I make three rehearsed sounds close together, it stops the fantasy.

The words "I'm going to shave you" circle in uncertain skies.

He shoves a pillow under my butt. I hear water running into a bowl.

Decision time. There's a long, long pause, an opportunity to stop what's going to happen next.

The uncertainty is almost overwhelming. The pillow under my hips offers me up. I have a prominent mound forested by black hair. I haven't been naked there since I was a girl.

I want his mouth, his tongue, his passion to explore me.

I remain silent, hear the snip, feel the cold metal of the scissors against me and the occasional warmth of his fingers, but never in the place wanted.

As he washes me, the palm of his hand presses hard in the way he knows I like. But his fingers border on sadistic in their inquisitive gentleness.

I writhe despite the ropes; a groan escapes despite the gag.

When he uses a shaving brush, the cream is cold or maybe I am hot. The brush makes brisk, circular motions with varying degrees of frustrating pressure. Then there's a long pause in the darkness before the first touch of the razor and the delicate sound of its scrape in the otherwise total silence. A subdued splash of water follows each razor stroke, intensified by the quiet.

When finished without a nick or mishap, he washes me again, then dries me with a soft towel, chaste.

I am truly naked, vulnerable, helpless, and completely at the mercy of the man I love.

Then a pause. I'm relieved the shaving is over and speculate again on what he will do next. I hear him taking away the bowl. Getting rid of the water. Taking his time.

I think—*hope*—he's going to fuck me now. Jed must be surfing on the crest of frustration, a superb balancing act. I want him inside me.

He kneels on the bed between my legs, then his hands are under my buttocks lifting me up, ropes or no ropes. Then he starts snogging me hard and strong as his tongue is fucking me. The strength of his hands is irresistible. The ropes are tightened even more and hurting but I don't care. The delirium of pleasure overcomes the discomfort.

I am soaring up the mountain as if riding a jet-powered cable car but then he drops me at the last moment back onto the bed. I'm throbbing, blushing between my legs, and if it weren't for the gag I'd have been begging.

I let out a groan of indignant irritation, frustration, and anger. He tears the tape from my mouth and pulls the scarf from my eyes.

Blinking in the light, I'm shocked to see how angry he is, how fierce. Even his dick looks threatening.

"Silence or you get spanked."

Uncertainty floods back but ebbs when the kisses are gentle, persuasive, though my lips are slightly sticky from the tape. These are not the best kisses I've ever had but the return of his gentleness is intoxicating.

One hand is working to release the knots while the other leaves warmth and pleasure wherever it touches.

He breaks the kiss, gets off the bed, releases my ankles. "Get up. Turn around and kneel."

I kneel in the center of the bed, nervous. It can't be a spanking because I haven't made a sound. He never cheats.

Jed leaves me and I watch as he fetches a wooden pole from under the bed. This is new.

"Now spread your knees as far as you can."

I drop forward doggie-style and move my knees apart.

"More."

Jed ropes my spread ankles to rings in the bar and I realize where this is heading.

He takes my wrists and guides them between my legs so that I topple forward, my cheek on the bed with my butt offered up, enormous and vulnerable.

I have never been in this position before, never so utterly vulnerable.

As he's tugging and tying wrists to ankles, I'm considering use of the safe code. But raw excitement fights against this. I cannot move. I want to ask about Skinink. I want to be fucked. I am so come ready, a puff of breath between my legs would trigger me.

His hands are moving up the backs of my legs, fingers fanning out over my butt, and then his love finger, torturer in chief, moves down through my crack, making me twitch.

There's something he does with his fingertip that works every time. It takes me to the razor line and leaves me there. And each time I'm confident that I will be able to just nudge against his exquisite fingertip enough to send me hurtling through to the next unique orgasm.

But he's not going to let me come. As the fingertip approaches my clit, my breathing gets ragged. It arrives, and as he touches me, time takes time off to watch for a moment and then—mission accomplished. Jed leaves me dangling there.

With this intensity of teasing I want the gag, need it. "Gag me." And now I'm going to get spanked into the bargain because I spoke out loud and asked for it.

I've irritated him. His actions are quick as he searches among all the ropes for what I know will be the ball gag. It's not my favorite and he knows it, but I don't care. I want him to realize that I can do the unexpected, even when helpless.

He pinches my nose roughly as if I'm resisting, shoves the ball into my mouth when I have to gasp for air, buckling the strap at the back of my head.

"Six," he says. And I get three on each buttock quick and hard, scarcely a pause between the sound of each slap.

Call that a spanking?

"Skinink." It was the last word he said to me Sunday night.

His finger returns, finds me, sets me off like a firework even as his dick slides into me. I jerk him off in moments with what little movement I have. My second orgasm is a shock. I don't often do second orgasms. It's wonderful. Sometimes an orgasm takes me to another planet, into a medical spasm or on a deep-sea dive. They're never the same. This one is like a ride through a hailstorm.

Afterward, he kisses my ass and then releases me almost as quickly as he'd restrained me. Much as I love bondage, after we've come I'm done with it and just want to get free and dive into the afterglow.

In the darkness, there are no words, just kisses, touches, warmth, sporadic outbursts of passion as we tumble down toward sleep.

"Lady Glencorra, would you like to order now?"

The words shake me awake. It's Monday again and I'm on the plane.

The steward is offering me a menu as I open my eyes. "Here is the lunch menu. May I bring you something to drink while you decide?"

I order a vodka and tonic. Movement makes me realize my panties are wet from the daydream. I don't care.

I watch the video as I eat.

Skinink is a transparent, electrically charged spray. It's temporary, lasting about twelve hours. It can respond to all kinds of stimuli, from sound to touch to variations in light and temperature. They call it the ultimate tease, renewable, repeatable, variable.

A scene shows a lover playing the guitar and the effect it is having on a naked woman.

But Jed doesn't play the guitar, he plays me.

The voiceover is quick to point out that it could just as easily be a famous rock star playing the guitar via the hi-fi speakers or through headphones.

I pause the video.

Last night we fell into an "unhappy" sleep.

Jed is rarely restless. Sleep to him is like diving head-long down a six-hour sleep chute that automatically tumbles him out into the morning needing nothing more than a shower, clothes, a comb, and food.

But this morning he wouldn't talk about Skinink at all other than to say that all my questions will be answered on the plane. We aren't committed. Nothing signed. It's my decision. A chance to be one of the first. The envy of everyone. The ultimate.

As he was leaving for the office, I said, "Jed, what's wrong?"

His deep-blue eyes showed hesitation. I knew he wanted to say something but stopped himself. "Nothing's wrong. Didn't you like last night?"

And he was out of reach again. Just like now.

On the plane, after lunch, the brochures have been read and the video watched. We'll be landing within the hour.

I use our private cell phone without much hope, but surprisingly, he answers. I'm tongue-tied for a second but say, "Jed, listen, don't think I'm ungrateful but Skinink isn't for me . . . "

He lets out a sigh.

" . . . Jed, I watched the video and realized something I've known pretty much ever since we met. You are my Skinink. A million dollars wouldn't improve what we've got. Don't be disappointed."

"Disappointed? I'm relieved."

The rich warmth of his voice is a stroke of pleasure.

"Corra, I wanted to offer you the ultimate, the thing everyone's talking about, the best money could buy. But then I thought what if Skinink could give you everything? They claim you might never need a partner again. Guess that's why I was angry with myself and maybe went too far. I got this voice in my head, goading 'What if this is the last time?' I should've handled it better."

"Jed, I loved Sunday night and everything that happened."

"Me too. Corra, why not stay on the plane when you land to refuel and come right back?"

A flood of possibilities overwhelms me.

In the pause he says, "I'll clear my diary, today and tomorrow . . . "

"Jed, that might not be enough time . . . "

He laughs.

" . . . but it will do. Okay, maybe I'll be the angry one this time, pick up where we left off?"

"Sure." He laughs again but I'm serious.

"I'll send you instructions, Jed."

The return journey is much more interesting, while I'm planning what to do with him, if I dare.

I change into my gray business suit to show serious intent but underneath the panties remain.

The house is silent when I get back. I'd sent the instructions off quickly so I couldn't change my mind, but now my heart is racing and my bravado faltering.

Jed might jump out at me at any moment and take control.

If he's obeyed he should be in the bedroom.

I walk upstairs slowly, letting my heels sound loud and proud on the marble staircase.

I push the door open and stand in the doorway, and my heart leaps at the magnificent beauty of him.

Jed is standing on the padded bench seat at the foot of our four-poster bed, his back against a post, blindfolded, naked except for the white swim briefs I won't let him wear to the beach.

He is superbly, cruelly erect. He has cuffed his hands behind the post and the tape on his mouth is much harsher than I would have dared. There's a bottle of champagne in a bucket of ice and a roll of tape on a small table. Our play-box is nearby. Everything as instructed.

I walk toward him, noting that the ice is still fresh so he can't have been "captive" for long.

The tight black blindfold is excellent because I can look at him, study him, not just the white bulge but the muscle tone of his chest and abs, the width of his shoulders—and I can touch, I can cause, not just respond.

And the height of the bench is wickedly correct. I thought it would be. With my hands on his hips I kiss the white briefs, slowly at first. The head of his dick shows above the merciless grip of the briefs. As my tongue defines and maps it, the cuff-chain rattles as he writhes and grunts. I snog him hard until he squirms.

I step back. "Take the handcuffs off and get down." My voice has an unfamiliar husk, my heart an alien rhythm. The handcuffs are the first we ever bought, just a toy, self-releasing.

I grip his arm and guide him off the bench.

"Now you will do as I say. Keep your hands to yourself unless directed otherwise. The blindfold stays on. Kneel down in front of me."

He obeys.

"Take off my skirt."

I take a step forward and his hands reach around me, feeling my butt. "Do it slowly."

He finds the zip, starts to draw it down but misses

the clasp on the waistband so his attempt turns into a clumsy tug that gets nowhere.

I slap his head and we are both shocked, but I manage to say in a firm, calm voice, which in no way reflects how I'm feeling, "There's a clasp at the top."

He finds it and the skirt gives and is coaxed over my hips. I love the feel of his slow hands on my thighs. I step out of the skirt, kicking it away, and lose my jacket and blouse, throwing them after it.

He listens.

"Take my panties off, Jed. I'm wearing two pairs, especially for you. Take them off one at a time and hand them to me."

He seems unsure but then his fingertips trace my belly and find the hipster waistband of the first pair. As he peels them down I think he is going to kiss me. "Don't." The word stops him. I step out of the panties. His hands grope around the floor and he picks them up and offers them to me.

I rip the tape from his mouth. He winces but makes no sound.

"Now you may kiss me, Jed. You may kiss me as hard and as soft as you like. I will let you know when to stop…" I am determined to not make a sound but when the assault of his mouth and lips on the thin, tight material begins, I let out an involuntary groan. His hands are on my butt, pressing me onto his face with delicious force, like an animal that has my scent.

I'd been wet and turned on before, but now it's getting out of hand.

I catch a bunch of hair and pull his head back off me. "Now take them off."

With some difficulty because they are so damp and so tight, he tugs them down and hands them to me.

"Thank you, Jed. Now open your mouth wide."

There's a brief wry smile before he obeys. I bunch the panties together and stuff them slowly into his mouth saying, "One tiny pair would never have been enough, would it?" I put tape over his mouth and kiss it tight. "Now get back against the post."

I guide him back up, turn him around, and say, "Hands behind." I get onto the bed and cinch his wrists together with a long length of rope, using the spare to wrap around the post.

I've tied him up before but he always gets away. Turn my back and he's free and then, hey, I'm the prisoner— but not this time.

I use another rope to pull his shoulders back against the post. He ties me this way too sometimes and it makes my breasts stick out and causes my nipples to tighten.

I bind his thighs to the post just below the bulge of his briefs, and then secure his ankles.

He now knows, if he didn't know it before, the only escape will be the one I grant. I knot the last rope and then go around front to look at him.

Truly magnificent. A captured hero from ancient mythology and I am the goddess.

He has the taste of me in his mouth. His eyes and his body are helpless.

I take pity on his dick, pulling the briefs off it so it springs free. I grope his balls and fetch them up over the elastic so they are on display. He does this to my breasts sometimes, getting them out of my bra so they rest on the cups.

His balls are hard and ripe. They are beautiful to touch with fingertips, lips, mouth, and tongue.

He gives a restricted thrust into my mouth, and I think he might be about to come. I withdraw. "Not yet, soldier. Do you think this feeling could be any better with the help of Skinink? We could use the money to build and stock a dungeon."

I leave him be, let him think I'm opening the champagne, making ice-bucket noises and clinking glass, but with my free hand I'm quietly going through the play-box and find a bottle of baby oil and the flogger. It's very small, with tails no more than six inches long. I place it handily and then pop the cork, fill my glass, and take a sip.

The sound of the glass being placed back on the table sounds extra loud. The swish as the black tails slap against his left nipple shocks his whole body. There's no force to the blow, more flick than blow, but as I know so well, it stings. But not for long and as it fades, it leaves behind a lovely, warm presence. I flog his chest and belly, then his thighs, straying as close to his balls as I dare.

"The flogging is for thinking you could ever lose me to some stupid fad like Skinink. What happens next is my thank-you for wanting only the best for me."

I leave as long a pause as I dare, then say, "I'm taking off my bra . . . " I shake the baby-oil bottle so he can hear it. I don't have to say any more. Jed knows what I'm going to do.

At last I take his dick captive in my cleavage and then do nothing, holding it still. There's no hurry. He tries to take control, jerk off, but it's not until I start working him . . .

The first gush misses me somehow, heading for the ceiling. The second gets me in the face, hot and strong, but I don't mind. He dances an ecstatic rope dance and then sags. It's as if the bonds alone are holding him up.

I join him on the bench, pressing against him, pulling the tape off his mouth. The panties spill out of his mouth as he coughs.

"Don't speak." I kiss his salty lips and let my tongue explore his mouth as my oily fingertips find his nipples.

I take the blindfold off and then leave him there, letting him watch me tidy up, naked, putting the panties in the bin, pouring a second glass of champagne and topping up mine.

He says, "You're beautiful."

I smile.

Now his dick is resting on his balls in a semi-slumber.

I set about releasing him. When he's free and down off the bench, I hand him a glass. He drinks it down in gulps. I refill it and propose a toast. "Here's to Skinink and all it has taught us."

He nods and although his face shows blindfold and gag marks, he seems more relaxed than I have seen him in a while, positively dreamy.

I say, "We'll take the bottle to bed, finish it, and then, when you've recovered, you can fuck me to sleep."

Jed grins and grabs the bottle. "Wonder how much it'd cost to equip a dungeon?"

The long good-night kiss makes me feel as if I'm flying at thirty thousand feet.

PAYING ATTENTION

LN Bey

He has this thing about posture.

My husband will tell me to stand perfectly straight, ankles together, hands at my sides. "Shoulders back and tits out," he will say. He will correct my errors with the thin bamboo cane across my naked ass and I will secretly crave another, or across the fronts of my thighs and I will not. But if I have an occasion coming up that will require me to wear shorts or a skirt, he will not hit my thighs. He knows my calendar better than I do.

It must be some kind of guy thing, this military precision. Not that Dan was ever in the service. I once dated ex-military, and while that guy was hyper-organized, he wasn't into all this standing at attention as something erotic. "It's all about the beauty of the female form," Dan will tell me, "and working to achieve its utmost potential." A slouching girl is just not as attractive as a statuesque one, her assets well displayed. Well, who could argue with that?

More than anything though, I think he just likes to make me *wait*.

He demands the same perfection when I am on my knees—kneeling up, back and shoulders straight—and when I am on my hands and knees, wherever he puts me: on the floor, on the coffee table in corset and garters, or even displayed for his amusement on the kitchen table, which makes me nervous as there is one angle from which our neighbor could see the whole show through our window.

Or on our bed. He will tell me to keep my legs spread wide, to keep my back arched and my ass raised high. "Chin up," he'll tell me. "You're my prize show dog. Show it."

Degrading? Spare me, because I know what's next: first the whip, yes, but then the fingers. He will slide two fingers between my open labia and massage my clit, his thumb wandering where it may. If—and only if—I can hold still long enough, he will bring me to an intense climax.

However, if I break my posture at all—rock my hips, bend my elbows, even drop my head in a moment's loss of concentration—the hands recede, leaving me alone and exposed and desperate. I am left to correct my errors while he watches, often for a very long time, which he knows drives me insane. If it was a minor failure, the hands will return. If it was major, though—say, breaking down and burying my face in the bed—I'll have to count strokes from the whip, five or ten, all while maintaining that damned perfect posture.

Then the hands again, or he'll circle around in front of me and take my mouth, or he just won't be able to take it any longer and will thrust his cock inside me and fuck me silly.

This isn't an accurate description of our overall domestic life, of course. When I'm dressed, he listens to me. We talk money and goals and lawn care and maybe dropping cable for Internet, and we usually disagree. But these are the moments I live for; this is why I married him. When he says stand naked at attention, I stand naked at attention—no matter how much I'd rather rip off his clothes and jump him.

This is not to say that I can't manipulate him, too, now and then. I mean, he is a *guy*. They're such simpletons, sometimes, even the smart ones. I'll check the weather forecast and if it looks like rain over the weekend, I'll suck him once or twice during the week, unasked, uncommanded, and then he'll almost certainly return the favor on a rainy, lazy Sunday afternoon, my favorite thing in the whole world.

Or, if I've got a deep craving for something darker, I'll slouch. Not when we're playing—just lounging, on the couch, reading a book. He can't really correct me; I'm just relaxing, reading. It irks him, though, just a little, and I know it'll come back to me in the best possible ways.

Another example: just this morning, I managed to pull off a little stunt that requires so much timing, listening, and sensitivity to mood that I don't even try it very often, or it'll become obvious that it's a ploy—because its success rate is so low to begin with.

My husband gets up for work before I do, and I sometimes loll around in bed, awake, and I'll get to thinking . . .

The first step is to listen and try to tell if he'll be leaving early, in a hurry. There's a frenetic pace to his footsteps, maybe something's wrong at work. The second step, if things sound more leisurely, is to try to discern his frame of mind, a very subtle task—taking in every creak in the floor, how fast the water is running through the pipes.

Today, while shaving, he made it easy. I heard him actually singing, slaughtering an old song: "Silk shirt . . . new shoes . . . every girl's crazy 'bout a . . . "

Bingo.

Now the timing part. I waited for him to hit the bathroom one last time before leaving, then made my move. I got out of bed and put on my long T-shirt, with nothing underneath. I paused a few beats until the timing felt just right, then I walked down to the kitchen, went to the coffee machine, and got a cup from the cupboard. I waited, leaned forward slightly against the counter, and poured my coffee.

That's all.

I heard him coming out of the bathroom and into the kitchen, on his way to the garage.

"Hey, babe," I said over my shoulder.

He stopped short and I knew I had him. I took a sip of my coffee.

"You're leaving early."

He said nothing, just stood there a moment. Then he came up behind me, slowly. I set my cup down when I heard his briefcase touch the floor.

He gently grasped my hips from behind.

"I know what's on your mind," he said. "I *should* make you wait for it."

But he lifted the back of my T-shirt, exposing my ass, and caressed it. I love it when I have the power.

He crouched down behind me (*yes!* He was going to do it) and gently nudged the inside of my thigh with his hand. I spread my feet. Then it all happened quickly, as it always does. I felt him kiss the left cheek of my ass, then felt his tongue, warm and wet. Up and down, finding its way—he *still* made me wait for it. As he neared his target I felt his hot breath, then I nearly melted when his tongue's warm softness found such a racy spot. I arched my back.

His tongue swirled, teased, pressed harder. I leaned farther forward on the counter.

Then the fingers, here they come. His tongue never left my ass, and I felt his hand slide up between my thighs until he slid his fingers around my clit. Massaging it. Using my slippery juices to lubricate it even more.

Not one word was said, but I couldn't help moaning, all this attention first thing in the morning. He kept licking and kept fingering, and it was all I could do to keep my balance. I spread my hands across the counter, trying to find something to grip, anything. I bowed my head, extended my ass out to his darting, swirling tongue.

It was too much. Finally it all built up to where I couldn't hold back and I came, full force, practically screaming my pleasure with each breath.

He stood up as I shivered and tried to catch my breath with my forehead on the counter—there wasn't much else I could do. He didn't bother pulling my shirt down; he preferred me uncovered. He reached around me to turn on the water in the sink and wash his hand.

"Window's open," was all he said, and I jerked my head up and looked out into the morning light. He headed out the door and I heard the car start and the garage door open, and I moved from side to side as I searched the yard next door.

Mrs. Koslowski always gardens in the morning. Had she heard? How could she not have?

Usually, the Morning Kitchen Ploy gets me through the day just fine. Fantastically, in fact. I will be the happiest shopper in the store, the only driver stuck in traffic with a big smile on her face.

Today, I wanted something more. I was feeling unusually confident. I wasn't about to let my husband know that I'd arranged the whole encounter this morning; then he'd never fall for it again, and it's hard enough to get it right to start with. There are mornings when he'll come up to me, but *does* make me wait until he gets home.

Yet, in my exuberance, I was feeling the need to show him that I could be in control, too, not just him, and that today I *liked* it.

We have a rule concerning our private life: keep it private. We live in a fairly conservative neighborhood, and he has a fairly conservative job, and there's no point in openly rebelling when we get along just fine doing our thing in private.

The biggest risk we ever take, this morning's screaming-fest excepted, is on rare evenings when he orders me onto the dining room table—his centerpiece, he calls me. The view out the dining room window looks out over the very back corner of Mrs. Koslowski's yard, where her garden is, but she usually stays indoors in the evening. There's a little thrill to being told to climb up there under the chandelier and pose naked, posture perfect, while he reads and pretends to ignore me as I balance obedience, impatience, and fear.

We keep our kinks to ourselves, that's the rule. We never bring it up with our friends, never even whisper a kinky thought at a party, never call each other at work with obscene phone calls where coworkers might hear.

I decided to call my husband.

"This is Dan."

"I got three compliments on my posture today." I could hear voices in the background. Men's voices, women's voices.

There was a long pause.

"Oh, yeah?"

"Yes. The first was Mrs. Jackson, you know the nice older lady who always walks that golden retriever puppy by our house every day? She lives two blocks from us, it turns out. She brought the little guy in to get fixed this morning." I work mornings at the animal shelter, and every two weeks a veterinarian, Dr. Reed, comes in as a public service. I used to have a better job, but didn't we all?

"We neutered the poor little bastard."

"Oh no."

"Yes. It had to be done."

"So what did she say?"

"When I walked out to call her name and I crouched down to pet the puppy, she said, 'My, you have such wonderful posture. You just don't see that anymore. So graceful.' I said, 'Thank you! I work on it, you know.' If she only knew how *hard* I work on it."

"Mm-hm." I could still hear voices in the background. "There's more, I take it?"

"Yes. Dr. Reed complimented me, also."

Another long pause.

"Oh really."

"Yes. He said I had amazing posture. That was all he said."

"And what did you say?"

"I said, 'Thank you...sir.'"

I bit my lip. I was pushing it. Dr. Reed wasn't half bad looking, and Dan knew it.

"You said there were three."

"I'm not sure you know her. Jenny McNeil, I know her from the gym. Gorgeous redhead?"

" . . . No."

"She brought in a little kitty."

He didn't say anything. I think he was still thinking about the doctor.

"She said she admired my posture, especially considering my shoes."

"Which ones?"

"The black stilettos."

He sounded almost indignant: "For work?"

"Not the ones we play in. The three-inchers. Still, though. She loved them. You don't know her? Very pretty redhead, works out a lot, adorable little pussy . . . cat? Loved my shoes."

I licked my lips and bit my lower one again, waiting for him to figure out what he could say at work.

All he could manage was, "Really."

"Yes. I just thought you should know, maybe brighten your day at work. People really do notice my posture, thanks to you."

"Well, I'm glad to hear it."

"Bye, honey."

Now it was his turn to wait. This *was* a thrill.

"Good-bye."

Who was I kidding—I was in for it.

My phone rang at exactly 4:45.

"Hello?" I said, as if I didn't know his ringtone, his picture on my phone.

"Dinner in Heels," he said. I felt a tightening in my stomach that I knew was not going to go away. Maybe I should have thought this through; neither foresight nor patience is one of my stronger virtues.

"Okay...Sir," I said.

He hung up.

Dinner in Heels means just that: dinner served in nothing but heels. It follows a very precise, prescribed ritual that evolved over time, until it reached what my husband felt was perfection and so it has remained the same since. It is rare—maybe once every three or four months, about as often as the Kitchen Counter Encounter. But they'd never happened on the same day before.

I kneeled naked by the front door, a vodka cocktail in my hands, smell of fresh basil in the air. I was waiting even before I heard the garage door open. On these occasions, he likes to come in through the front door, Ward Cleaver–style, and walks around the house as the garage door closes. It's more formal, somehow.

I straightened my shoulders as the doorknob turned, and he opened the door.

"Hello, husband," I said, and offered the drink up to him, holding it above my bowed head. The ice clinked in my shaking hands.

"Hello, dear." He petted my head, ran his hand over my hair, and took the drink.

"How was your day?" I asked, and bent down to untie his shoe.

He hesitated, and I knew there was tension—was it work, or me?

"Not bad," he said, as he lifted his foot from the shoe that I held. "A few problems. Nothing that can't be corrected."

I untied his other shoe and couldn't think of what to say. He pulled his foot from it, too.

"Smells good in here," he said. "Is dinner ready?"

I nodded. "Yes, Sir."

I can only blame myself for having to call him "Sir" during Dinner in Heels. It is the only time I call him that—not even when he's whipping me, disciplining my posture, making me come. (And now you see why referring to Dr. Reed that way got him so riled up.)

These rare nights of serving him dinner naked are the only times we mix daily life with our...thing, and it somehow makes it all the more intense, like I'm an actual slave girl. I once called him Sir, on my own initiative to see what he would think, and let's just say he liked it.

He sat at the head of the table while I brought him his dinner on a little silver serving tray. I wore the

five-inch heels, nothing else, and I kept my posture
perfect, the click, click, click of my shoes the only sound
as I exited the kitchen.

I always fix one large portion only, and I always keep
it light and very neat—penne pasta, salmon maybe—
because I am to kneel beside him while he eats, my back
straight, and he feeds me off his plate. I don't get as
much to eat as usual, but I'm barely hungry anyway.
My stomach is usually in knots doing this, and tonight
it was especially so.

He always begins by asking me "How was your
day?" and the ridiculous twist on domesticity, having
such a mundane conversation while he slowly reaches to
my open mouth with a forkful of pasta, is an exercise in
anticipation, a lesson in patience, in waiting.

Tonight he didn't say a word. He ate, and he fed me.
My one consolation was that the crotch of his trousers,
always swollen during this ritual, was stretched tight
tonight as well.

His breathing was heavy. I ate the food he fed me,
barely tasting the marinara I had cooked from scratch,
without saying a word. Finally he was finished and
decided I was, too.

"Clear the table, put the dishes in the sink. Then
report back here immediately."

Well, of course I would. What else was I going to do?
I wanted to kiss his feet, suck his swollen cock. I wanted
to apologize for the phone call.

"Yes, Sir," I said.

"Do not dawdle."

"No, Sir."

"Up on the table," was all he said as I stood before him. He looked up and down my naked body. This was not usually a part of Dinner in Heels, but this was a command, not a request. I stepped on a chair and climbed up in silence.

When I am not naked, I have opinions, often strong ones. But when I am, I speak only when asked a direct question. And I am perfectly fine with that. I will just go ahead and admit that right here.

I assumed the Dinner Table Position: hands and knees, legs spread, all the goods exposed, chin held high. I was his prize show dog. I raised my ass and head as high as I could, arching my back. I was going to get a whipping later anyway, for my prank, and I didn't want to give him a reason to start early. My posture was *perfect*. I waited patiently (no, impatiently), felt the hard wood under my knees.

He stayed seated. He watched me carefully, waiting for any move, searching for any error in posture. He said nothing, didn't pace around the table like usual, like I was some sculpture in a museum. He just sat.

I heard him dial his phone.

"Mrs. Koslowski? This is Dan, your neighbor. Yes, how are you? Oh, good. She's good, too, thank you. Oh, really—no I hadn't heard that, I hope she's okay. Oh good. Good. Well, I'm glad to hear that."

What the hell was he doing? Besides listening to our neighbor talk about her grandchildren, that is—god, that woman could go on. At least I knew this wouldn't have anything to do with me posed motionless and naked on the table—private stayed private, that was the rule.

The rule I'd broken this afternoon.

"Well, listen, Mrs. Koslowski. The reason I'm calling, I've been noticing your wonderful garden, over the fence there."

Oh, no.

"Yes. Well, you've got such a wonderful crop there, especially this late in the year. You really have such a green thumb. Oh, you're welcome. Second crop, you say!"

He wouldn't.

"I was wondering if I might be able to buy some vegetables from you. I noticed the yellow squash are looking especially nice. Zucchini? Yes, I'd love some zucchini. Oh. Well, now, you'd—yes. No, you'd *have* to let me pay you. You just can't get vegetables that fresh even at the farmer's market. No, I insist. Well, are you sure? Okay, then. You'll at least let me trade some of my wife's cookies for them. I'm sure we can work something out."

He looked at me, I saw at the very edge of my vision—I was looking straight ahead, not moving a muscle.

"Are you busy right now? I could meet you at the fence. Okay, sure, I'll come around, then. Be right there. And thank you!" He ended the call.

He stood, looking out the window at Mrs. Koslowski's garden.

"It's getting darker earlier this time of year, isn't it?" he said, to me.

This was a question.

"Yes, Sir," I said.

He turned and smiled, a little. This was the first time I'd ever called him that after Dinner in Heels—had I just started something new?

He reached to the light switch and turned on the

chandelier above the table, above me. The room was now brighter than it was outside, making me all the more visible from out there.

My only movement: my jaw dropped open. He was breaking *the* rule—what was this?

He must have been angrier than I'd realized, to risk not just a flash of my flesh but his entire reputation around the neighborhood—Mrs. Koslowski loves a good bit of gossip, and this would be, to say the least, somewhat interesting news.

He works in *risk management,* for crying out loud. Why was he going to such dangerous lengths to drive the point home, over such a silly little trick?

"Just so you know," he said, "I couldn't get up from my desk for a good fifteen minutes after your call. I was like a teenage boy. I ended up late for a meeting—*my* meeting. But I couldn't very well get up there in front of everyone with my dick tenting my pants, now could I?"

Question? Or rhetorical question? I couldn't decide whether to answer him or not.

He turned on the recessed lights along the wall to brighten the room even more.

"Be right back," he said.

If she saw me, she didn't let on, which would have been quite a feat. Perhaps it was because I never once moved that she didn't turn her head, open her mouth in shock. I watched carefully as she and my husband joked and gestured and talked about vegetables. I knew that *he* saw me; he looked directly at me several times. I brought my eyes directly forward each time.

He returned, set the basketful of vegetables on the

counter and said, "I'd like another vodka tonic." He went into the den in the back of the house.

I climbed down and made his drink.

The den is the only room we haven't remodeled, all heavy '50s ranch—stone fireplace, low beamed ceiling, big sliding glass doors leading out to the backyard. We had no choice but to decorate it mid-century modern.

He had a baseball game on the TV.

I kneeled to serve him and he pointed to a spot on the floor, and I knew that I was to stand there, at perfect attention, until he told me to stop.

This too was not entirely new. He sometimes has me stand straight and at the ready while he pretends to ignore me because he knows it drives me crazy and because he likes the way I look that way—shoulders back, tits out, as he'd say. The twisted incongruity, the casual obscenity of my nakedness versus the comfortable husband watching a ball game in such an old-fashioned room has always held a certain perverse, anti-liberated thrill for us both, my increasing impatience and frustration a part of our game. At least the ball game was nearly over.

The game went into extra innings. He said nothing to me the entire time, only shouting out occasional frustrations or satisfactions at the players and umpires on TV. His team won, with playoff implications.

He turned the TV off and stood, walked to the wall and pulled the cord that opened the curtains that covered the big, double sliding doors. It was now completely dark outside, and in the interior light I was fully exposed to the outside world.

He wasn't exactly parading me around the neighbor-hood. Neither neighbor could really see from where this room was set. But we had no privacy fence—anyone walking their dog behind our subdivision or still biking on the trails by the woods or, if their vision was truly sharp, driving home on the freeway off in the distance, could stop and watch as long as they liked. I was free for the viewing.

I wanted to cover myself and hide, but I held my place as I watched my reflection in the glass. I looked my own body up and down, as Dan had done earlier and was doing now: breasts, stomach, hips, thighs. He was right—a girl *does* look better standing straight than slouching. How'd he put it? All my assets properly displayed. I pulled my shoulders back a little farther—this *was* a punishment.

But then he turned, not saying a word, and went upstairs to our room, leaving me alone without telling me I could move. Oh, this wasn't a punishment—this was just a big damn tease, was what this was.

Once again, it was my turn to wait.

I am waiting here still. It seems like hours, though it hasn't been, and my feet are starting to hurt in my heels, but I am aching even more with desire. At least he is not one to leave me here all night—his crotch was as swollen as mine was wet. *Is* wet. I want to move my hand toward it, but my reflection reminds me not to.

I calm myself with the knowledge that his patience is also limited, up there by himself. There is a whipping or perhaps even a caning to be administered, which I know he is dying for because I can hear him pacing above me, and then he will fuck me into sweet oblivion as I hold still for it and then, yes, he will massage my sore feet.

I want to go upstairs to him, but he knows me too well. With any other man I've known, I would have quit this ridiculous pose long ago, demanded fair play, slammed the door of our room if he refused it, told him to sleep on the couch.

Yet here I am, at perfect attention, watching my own naked reflection for any slips in posture as I wait to be called up, while yearning for release from this torture of endless anticipation that I myself have caused.

How many women would marry a guy *because* he makes her stand naked while he watches a few innings of baseball and then leaves her to simmer in her own juices, ponder her mistakes?

This gal would raise her hand in the air, if she hadn't been ordered to hold perfectly still until further notice no matter how insane it drives her.

You?

THE HANGING GARDENS OF BABYLON

Valerie Alexander

Tell me what I want."

The man in the black suit sits across the table with an impassive face. I'm on my first date of the night, a private session, and my first time with him. His handsome face is composed, his black hair laced with silver. He's probably a wealthy executive visiting the local biotech corporation. He's not a club regular or that would have been noted on the date request. All Babylon performers get intel on the men and women who bid for our services, so we can decide if we want to accept or not. His only contained a headshot, a bid, and his sex requests. *Private session, straight sex, some roleplay, bondage, Dom-switch.* And because I like a bit of mystery, I accepted.

"You want me to crawl. You want me to beg for your cock." These executive types usually need to feel worshipped for at least part of the session.

"And?"

His pale eyes are cold. But I know what he wants.

The Hanging Gardens of Babylon is known for its beautiful performers: angelic-looking boys, heartbreaking girls. The club is also famous for its elaborate bondage and suspension performers—unusually flexible, able to be tied up in strange contortions for long periods. But I've become known as an expert Dominatrix as well. And despite the client's patrician aloofness, I can tell he's looking to grovel.

Outside our private lounge room, the club music is booming. I slide off my chair and get on all fours. My stockings will rip and my long hair hangs over my carefully made-up face, but I crawl around the table and look up at him like a pet jaguar who could purr against his knee or tear out his throat.

"And you want me to suck you like this."

I push down my corset to show him my nipples. His eyes lock on my tits and he swallows visibly. Definitely an overworked executive in one of the top firms. Maybe he's older than he looks, one of the customers who still aren't used to brothels being legalized. The older ones have never gotten used to these fantastic new clubs where they can buy dazzling boys and girls to fulfill their dirtiest fantasies.

On to his zipper, where I'm rewarded with a hard, smooth cock. I suck his entire shaft into my mouth, undoing his last vestiges of control, and work him over until he's panting—and then I jump to my feet, take his wrists, and swiftly lace him into an arm binder behind the chair.

He groans with anticipation. I turn his chair until his face is eye level with my hips.

"Please . . . "

"No."

"Can you at least . . . show me . . . "

I slide my panties down just enough to show off my hip bones and the smooth skin right over my pussy. Then I stop. "You have to earn it."

I tease him like he deserves, ordering him around until I relent and permit his tongue entry into paradise. But it's all pretty routine for me, and so I'm mostly watching the main club floor through the private lounge window. The nightly floorshow is going strong, with two men headlining the stage: dark-haired Ryder, considered to be the most beautiful young man at Babylon, and his best friend, Nick, a rambunctious boy who's only been here five months. Since Nick's arrival, they've teamed up to become the top attraction at Babylon—partners in crime whose popularity has made them unbearably cocky.

A competitive envy flares up in me as I watch their admirers toss flowers and money on the stage. But I try to focus on my client.

"And now you want me to use you like the filthy whore you are." I'm on top of him now, engulfing his cock. Fucking him smooth and hard, holding him by the throat and squeezing to let him know who's in charge and it's not him—he's just the desperate executive who came to Babylon tonight to pay for this while I'm the blue-lit goddess of his dreams. He's just another customer, someone I'll never remember, while he'll remember me and this night forever.

He struggles against the arm binder, just the way I like. Definitely one of the better clients I've had to take my mind off Mira.

* * *

But the next morning I wake up late to the sound of rain, and she floods my mind again. I drowse in bed, imagining that Mira still works at Babylon and she's going to open the door with a tray of pastries and crawl into bed with me. Since she quit the club and went back to school four hours away, it's becoming clear that our feverish affair can't survive the separation. Instead I content myself with imagining her showing up here alone, dressed in a man's suit and a fedora pulled down over her beautiful almond-shaped eyes. Sneaking into the Velvet Room with its luxurious sofas, all the time in the world to enjoy each other.

I get out of bed, cringing at my reflection in the mirror—a pretty-wrapped wreck in peach chiffon, nice legs, a tumble of long reddish-dark hair, and puffy eyes that are beginning to show too many late nights. My comm device is already blinking blue with date requests. Clients enter their preferences—a group or private session, spanking, voyeurism, and so on—and enter their bids. Performers choose based on money, type of sex, the client's appearance, or any other whim. For tonight I choose a two-hour private session with a young blonde client my age. She wants me to dominate her. Easy enough. If our session isn't too strenuous, maybe I'll do a show on the main stage afterward. Emerge in full makeup and sexy costume and do my famous hanging rope dance to remind the audience how much they want to book a date with Gisella Romand, the best bondage performer at Babylon.

On my way downstairs to brunch I stop at the arched windows. Some of the boys are playing football, enjoying the rain on their bare torsos. The tallest one throwing the ball across the grass catches my eye: Ryder, all broad shoulders and long legs, with black hair sweeping over his eyes and a slow smile that inevitably turns into a smirk. Allegedly he has a beautiful cock too, not that I would know. We've never been requested for a group session together in the year we've both worked here. And unlike a lot of performers, he doesn't get naked onstage, which forces clients interested in his cock to pay for sessions. I've always been curious to know if he's skilled sexually or if he just lets his looks and his muscles earn the money.

Nick snatches the ball up from the grass. His blond hair is darkened with rain as he lets out a war whoop that pierces the air. He's popular with clients who like that mischievous boyish energy. Sarcastic and kinetic, he's too fond of pranks for my taste.

Ryder goes down in the wet grass, tackled by Nick. Covered in grass and mud, they wrestle—until Nick looks up and sees me in the window. He blows me a kiss and I turn away, annoyed they caught me watching.

Downstairs, girls are gossiping about a scandal at another house, while other performers are getting their makeup applied and their hair done for outcalls. Others are getting photographed from multiple angles to send out nightly photo cards to entice business.

I'm reaching for some blackberries in the dining hall when water sprinkles my back. I turn to see a still-muddy Nick flick his wet hair at me, snapping his head forward like a genie. "Stop it."

He does it again. "I've got a surprise for you tonight," he announces. Ryder smirks behind him.

"How titillating." I reach for more berries to show how unconcerned I am.

"Don't pretend you're not curious," he calls as I walk away. But I'm only doing the private session tonight so it can't be a group scene he's referring to. I refuse to react.

The main stage is always a spectacle, with light shows, music, trapezes, cages, and more than two dozen dancers entertaining the three hundred seats in the audience. I bypass it for the corridor of private lounges, where the club booker has assigned me for the next two hours.

The client is waiting on the couch. She's cuter than her picture, with big blue eyes and a red corset with matching collar. Her blonde hair is in a ponytail.

"Do you remember me? Lily. I was here three nights ago."

Clients always want to be remembered. I take her breasts in my hands. "If you think I could forget these…" But I remember now. She was the submissive of a beautiful but menacing mistress who tried to buy me for a lap dance. I'd refused and her mistress had been indignant.

She smiles bashfully. "Thank you. You're so pretty and I felt like we really connected."

If there's one thing I've learned as a performer, it's that connection is in the eye of the beholder. I can turn out a shamefully lifeless performance and the customer might find it to be the fuck of a lifetime. And there have been times when I was on fire, only to have the customer shrug me off as forgettable.

"You understand that you're my slave for these hours."

She nods excitedly. These are the women I always draw to me—submissive, giggly. I prefer the Miras of the world, quick-witted and clever. But it's refreshing to be the voyeur, not the show. To sit back and order her to spread her legs and play with her pussy for me. I stroke my clit slowly as I watch her.

I don't come with clients. Even when Mira and I would perform together, we'd put on a wild show for the client and later finish each other off in private. Partly it's about focusing on the client's preferences, but it's also about vulnerability. Getting lost in euphoria changes the power dynamic, lessens my authority. It's my job to stay in control and that's what I do now, telling Lily to slide three fingers in her pussy.

She's writhing on the banquette when the door flies open and her mistress from three nights ago snaps, "Stop that. Now."

I stand up. "This is a private session."

"I'm Mistress Ellina and Lily is my slave," the woman says. She's tall with long, ice-blonde hair, high cheekbones, and high boots: the picture of the imperious Dominant. "You'll report now to my group session. Your booker told me I could interrupt."

This is unprecedented and I will definitely be chewing out that new booker. But I don't protest as much as I might otherwise because Nick's wavy blond head appears behind her, then Ryder's dark head. Both of them are shirtless. They're apparently part of her session tonight.

"I decide what sessions I will join," I say. "I don't know what kind of houses you're used to, but at Babylon the performers decide who we work with."

"Please say yes, Gisella," Lily begs plaintively.

Her mistress sighs heavily. "I'll pay you quadruple whatever Lily bid for the session."

Nick leans against the door frame, watching me intently. Mistress Ellina's eyes are cold. She's going to make me earn that high rate. But Nick and Ryder have piqued my curiosity. So I agree and that's how we stop arguing and move on to their private lounge.

Pink lights shine down from the ceiling on the black couches, the spanking stool, and the stockade. A boy I've never seen is bent over the stool, his hands and ankles shackled to its iron legs. But the real spectacle is the naked and voluptuous girl suspended in the room's elaborate pulley system. Her arms are above her head, her legs spread-eagled with high heels off the ground. Her breasts are so luscious I can't help staring at them. What a shame she's in private service to this abrasive mistress.

A light hand caresses my neck: Lily, my submissive client. "I'm sorry we got interrupted."

I shrug. Being aloof is like catnip to sub clients; they keep paying and paying to elicit real interest.

Ryder and Nick move to the boy bent over the spanking stool. Nick spanks his ass hard, and Ryder laughs. "Break's over, you little slut." They were taunting him before I arrived, apparently. It's a hot scene, but I'm distracted by the blindfolded girl suspended like a voluptuous sex cake for the taking. Maybe both boys are going to fuck her. Instead Mistress Ellina picks up a crop and deals out flushed welts on the girl's creamy skin.

Lily circles me like a python. I sit in a throne-styled chair and lift my skirt. "I believe you owe me."

She kneels at my feet and begins licking my pussy. I watch Ryder and Nick. Their cocks are both bulging in their pants as they taunt the whipping boy. They're going to jerk off on him, maybe, or fuck him up the ass. And that's really why I came here: to see them in action at last. But as Ryder unzips his pants, I can't quite see his dick in the dim light at this angle.

He shoves it into the boy's mouth. "Suck it like the filthy whore you are. And if you can't fit us both in your slut mouth, you'll be sorry."

Lily's blonde head continues between my legs, licking me skillfully enough to spark a heat spreading through my blood. The boy squirms on the stool. His hands are tied to the stool but blowing Ryder is clearly exciting him because he's grinding his dick against the leather, his muscled thighs shaking.

The blindfolded girl doesn't move. Her mistress has trained her well because she retains a certain dignity in her binds, naked and on display as the crop lashes her skin. I should be degrading Lily but I'm more interested in watching Nick, who's now pushing his shaft into the whipping boy's mouth. He's watching me and Lily, and Ryder has neglected the whipping boy entirely to study our scene. Showing off, I open my legs wider, grinding into Lily's face. My corset is unlaced and slightly loose, showing everything but my nipples. This is the most the boys and I have seen of each other in action, but we're still not seeing it all.

Then Mistress Ellina steps back from cropping the voluptuous sub. Her arm drops as she looks at me, then at Nick and Ryder.

"What's this? Three Babylon performers have a little crush on each other?"

A good Dominatrix, she's missed nothing. I should have focused more on Lily, who is the paying client. Clients hate it when the performers pay more attention to each other.

Nick has paused mid-thrust, his dick still in the sub's mouth.

"Well, well." Mistress Ellina smiles, looking both amused and cold. "Here I thought this was *my* session. Apparently you think you're here for each other."

She's going to rebuke us. Crop us. Or something horrible. This is a Domina who has no reservations about using her authority.

She walks up to me. "So which one do you want?" she asks. "You're obviously pining for one of them. The black-haired one or the blond?"

I can't answer that. Whoever I don't pick will resent me forever, while the one I do pick will be unbearably smug. I glance at the blindfolded sub, but I can already tell her services are not an option tonight.

"Answer," she says, her tone going colder. But I hesitate, trying to think of who is the lesser evil, and her crop lashes out on my exposed thighs. "Both then. Lily!"

At the bark of her name, Lily scrambles over and frees the beautiful sub from the suspension. Oh, no. This can't be going where I think it is.

"Gisella." She says my name so bitingly. "I've heard you are quite flexible. That you can be bound for long periods."

This is going exactly where I think it is.

"Ryder. Nick. Get Gisella rigged up. I'm going to teach all three of you a lesson."

This is the moment for me to decline. I only agreed

to the group session, after all, not the actual bondage, which is normally negotiated in advance. But Nick and Ryder are watching, and I don't want to admit I'm intimidated by their presence. Because that's really what's stopping me, not the brutal mistress and her head games and riding crop. Getting naked with clients is one thing. It's an acting job, most of the time. But being tied up and stripped and fucked by the same performers I train with and eat breakfast next to is a much more sensitive, vulnerable feeling.

I stand up, straightening my skirt with as much dignity as I can. Ryder steps up behind me and brings my wrists over my head. His torso against me is hot and damp, his heart thudding with excitement. "I'll do the honors," Nick says boldly and yanks my unlaced corset down, grinning with adolescent glee like he doesn't see naked breasts onstage every night.

Ryder expertly unbuckles my skirt and throws it aside. Now I'm naked. He presses up close and laughs a low, sinister laugh in my ear. "We're going to fuck you so hard," he says, and it sounds like a menacing statement of triumph.

"That's only partly correct," Mistress Ellina says. "Apparently all three of you need a reminder that you're here for me, not your own pleasure. So yes, I want all three of you to show me a wet, hot, screaming fuck— but none of you are allowed to come."

The boys go quiet. I swallow. Normally this wouldn't be an issue. Not coming with clients is the easiest thing in the world. But it's the boys and me together for the first time, and with the way they're eyeing me naked, the air between us is already electric.

"In fact, anyone who does come," Mistress Ellina says, "will owe me a very challenging night of submission."

Ryder adopts an uncharacteristically humble tone. "Mistress—ah, when will we know to stop?"

"When I say so," she snaps and lashes his shoulder with her crop.

The boys and I look at each other. She's not going to stop us until someone loses by coming. At that moment, the battle of wills is on to push each other over the edge.

Ryder begins it by turning me around. Our eyes meet right before Nick undoes my hands and pulls them behind my back, roping them together. He fastens my ankles into the pulley cuffs. And then I'm being elevated and bent over a suspension bar, spread-eagled in the crudest way possible with my ass and pussy on display.

The crop catches me on my right cheek. I twitch in the ropes. A low laugh; Mistress Ellina has given Nick the crop because she understands that being cropped by a fellow performer is far more humiliating for me than if she were to do it.

Nick lightly drags the leather tip up my inner thighs, then across my clit. He's going to tease me until I beg to be fucked. But then Ryder walks around to face me with an evil smile. He slides down his pants and shows off his legendary thick and gorgeous cock.

"I always wondered what it would be like to fuck your mouth, Gisella," he says right before he pushes in his swollen crown.

The taste of his precome makes my head swim. Ryder winds his fingers into my hair and begins thrusting in and out of my face, slowly so I can still suck him. It's kind of dreamy, actually, and Nick must sense it because he drops the crop and takes me by the hips. His dick drives into me a second later, his balls resting against me, and I almost choke on Ryder's cock. It feels so good, both of them inside me, Nick driving in and out in a perfect rhythm while I'm captured tight and powerless in the ropes.

But I can't lose control. This is just another client session, I remind myself. The money, that's what I need to think about, and not how I'm utterly naked in Nick and Ryder's control.

Ryder releases my head and slides his hands down over my breasts. I look up at him, using my mouth as artfully as I can to break through his performance buffer zone. He pushes in deeper and as our eyes connect, his whole body shudders. He's succumbing to my tongue. He's going to be the first to come.

But then he abruptly pulls out and walks away. "Let me fuck her," he says to Nick. They say something I can't quite hear and then Ryder's cock pushes into me, just slightly too big for me until my pussy relaxes and fills with electric sensitivity. A raw and broken cry escapes me.

"Losing control already," Mistress Ellina sniffs.

He fucks me at a steady pace, controlling his thrusts. I wish we were fucking each other in private; I wish I had never accepted Lily's date request, because my skin is filling with heat and my clit feels more sensitive than it has ever been. I'm turning delirious, the euphoria in my blood going higher. Nick takes my tits in his hands and begins teasing my nipples, and I'm cursing them and glorifying in it at the same time when a commotion behind me distracts me.

I look over my shoulder as best I can to see the whipping-stool boy being unshackled. He stretches and ambles naked across the floor, more handsome than I would have expected. There's a flash of his smile in the dim room and then Lily hands him an object: a slender silver vibrator.

Oh no. Ryder rests it against my anus, its coolness welcome on my hot, flushed skin. There's a squirt of lube, and he begins delicately playing with my rim. I know what they're doing—they're controlling their own excitement while deliberately frustrating me to a fever pitch. Then they'll unleash the real fucking and drive me into a screaming, twisting orgasm.

He's still fucking me in a measured rhythm as he slowly slides the toy into my ass. It's an unfair advantage on their side but it feels good, so good, being paralyzed and stimulated relentlessly. Everything is being touched perfectly, my nipples, my pussy, and my ass, and then the whipping boy kneels under me. His tongue washes over my swollen clit.

I groan. But I have to fight this, I can't give in. Lily fingers herself on the divan, watching with a dreamy smile.

They change places and it goes on like that for a while, one cock after another in my pussy. The boys are panting now, their sweat dropping on my spine as they try to fuck me past all self-control. I know they want to hold off; making me come will give them bragging rights for all time, but they're close themselves. It's too real now, not a performance at all in the way they're fucking me and touching me, responding to the swollen wetness of my pussy and the heat of my breasts in their hands.

Sweat is soaking my skull. I try to think about other clients to cool my fever and buy me time until one of them comes. But Nick is now playing with my breasts and sucking my nipples and I'm twisting in the ropes, almost out of my mind. And then a guttural groan fills the room—the whipping boy, whose come fills my tongue. Then Ryder makes an odd noise like a plea as he begins fucking me super fast.

"Don't!" Nick says to him. But Ryder's leaning over me, squeezing my tits and banging his cock into me as hard as he can in what are obviously his final moments. Nick slides down to my clit, licking me ferociously to make me explode first. But his own cock is stiff and dark, and the whipping boy greedily sucks it hard, a wet, sloppy blow job as Nick groans into my pussy. And it's his loss of control that slams me with a throbbing, forceful orgasm and I come screaming and squirting all over the floor as Ryder shudders on top of me.

I'm a wet, shaking mess. Lily jumps up to unbind me. I collapse onto her divan as someone tenderly pushes my hair back and holds a cold glass of water to my mouth. It's the beautiful sub. Without her blindfold, she is exquisite.

Mistress Ellina is sneering at us, telling us that for the top performers at Babylon, we're no better than animals, that she's going to discipline all three of us severely next time. But no one's listening to her. Instead Nick says to Lily, "We owe you a freebie," so quietly that Mistress Ellina can't hear. I'm curious what that means until the mistress says contemptuously, "Not a very challenging first night at Babylon for the new girl. But I'll have her another night."

I understand it then: the beautiful sub is a new Babylon performer and she was intended to star in this bondage scene. But Ryder and Nick somehow engineered Lily's date with me to piss off her mistress and get me in the ropes. They are clever bastards, I'll give them that.

I say to the new girl, "Welcome to Babylon. If you want to have brunch tomorrow, I'll show you around."

Nick is fidgeting by the stockade, waiting for me to acknowledge him. Ryder's eyes are locked on me. They want to be praised, petted. They want to know how I feel about our new status. But there's time for that later. The new girl laces me back into my corset and I go upstairs for a long, cool shower. The club is still hopping five floors below me when I fall naked and wet on my bed. Then I see my comm device is blinking. *I think I can visit next week. Don't forget me. Mira.* Maybe she'll come, maybe she won't. I'll be fine either way.

THE PRICE OF PATRONAGE

Eve Pendle

She got a brief impression of wide shoulders and red hair before he spun around as she entered her parlor. "Good morning, Mr. Merridon."

"Lady Charlbury." His chest swelled as he took a deep breath. "Thank you for agreeing to see me."

A shine of metal announced he'd followed her direction to set up his machine on a table just to the side of her favorite chair, with deep cushions and arched arms. As always, the fire was burning high, warming the air of the spring day outside.

She studied him while she sat and arranged the crinoline and petticoats of her Perkins mauve–silk dress. He'd worn his best suit to this meeting and it didn't seem comfortable. His cream waistcoat had a pattern of pale-pink flowers that suited neither him nor his abruptly angular machine he'd brought to show her. He had short, red-ochre hair, with a slight curl. His freckles were so close together that across his nose they almost joined up to create the illusion of dark skin. As a child, he was probably teased for those freckles and red hair. Now that he was grown, anyone would see his bulky shoulders and think twice about teasing him thus.

The square set of his jaw gave him an impression of firmness that the rest of his countenance, when simply described, wouldn't indicate. Pale-blue eyes, full of a maelstrom of fear and hope and eagerness, were what really caught her attention though. "Tell me about your implement, Mr. Merridon."

"Um." He closed his eyes for a second, apparently composing himself.

"What does it do?" she asked encouragingly. Some nerves were understandable. Her patronage was not just access to money that could launch his idea into the world, but also her scientific contacts, influence, and advice. Men couldn't always manage to take a blonde lady's brain or wealth seriously, even though she was a baroness. Aside from being her favorite pastime, these little demonstrations served as an important test.

She'd had some of the most talented scientists and inventors in England visit her to demonstrate their ideas. She was generous with her late husband's wealth.

Sometimes the meetings took an even more fun direction. She certainly wouldn't object if Mr. Merridon, with his lovely physique, were interested in that.

He took a deep breath. "It is a method of providing perfectly formatted writing, in the manner of type as is used by printing presses, available in the home." He looked at the machine rather than her, as though it needed informing of its purpose. Despite all his height and muscles, he was struggling to look straight at her. "I believe it will be useful for many businesspeople in making their correspondence more legible and professional. In particular, it will help in preventing mishaps and misunderstandings arising from poor and fast handwriting."

Now that he was talking about his machine, he seemed calmer. He'd practiced this speech and he was confident in his invention. Was there anything sweeter than a burly, clever, shy man?

"Like a typographer." She'd seen this sort of machine before, though this was much more attractive. "It might also be useful for lovers not wishing for their identity to be revealed by their handwriting."

There was a beat of silence. "I suppose that would be an advantage." He seemed frozen, his hand on the table, almost leaning on it for support. He was too still to not be thinking through the implications of what she'd said. "If the device were common enough."

Perhaps she'd turned him to stone with her scandalous implication. But if he'd wanted a patron with an untarnished reputation, he ought to have asked around a little more. She was no Lady Worsley, but her ex-whore maids, lack of gentleman servants, and whispers of being a merry widow were well-enough known.

"This is the whole machine?" It was like a miniature piano, with three tiers of keys, each with a letter written on. "It's rather a small thing, isn't it?" It took up only about half the size of a page of foolscap.

His intake of breath brought her gaze up. He was pinking in the cheeks, his eyes bright. Interesting. He'd given her words a meaning she hadn't intended at all, but if that made him so flushed with excitement, she would certainly work with him.

"It's compact, m'lady, but it does the job." He took a blank piece of paper and placed it into the machine. A few key presses and he retrieved the paper and handed it to her.

She could feel his gaze on her as she read. Her name was written in even, book-quality type. *Belinda Estherby, Baroness of Charlbury.*

"Ingenious." She smiled. "And portable too, I suppose. When William Burt showed me his, it was much larger."

"Yes." He gulped and his cheeks flushed red. But his shoulders were straight, as if he was preventing himself from leaning toward her.

Oh, he was deliciously embarrassed. Was he beginning to be aroused? The revelation sent a frisson down her spine. A flirting, sweet tease could be so much more exciting than direct compliments or lust.

"Can I touch it?" she asked in reverent tones, looking at him from beneath her lashes with soft, bed-me eyes.

"Yes," he breathed quickly.

She reached across and ran a finger along a gleaming key with all the sensuality she would give to a man's lips or nipple. "It certainly catches the attention, for all its lack of size."

He shifted over closer to the table and mumbled a reply.

Hiding an erection, perhaps, but his fashionable trousers were rather tight and his suit fit him ill. It wouldn't do to be caught getting hard by the lady you were trying to persuade to sponsor your writing machine.

"How much will you need to put this device into production?"

He gulped and raised his gaze to hers. "Ten thousand pounds."

"That's a lot of money." She sat back into her chair.

"I have a full list of—" He reached across the table.

"I'd like to see what I'd be funding a little more fully."

He stopped.

Deliberately, she examined him from foot to forehead, lingering at his waist as though she could see through the table he stood behind and the clothes covering him.

He was well built. She imagined that under the suit he would have pale skin and downy blond hair across his muscled chest. Lower down it would become coarser and darker. "Please take off your clothes."

His lips fell open in a sweetly lewd gesture, revealing his soft-looking mouth, but he didn't move. She wanted to run her finger over his lips and feel their velvet warmth. Would he be good with his tongue? Men who worked with their hands could be remarkably skilled with other challenges requiring dexterity. But tongues were another thing altogether, and it was tricky to accurately predict whether a man was good at licking a woman out. She preferred to know in advance. Perhaps he'd be amenable to a trial with her maid Louise, who sometimes aided her in such matters. A man who made an enthusiastic job of licking out a housemaid was worthy of consideration.

She slanted one eyebrow upward. "I'm waiting."

He flushed scarlet. "I must have misheard you, m'lady."

"I don't think you did." His face said clearly that

he'd heard exactly what she'd said but couldn't quite believe it. The angle of his body, tilted toward her now, spoke of his eagerness, even as his mind protested.

Their gazes locked for a long second, then he looked down. She could swear she saw a glimpse of a smile as he shrugged out of his jacket.

His shirtsleeves were revealed, and with them that he'd borrowed the whole ensemble from a slighter man. She nodded approvingly. "How small your..." She watched as he squirmed. "Shirt is."

She raised her hand and flicked her fingers, indicating for him to move away from the table. Watching him shift reluctantly across, she saw she'd been right. He'd been concealing an erection, his trousers pushed out, as unmistakable now as when he'd tried to hide. It had been a while since she'd last had a project like this.

There was only the rustle of fabric and the sound of his breath, a little shallow, as he unknotted his cravat and slid off the cream waistcoat. He laid each garment carefully on the table, to the side of his machine.

His hands were unsteady as he undid the buttons on his shirt, revealing a trail of chest hair leading enticingly down. When he shrugged out of the shirt, she had to stifle an intake of breath. His chest and shoulders were stunning. He was strong. There had been no hiding his muscled physique under a neat suit, but out of it he seemed even more powerful, like a Celtic god rather than an inventive engineer. Heat bloomed between her legs. The view of his shoulders was further improved when he knelt to take off his boots and stockings.

He rose and reached for the falls of his trousers. She

had to stop herself from leaning forward with anticipation. Would his other hair be as red? Would there be more freckles? Oh, but maybe she could make this even sweeter for both of them. "Is it red?"

His hands stilled and his blue gaze flicked up to her.

"Your . . . " She lowered her lids a little to show him she was looking at the bulge between his legs.

His eyes widened. Was he thinking of the swollen head of his prick or the color of the hair surrounding it or the delicate rosebud behind?

"Yes," he whispered.

"Show me then." She couldn't wait to see his cock, jutting up. He opened and let his trousers fall in one motion, as if taking them off gradually would be painful and it was best to get it over with. She had a glimpse of his thick cock before he leaned over and yanked the trousers off his ankles, before holding them in front of himself while he folded them. Very slowly. He fussed over getting the creases straight. Then he fiddled with a button.

"Drop them now."

The cloth pooled at his feet.

His instant compliance made her smile. She wanted to look at his face and check if he was mortified or aroused or both. Instead she tilted her head, as if considering whether his cock would do.

"My, is that all?" He was actually a rather good size. It was enticingly solid and would stretch any woman, maybe even painfully. But in length, though it wasn't small, it wasn't as intimidating as the rest of his frame would suggest. On his massive frame, an average length cock looked out of proportion.

"I'm sorry, m'lady." He licked his lips.

"It is a little cold in here," she pretended to reassure him, shrugging as if she couldn't feel the roaring heat from the fire. She was enjoying his embarrassment almost as much as he was.

Spots of pink appeared on his cheeks again and he rubbed his chest self-consciously.

As she'd guessed, the hair that surrounded his dick was dark ginger. His balls were large and hanging away from his body in the heat of the room. Her hand clenched with the want to trail her fingers down the path of his hair on his chest all the way to his hardness.

It was tempting to revel in him. The urge to order him to be motionless while she explored his body with her hands and mouth was strong. But he'd told her, not in words but with the heat in his gaze, what would seduce him more. "Stroke yourself."

He didn't hesitate this time, wrapping his fingers around his stem. His big hand covered the majority of his cock, and she understood a little better. He eased his hand up and down with the same smooth precision as his machine.

There were too many places to look, all at once. His unabashed nakedness, shown in his straight back and high chin, even as his breath hitched with pleasure, was mesmerizing. She wanted to focus on the hard cock between his legs, but her eyes kept wandering, taking in the muscles in his forearm flexing as he moved, his taut calves holding him still, and the planes of his stomach. It was odd that a gorgeous man had gained a penchant for being teased. "Who told you that your dick was small?"

"Oh, I, er." His eyebrows pulled inward momentarily. "You know."

"Ah, you saw other men." While washing perhaps. She could imagine him glancing sideways at his friends and wondering what they'd look like hard.

He nodded, but she could see his fist tightening over the head of his cock as he tugged.

She waited a moment, to let him think he was off the hook. "Who else?"

"No one." His hand had sped up.

It was much too quick a denial to be true. "Slow down please."

He let out a groan but slowed his pumping wrist.

"Now, do I need to stop you, or are you going to tell me now?" It was unconscionably fun to force him into disclosures so enjoyable to them both.

He made a choking sound. "A whore."

Clever lady. "What did she say?"

"She." He gulped. "She said if I went to another lady at that establishment that she'd laugh at my... She said they'd laugh about it together when I left."

She didn't repress her chuckle. Professional women could be very insightful. "And you went to see another whore, I presume."

He made a drawn-out noise like an animal in distress. "No."

Understanding dawned in her. "But she continued to threaten."

He nodded. And he'd liked that a lot. His cock had definitely grown even thicker in the last few minutes, under his frantic ministration and her mischievous enquiry.

"Not too quickly, Mr. Merridon. I don't know if that tiny thing can take so much."

The sides of his mouth creased, as if it was physical pain to slow the progress of his orgasm, just as her word "tiny" caused him to surge with need. But he eased to a torturous up-and-down beat. Precome beaded at his tip.

He was magnificent. Her pussy squeezed with the desire to have him, with all his banked control and passion for her approval, in her. She was flooded with wetness at her juncture, entirely too ready for him.

He'd willingly fuck her with his nicely proportioned cock and his oversized body. He'd pinch her nipples when she commanded and go deep and slow to tip her over. Then quick and hard to make him spill inside her. Another thing she suspected would embarrass him wonderfully, if he came without permission.

She needed to come. But satisfying though fucking him would be, it wouldn't keep up their game, which they were both relishing. It would leave them less to anticipate. Moreover, his shaking and desperately leaking cock suggested he might not last long enough to fully enjoy a coupling. Thus she said, "Stop."

"M'lady?" He was panting, his expression dark. But he abated, pale-blue eyes focused on her.

She wriggled back into the cushions of the chair. "Put your hands behind your back."

His face crumpled momentarily. He'd been so close to climax and was understandably reluctant. He obeyed as if his hands were heavy iron and he was resisting a magnetic pull.

With unhurried ease, she stroked across her silk-covered thighs and down to the hem of her dress. His eyes widened as she lifted her skirts to her waist, and she smiled to herself. She wasn't wearing any drawers and thus he'd be suddenly able to see everything, like a cloth whipped from a surprise cake. The cool air hit her bare legs and cunny and she basked in his slack-mouthed stare.

As she slid her hands down the smooth skin of her inner thighs, he watched intently, following her action with his chin and leaning forward in his eagerness. Oh, this was going to be so fun. She teased around her wet slit. He'd want to see more, quickly, and in truth, she wanted to gratify herself. But after so much time already, it seemed wrong to dive straight in. She opened her legs but used her hands to hide and reveal all the treasures between her legs.

Working by feel and his hot gaze alone, she worked her way inward in little insistent circles with her right hand. The first slick movement over her clit made her gasp, though she knew it was coming. With her left, she fingered suggestively at her hole, dipping lower as if she might sodomize herself with a finger.

His cock bobbed. There was hard desire and covetous need in his eyes. Good to know this was making him insane too.

"You'd like to fuck me, wouldn't you?"

He groaned, and somewhere in the noise was an affirmative.

"You'd like to put that little cock of yours in me and try to prove to me that size doesn't matter."

"Yes, m'lady. Please." He took an involuntary step forward and she quashed him with a raised eyebrow. He stepped back.

He wanted to fuck her, but he wanted more to be

denied. His body was close to perfection, with just enough insignificant flaws to make him vulnerable to teasing. Strong arms, broad shoulders, and sharp eyes might all make a man gorgeous, but they could give a man the inflated idea of his own importance and make him a lazy lover. A man who could enjoy being teased knew his true value so deeply he could enjoy what would injure the pride of a lesser man.

"I don't think I need your diminutive implement to help me." She licked her upper lip as she slipped one hand to her entrance as her other continued to glide over her nub. It was an awkward angle momentarily, but she pushed two fingers into her entrance, curling them upward to press against that sensitive spot. She moved her fingers in tandem, each sensation enhancing the other. And best of all was the view while she was pleasuring herself. He was really a glorious sight naked. Standing still but intent, his eyes flicked between her face and the filthy, wanton things she was doing between her thighs.

He was leaning forward, greedy to see her. His hands were clasped behind him, holding himself back.

She increased the circles around her clit so he'd be able to see her pink nub appearing and disappearing. The lips of her sex were generous, made to be watched. The moan she let out as the pleasure built inside her was entirely genuine, but his answering groan of need made her wish she'd played up for him.

She stroked around her nub, revealing herself and then obscuring as she pushed and eased to hold her orgasm away, then pull it forward.

Then she couldn't resist. A little too hard, a bit too fast, and she spilled over, despite her intention to draw the sensations out. She closed her eyes as the peak of sensation washed over her, pulsing out from her core.

His breath, fast and deep, must have been audible all this time, but it was only as the pulses between her legs ebbed away that she became aware of it. His wild, pale irises were the first things she saw when she lazily opened her eyes.

Her mouth curved into a smile. He hadn't broken posture, or come. He'd waited for her approval.

"Perhaps I'll leave you thus," she mused aloud, stroking one fingernail over the lips of her sex and easing out her fingers, dripping with her juices.

"Oh." There was a brightness in his eyes. Excitement. His cock was still as hard as ever. "Please don't leave me."

"Very well."

He stepped toward her, hope sparkling in his eyes.

"You may resume." She nodded at his waist.

He understood and dropped back, his hand immediately on his aching cock. He pushed up and down, the head revealed then hidden by his foreskin, then his fingers.

But there was a price to pay for any indulgence. "You will spill on the floor."

His expression collapsed into outright trepidation, but he didn't stop. With all his neat machinery and tidy clothing, this would be at least as difficult as being denied. All the muscles across his belly were tense with the effort of preventing himself from spilling, making them seem like an immovable Greek statue, even as his whole body twitched with need.

"I could still order you to put your breeches on over your cockstand. I could send you into the street with your cock pushing out. My maids would see you and titter. They'll tell their friends and giggle about the ginger-haired man, with his freckled face, who got hard speaking to their mistress."

He was frigging himself really hard now, legs firm even as his head tipped back.

"Are you imagining it?"

He was, she could tell by the rough look in his eyes.

"Yes."

"One of the pretty married ladies who lives in the square will notice and look away with a smirk."

He bit his lip hard enough that it went white.

"Come. On the floor."

His gaze searched for somewhere to spill that wasn't the floor or his hand, where it would make a mess. His seed would end up all over the floor, his trousers, possibly her thighs and dress.

He leaned forward, his muscled body tense and his eyes trained on her face, despite the pretty tableau of her pink, wet sex.

Then his face was loose and reams of white were over his stomach and falling onto the floor. Somehow, he managed to avoid either of their clothes, even as he moaned and shook. There was nothing like watching a strong man overcome with pleasure.

She smoothed down her skirts.

His eyes were still open, but he seemed to gradually regain his ability to see, and looked away. He grabbed at his clothes and hurried to dress himself.

She turned her attention over to his machine. It was a good design, and the intricacy of the mechanism meant it would be welcome in many homes. He'd managed to cover that glorious chest by the time she looked back. The tails of the shirt fell over his still-hard dick. His movements were jerky with panic as he picked his crumpled trousers from the floor and yanked them on, then hastily tied his cravat.

"I'm very impressed, Mr. Merridon. I'll give you the money you need to progress your writing machine."

He looked up as he shrugged on his coat, possibly more shocked than when she told him to take off his clothes. He fumbled with the buttons of his coat.

"I . . . thank you, Lady Charlbury." He didn't look happy though. His mouth was bowed with disappointment.

What did he expect? A marriage proposal? "I'll have a maid bring over the money next week." Louise might enjoy that task.

His mouth sank into being fully downward. He was so adorably transparent. Unlike some men of science or men of rank, he was utterly without guile or arrogance.

He fussed with his cravat, making it less straight, not more.

"You may visit again when the writing machine has progressed." She'd found a visit to be valuable further inducement for the men she sponsored not to waste the money she gave them. "I think there is a risk of the ink smudging in its present design. I should like to see it again in two months' time. And you with it, obviously."

His vivid imagination found a host of delicious things she might mean and made him blush again.

Perhaps she'd strip him naked every time she saw him, just for the joy of seeing him thus.

DAILY DENIAL

TammyJo Eckhart

'm alone on a Sunday morning.

I can feel the remnants of his presence starting to fade away, but I won't simply wait for them to dissipate. I sit lotus on the cushion after the candles are lit. I begin with silent, short commands.

Close your eyes.

I can feel my eyelids slowly close, the light from the window I'm facing creating a murky gray in my field of vision. Tiny sparks occasionally play across the gray as my mind struggles to find something familiar in the blandness. I push aside the memories of yesterday and let the gray take over.

Center your body.

I lift up my shoulders and roll them back. I adjust my hands, resting them palm up on my thighs. I wiggle enough to ease the stretch on my hips. I feel the light air from the ever-running fan brush the air over my arms and stir the hair that has come loose from my bun over my neck and shoulders. I feel every trace of his touch float away. I force my fingers to relax and my chin to lift upward.

Breathe in.

I can feel the sharp tickle of air slip through my nose and slide down my throat. My chest expands slightly and I have to straighten up so it can grow more.

Breathe out.

I can feel my tummy expand as I push air out, rushing up my throat, fluttering through my mouth, then flowing out over parted lips.

Deeper. Take deeper breaths.

The air dives through my throat into my lungs. My nipples brush against the soft silk top I'm wearing, and I direct that sensation lower. By the fifteenth breath in, I can feel the warmth and swell of my clit. I pause, holding that air until warmth moves outward.

I repeat for another ten minutes, challenging that desire back upward until every part of me is warm.

I open my eyes and smile as that energy settles into my brain. "Better than coffee," I say, chuckling softly as I stretch out and rise to my feet.

As I have breakfast I start a new entry in my journal. Phrases about light, dark, air, and skin.

Monday I focus my mind for a moment as the meeting breaks up.

Today's target is Brian.

He is wearing a rust-colored tie with three vertical baby-blue lines an inch under the basic knot. Each line has another line's width of space between it and the others. His shirt is baby blue, the buttons hidden by the tie until he leans forward to snag his cup after standing up. The buttons are the same blue color. When he straightens up, the light from the conference room windows reveals flat, dark nipples and the fact that he isn't wearing an undershirt.

I force my gaze to move over to a shoulder and down a sleeve. There at the mid forearm are wrinkles indicating he rolled up his sleeves before the meeting. He's our system administrator, so he spends a lot of time in the computer center, which gets even warmer. The computer team has more leeway in how they dress, but corporate Monday is still formal business wear.

Unlike many IT folks, his skin is a healthy hue, not darkened by too much sun or pale from days upon days indoors. He has a single gold band on his left ring finger, and his veins become visible when he grasps the cup.

I trace my eyes from the cup over the shiny tabletop back to Brian's body. He's wearing light-gray trousers and a slightly darker belt, with a rainbow buckle that pushes the boundaries of allowed personal jewelry regulations. His pants are wrinkled from sitting for an hour, but the fabric is neither bunched nor stretched to show what he's wearing or not underneath.

I pull my gaze back and gather up my own notebook and files, logging a few ideas into my mind about colors and light.

I smile at Sandra as she puts a hand on my arm to double-check that our Monday lunch date is a go. "New deli across the street needs our seal of approval," I tell her in a firm but friendly tone.

While she's in the ladies' room, I take out my journal and make a few more notes about fabric, boredom, identity, and newness.

* * *

The water parts beneath my vertical slice as I follow the aerobics instructor's directions Tuesday evening at the gym. Jodi is breathing hard beside me, so I just give her a glance and a smile. The water resists but parts for my hands, my knees, and my torso as I move through the twice-weekly workout. It warms with the movements and body heat of a dozen students as we push ourselves for an hour to the sounds of gentle pop, energetic club, pounding techno, and soft jazz.

Jodi's breathing peaks at one point, and I hear a gasp from her. I turn to her again and whisper, "You can do this. Breathe." I smile as she complies, and her breathing returns to regulated levels.

I look at Jodi's flushed face as she climbs the ladder after me. My own body is tired, but I keep my eyes on her, an arm ready to steady her should she need it. We walk side by side to the women's locker room.

"Good job, ladies," our instructor says to us as she walks past us to go log the hour and the attendees on the clipboard hanging just outside the pool room.

Jodi brushes against my arm before settling her hand under my automatically offered elbow, resting her fingers around it. "You never make fun of me at the end of the workouts," she says with a sigh.

"I'm your friend. Your coming with me helps me stay in shape," I insist.

"How do you know when I'm having a rough time?"

"You're my friend; it's part of my job to be aware of you. Just like you are of me."

Jodi pauses, then nods her head sharply before we continue walking.

I note Jodi watching me as we hop in the showers, struggle out of the bathing suits, and then quickly soap up and wash out our hair. She looks away when I make direct eye contact. That shyness sends a tickle out of my head, down my throat, through my torso, to warm my clit. I bite my tongue just enough to dampen that reaction.

The cooler and far less humid air of the gym outside the locker room makes us pause and take deep breaths. We wave to the staff and the other members as we leave. In the parking lot we hug each other good-bye, and I feel Jodi's breathing increase again.

I reach into my gym bag to take out my journal as she drives off first. I jot down a few phrases and words about exercise, water, sound, and embarrassment.

That is because you suck, you stupid cunt!, the idiot we allowed into our ranks for the dungeon mission lashes out on Wednesday evening. I count out one, two, three, four... The secondary tank is booted out of the team by our house leader, RavenHorde, so I don't need to do anything but smile when I see a banned notice come up on my screen.

Would you see if Steal is on yet, CocoaScout? Raven-Horde asks me.

On it, I reply as I use my privileges as subcommander to look at our roster. *Nope, but CrescentMoon sent us a request to join ten minutes back and is only fishing*, I report.

CrescentMoon?

We did Highrealm, the WaterTanks, and some older dungeons with him, SlipperyEel pipes up to remind us.

We haven't seen him in a while, RavenHorde replies.

She had a baby, I think, DawnsAngel tosses out.

She, yes, right, she, SlipperyEel sighs. *I know, I know, I'm a sexist pig*, he mumbles halfheartedly.

Shall I invite her? I ask.

Within a minute, CrescentMoon is with us and chatting with BrunoMounds, our main tank.

I take those moments to jot down a few things in my journal before I feed my dinosaur and my snakes and get ready for another attempt at the second of three bosses we want to take out tonight.

From my place in the back, I can see the entire battlefield. I bark out simple words warning of pending attacks or highlighting goons for us to pick off while the frontline stays focused. At the end of each success I add in a "Good job" or a "Nice work" before the next crisis demands our attention.

Once we've won and divided up the loot, DawnsAngel sends me a private message. *Thank you for always staying positive. You are the reason I stay in this house.*

I feel my jaw loosen and a brightness grow in my eyes as I bow to her and then portal back to our house. I sit for a few moments to look at my character on the logout screen. If I were a dwarf I might look like that. Calm but serious expression, hair pulled back into a few braids, bright eyes glancing around casually. I log out and turn off the system.

I push back from the desk as my computer powers down. I do a few stretches as I walk to the kitchen table. I pick up my wineglass and sip as I jot down notes about teamwork, positive feedback, sexism, and pets in my journal.

* * *

I toss a piece of popcorn into my mouth as the heroine onscreen spins around and plants her boot firmly into her enemy's torso, sending him skidding backward. Thursday is movie night after water aerobics. Just me watching at home—streaming, something DVRed, or one title from my collection. Her outfit is ridiculous, more annual swimsuit edition than warrior maiden, but at least she hasn't had to turn to any men for help yet, and the movie is almost over. Does that little boy who led her through the woods earlier count as relying on men? I shrug and eat some more popcorn.

I am not watching alone, though.

A text message pops up on my phone, and I read it. *Is her armor getting smaller with each fight, or am I just horny?*

Both, I send back.

Miss you. Wish it was Saturday.

I look at the message, turn from it, and focus on the continued fight. In those seconds I glanced down, the villain has turned the tide, and the warrior is on her knees struggling to keep his sword from impaling her. Now the bad guy is monologuing about how the heroine would look really great with her mouth full.

Wow. Can we get any more direct and still get a PG rating?

The warrior smiles, licks her lips, then pulls a dagger from her boot and drives it up beneath the baddie's legs.

Yup, we can get more direct.

Another text comes in so I glance down at it. *He deserved that.*

I look back at the screen. The villain has risen up

onto his toes as the warrior stands, urging him upward with that dagger. She makes some comments about freeing the world from future generations tainted by his blood before making a jerking movement that has her foe screaming and the screen turning gray briefly before switching to another scene.

My phone makes a beep, so I look down. *Have you thought more about knife play?* the new text message reads.

I frown and take a deep breath, closing my eyes for a moment, channeling those feelings through my body, releasing tension. I text back, *You don't dictate what we do.*

Within seconds he replies, *Yes, Mistress. I apologize.*

I feel my heart race and my groin clench in reaction to that title and how quickly he backs down. Five days since our last session without orgasm; denying myself the pleasure of even riding a wave of desire farther than the warmth of pleasure makes the reaction stronger. I text back, *Good.*

There is a pause in the texting as we finish the movie's final sequence. The warrior returns home to proclaim her village free from threats. She gets a parade, a victory speech, and a welcoming man back home who sinks to his knees before the end titles roll.

My clit throbs, so I stand up suddenly, yanking up my pajama bottoms to crush into it and deaden the reaction with a bit of pain. Luckily, I'm not a switch, so that always does the trick for me.

I glance back down at the next text message. *Time for another one?*

I look at the clock and gauge the time, run through

the titles on the streaming queue, and think of something cold. *Ice-cream break, then next movie*, I text back.

I head to the kitchen and get out a pint of brownie bliss. It sits open to warm up to the way I love it as I open my journal and take a seat. *Amazons, bossy men, fight, and boots,* I write down quickly. I glance up the page over the other words I've been inspired to jot down.

When I return to the couch, ice-cream pint in hand, spoon sticking straight up from it, I snap a photo of the dessert, only my hand visible in the image. I send it to him.

In a moment comes his return photo, showing him putting a spoonful of his frozen treat into his grinning mouth, making me smile. I want to send something back to tease him, to make him think about Saturday, but I don't. The week is for me to prepare and for him to merely speculate.

Instead I type out *start*, then hit SEND a moment before I hit PLAY on my remote.

"We have a few new items you might be interested in," the store owner I always talk with tells me as soon as I enter the thrift shop after work on Friday. This has become my routine.

This isn't about him. I could just cycle through the same three outfits, mixing up pieces from them, and he'd react like it was something I just bought that cost a hundred bucks or more.

I like to find something new so that when I look in my mirror I'm inspired. Doing that for most Saturdays would make an expensive year, but this place makes it doable without guilt.

This shop is known for being more eccentric about what you can bring in for them to sell, so the clothing and accessories vary. Last week I bought a pillbox hat and lace gloves, so we had a twisted tea party. A month ago it was a bit for a "tiny horse" that got us out into my fenced-in yard for an hour of pony play.

Tonight the proprietor takes me to the same dressing room where she's laid out a half-dozen things for me to look at and try on. "Two funerals last week resulted in some unwanted items from a grieving family, and I pulled these, thinking they might interest you. I'll give you a few moments to look at it all."

I wait until she steps out, then hang my clutch on a free hook so I can thoroughly look at the items laid out on the bench and hung on two other hooks. I look at the clothes first, my eyes pulled to the flapper-style cock-tail dress in a sparkling red color. Some of the beads are missing, but it looks like it might fit. Then there is a nearly transparent gray shawl hanging next to it. I think back to the movie's Amazons, to my colleague's trousers, and to my friend's rapid breathing. I feel my clit twitch, and I smile.

The items on the table include a fan with a green bamboo design that I quickly dismiss because I have three fans already. There is a string of pinkish beads that might be from the same era as the dress, but the color feels off to me. I'm just not a pink sort of gal. There is an elaborate ring with an elephant on it, but it slips around on my finger a bit too much for comfort.

I smile when I recognize the final object. The narrow box has faded from its original black to gray, and the ends show signs of wear, but inscribed is a row of little starbursts that make me glance back at the dress.

In twenty minutes I'm back in my car with three new tools beside me. I take out my journal and jot down *power, mystery, punishment,* and *shine* before driving home.

A couple of hours later I stand in the door frame of my dedicated dungeon room that my realtor called a "craft room" when I bought the house. I'm in cutoffs, a T-shirt, and tennis shoes, my hair up in a ponytail. I'm breathing a bit too loudly, so I close my eyes for a moment.

I breathe in and out, channeling the strain and drain of setting things up out of my limbs. I take the journal from my back pocket where I stashed it and a pen. I hold them in front of me like an offering. I shake my head once, then open my eyes.

I look over the layout and check off the words from my journal. *Dark. Skin. Fabric. Boredom. Sound. Embarrassment. Sexism. Pets. Amazons. Boots.*

I let my mind go through the setup, the plan, the possibilities. Each second warms my mound, making me slick, speeding up my breathing, until I'm almost kneeling before the elegant chair I've set up on a platform.

"Wait," I whisper. I breathe in and out. I unclench my fingers, loosen my grip on the seat, and bite the side of my mouth just enough to dampen the desire. In a few seconds I pull myself up and look down at the chair draped in shimmering scarves. With one slow deep breath, I make myself turn and descend the two steps.

I glance down at the attachment point a couple of steps away and pinch my arm to keep my focus.

I shut the door behind me and lock it without looking back.

I want to just lean back and slide down the door, one hand between my legs, but I march back upstairs to take a cold shower.

"Oh!" he exclaims when I slip the blindfold over his eyes as soon as he shuts out the light the next morning by shutting the front door.

"You can't sneak into our city, seed giver," I snarl at him.

He swallows and drops the backpack he brought with him while reaching up with one hand to push the blindfold off. He gasps when I snap his backside with my riding crop.

"Any attempt to escape will result in a fate worse than death," I warn him.

He works his jaw for a moment as I wait to see if he'll follow my lead or try to steer things. I strike at his ass a handful of times to clear his head until he's promising to do what I want.

My clit is already warm and wet, but I kick aside his backpack and focus on the scenario. "Take off your clothes. All of them."

It takes him a while to shed what he's wearing, because he always comes well dressed. He was once horrified to discover that my plans started with dinner at a fancy place in town; he had to borrow a tie and jacket from a miffed maître d'. I urge him on by holding tightly to the back of the blindfold and snapping any covered skin with my crop. By the time he's naked, his breathing is heavy, and I silently run through my mantra to keep mine steady.

"Move it, pig!" I order with a push toward the basement door.

"Hands out to your sides; grip the railing," I command once we are at the top of the ramp leading downward, a bonus feature I was willing to pay more for on the house hunt years back. I watch his careful steps, his grip on the railing, the clenching of his firm ass as he walks down.

"May I?" he gets out before I cut off his words with another swat of my crop.

His groan makes me shudder, but I breathe in and out, focusing on each step as we keep moving.

"In here!" I grab one of his wrists and pull him into the space and along to the spot I have prepared. "Kneel! Good boy," I growl at him as he goes down onto the thinly padded floor with a pained grimace. He pauses then leans toward me, so I crop him across the chest, forcing him to straighten up to move away.

"Don't move, or you'll lose something valuable," I tell him as I step to the side and snatch the wide collar from the nearby box I've covered with black cloth. He still flinches a bit as the leather touches the front of his neck but relaxes when I put two fingers between it and his flesh before locking it on. I reach down and bring up the chain I had set in the attachment point on the floor so I can fix it to the D-ring in front. I give it a good yank to demonstrate that he can lower his head but can't raise it much farther than a formal presentation kneel allows.

"Wait and be silent. If you say anything, I will gag you!" I snarl into his ear before I stand up and step back.

I count my breaths in and out, roll my neck, flex and relax my hands, and watch him try to be obedient. I can see every muscle and bulge of his body, lightly tanned from his work at a nursery and landscaping company. I recall every scent, hair, taste, and movement I've enjoyed with that body, but I channel that desire up and into my role for the next several hours. I know he turns toward the sound I make as I move away, but he doesn't make a sound.

I go into the attached full bathroom and slip out of the shorts and T-shirt I'm wearing. I look at my nude body, tracing my curves from muscle and fat, feeling the smoothness of my skin, and I smile watching my nipples pucker when I think of what I'm about to do. I slip on the garter belt and flesh-tone nylons. I pull the black riding boots on and run my hands up their leather to the silky fabric to just brush my trimmed mound. I let the heat descend slowly from my mind downward but keep breathing.

I put on the lacy black bra, adjusting my breasts to rest in each cup, tracing the straps and band to ease out any fold or crease. I run my hands under the cups and move them a bit more to give just a hint of skin. I breathe out jaggedly, closing my eyes for a moment, pinching a nipple when my clit throbs to turn the heat down.

I slip the flapper dress over me. The underslip is silky smooth, cascading across my shoulders and torso to fall just above my knees and the boots. I pull the left side of my hair back, clip it with a simple barrette, and adjust my curls so they fall over my shoulders.

I don't wear much makeup, and when I do it is always very natural, so when I pick up the kohl pencil and make marks around my eyes, it is dramatic. I add a few spots of sparkly red on the outer edges and feather it outward to my hairline. I put one blood-red dot on the center of my upper lip, making the crescent dip more pronounced. Finally I add some glitter powder over my cheeks, neck, chest, and shoulders to create an unearthly appearance.

I walk back out to the main room, and he turns his head toward me again. His mouth opens, then snaps shut. Even in this role of captive he is innately submissive, but I say nothing as I climb the two steps to the chair. I turn to face him and frown.

His blindfold is still on, but it has slipped a bit or perhaps he peeked. "Bad boy!" I growl out, and he jerks back.

I stomp down the steps, grabbing the gray transparent shawl as I go. "Do not remove this!" I order as I drop it over his head so it falls down to his waist, covering him further. I stomp a few steps away, then move as quietly as possible back to the chair.

I lift the edge of the dress then sit down, my butt on the edge. The cushions I placed help me keep my pelvis tilted slightly upward as I spread my legs wide. I reach out to the thin wand vibrator I've placed nearby and hold it on the edge of my labia for a few seconds.

I look at him and count out several heartbeats before I speak in a calm, regal tone. "Remove the blindfold but nothing else. Put your hands behind your back. If you do anything else, I will stop and my guards will take you away."

He brings up both hands and fumbles with the shawl, then finds the edge and moves under it so he can pull the blindfold simply down to his neck. I hear him gasp as he looks up at the queen seated above him two arm lengths away, even if he strains at the chain.

"This is my queendom," I tell him. I flip on the vibrator and the switch to the built-in stereo, the buzz blending into the drumming. I let my breath go and ride the week of ideas into orgasms over and over until I let the tool fall to the seat.

"Clean me up," I order him.

He quickly releases the chain but keeps the shawl over him as he crawls forward. He looks up at me, eyes wide, but makes no move to remove the fabric. "Down," I dictate.

His tongue through the fabric over my clit and lips adds enough variety to help me come until I've surpassed the times I've denied myself throughout the week.

I'm alone on a Sunday morning.

THE JOY
OF SOCKS

Elizabeth Coldwell

W hen was the last time I treated you?" Suzanne asked.

I glanced from the array of fancy cakes and finger sandwiches on the stand in the middle of the table to the glass of prosecco in front of me. "I thought this was my treat."

"Oh, Poppy, I love it when you play the innocent." She laughed. "Darling, you know exactly what I'm referring to."

"You mean, when did you last buy me something for the chest?" I reached to help myself to an egg and cress sandwich before correcting my behavior. "Pardon me, Miss, but may I?"

Suzanne nodded. "Of course."

She didn't say anything more, but I knew from the look in her eye that by asking for her permission I'd just avoided a demerit mark. Not that it mattered. If she wanted to punish me, it wouldn't take her long to find some other fault in my manners. She always did.

I took a bite of my sandwich and considered the matter of the chest. It was a grand name for what was, in truth, a box that once held a rather nice pair of knee-length leather boots. I'd covered it in purple wrapping paper and decorated it with an array of gold and silver stars. Inside it I kept the various things Suzanne had bought me over the years we'd been seeing each other. Belts, a wooden-backed hairbrush, a string of chunky plastic beads. All innocuous enough on their own, but the uses they could be put to when she wanted to tease and torment me...

"Excuse me." The voice at my ear was polite, with a distinct Eastern European accent. "But is everything all right with your afternoon tea?"

Interrupted in my musing, I turned to smile at the waitress. "Yes, thank you. It's all delicious."

"Can I get either of you ladies anything else?"

"No, we have everything we need, thank you." Suzanne's tone was polite but dismissive, making it clear we didn't want any further interruptions. The waitress nodded and walked over to check on the nearest occupied table.

"The service is very good here, isn't it?" I said. "I hate it when you're in a restaurant and they wait until you've got a mouthful of food, then they come over and ask you how you're enjoying your meal. It's like they're totally aware of the moment you start chewing."

Suzanne sipped her tea. "The chest, Poppy..."

"Oh, yes. You wanted to know about the last thing I got for it. It was that silk scarf, the green one you said matched my eyes."

We'd found the scarf in an exclusive store on Bond

Street, one of those places where unless you walk in dressed in a mink coat and dripping with jewelry, they treat you like something they've scraped off the sole of their shoe. Suzanne always looks the part, in her neat knee-length skirt suits and designer heels, but as for me—well, I have a bratty side, and when I'm with her I dress to emphasize it. I like skirts so short they threaten to expose my panties and thin white blouses with a black bra all too visible beneath them. Today, I'd made a concession to my surroundings and opted for a demure-looking tea dress, but somehow, in the rush to get out of the house in time to meet Suzanne, I'd forgotten to put on any underwear. If she had noticed the outline of my nipples pushing hard against the floral chiffon, she hadn't said anything.

The day of our last shopping expedition, I'd been favoring the overgrown schoolgirl look, with my hair in pigtails and a wad of bright pink bubblegum in my mouth that I'd chomped with loud smacking sounds as we'd taken the escalator to the second floor. I'd behaved well—or well by my standards, anyway, as Suzanne had asked the snooty assistant to show us a selection of their most expensive silk scarves.

"Which one do you like, Poppy?" Suzanne had asked.

The assistant had looked on as I'd pawed at the filmy scraps of material. Her face was a mix of conflicted emotions, most of them caused, I'd guessed, by my choice of eye-watering neon-yellow nail varnish. "This one's pretty," I'd said at length, holding up a plain, moss-green scarf.

"A good choice. Very discreet," the assistant had remarked, fixing me with a look that clearly said *though you wouldn't know discreet if it bit you.* She'd wrapped the scarf without further comment, and Suzanne had charged it to her card, not even blinking at the three-figure price tag. But please don't go thinking that I'm only with Suzanne for her money. I may be a brat, but I'm no gold digger. Suzanne has the ability to deal with my sulky behavior and occasional public tantrum better than anyone else I've ever met. Not only do I like to have my desire kept on a slow burn, I need to be treated with a firm hand. And she knows just when and where to apply it.

From the department store, we went straight back to Suzanne's apartment in Holland Park, where I wore my present for the first time. She wound it around my wrists as I lay facedown, clutching her ornate wrought-iron headboard. Once she'd knotted it, allowing just enough give for me to wriggle, she administered a hard spanking that left my bottom red and sore. Every time I opened the chest and admired that scarf, I recalled the feel of those firm, relentless swats on my bare ass and the way I'd writhed against the bedcovers and begged for her mercy.

"Yes, the scarf." Suzanne's voice brought me out of my pleasant reverie. "And thinking about it this morning made me realize I haven't treated you for quite some time. So, once we've finished our tea, I intend to put that right."

"Thank you, Madam," I said, hoping she wouldn't notice that my good manners had been a diversion while I helped myself to the last of the petits fours.

* * *

After the genteel hush of the tearoom, it was a shock to
step out onto the busy shopping street. Suzanne wove
her way through the knots of dawdling pedestrians,
with me half a pace behind. I had no idea of our even-
tual destination, but I assumed she was heading for one
of the expensive department stores she favored. Instead,
I was surprised to find her walking up to the doors of a
shop selling discount sporting goods. The windows were
plastered with huge red-and-white banners announcing,
SALE–EVERYTHING MUST GO. Bass-heavy pop
music blared from hidden speakers as I followed
her inside.

"Are you sure about this?" I wanted to ask, but I said
nothing as we made our way past racks of replica football shirts, yoga pants in bright, geometric designs, and
sweatshirts emblazoned with the logos of all the well-
known sporting goods manufacturers. I'd never have
guessed she would have heard of this company, and I
was surprised that being so close to so many synthetic
fibers wasn't making her physically ill.

"Ah, here we go."

She had led me right to the back of the store, where
we were surrounded by all manner of tacky, cut-price
accessories. Wrist and ankle weights with fetching pink
trim, water bottles decorated with the cross of Saint
George and the Scottish saltire, gold medals made from
chocolate, furry earmuffs in pastel shades. Mentally, I
filed a couple of the items away in case I had to buy
a Secret Santa present for someone I hated. Suzanne
bypassed them all and came to a halt in front of a
display of sports socks.

"Yes, these should do the trick." She took a pair of plain white knee-high socks from a rack and made a brief show of checking them over. "Now, where do we pay?"

We queued at the counter behind a woman with bottle-blonde hair, wearing fuchsia velour leggings. She was buying a large wheeled suitcase and a pair of dumbbells.

"So either she's going to hit her husband over the head with the dumbbells and stuff his body in the case, or he's already dead and she needs something heavy to weigh him down when she throws him in the river," I commented, loud enough for everyone around us to hear. When the woman turned to glare at me, I flashed her my sweetest smile. As she returned to the task of keying her PIN into the card reader, I addressed Suzanne in a stage whisper. "I'm remembering her face in case the police start investigating his disappearance."

Suzanne fixed me with a look that managed to combine disapproval and fondness. "That mouth of yours is going to get you into a lot of trouble."

Desire prickled all the way down my spine, and I grew hot between my legs. I clapped my hands together. "Ooh, goody."

The woman in front of us finished her transaction and lugged her purchases away, glaring at me as she did. She didn't know it, but she'd got off lightly compared to the comments I'd once made when Suzanne and I had been waiting for a couple to pay for a turkey baster in a kitchenware shop. It seems it isn't polite to speculate that someone might want to try out an unorthodox method of making a baby. But the spanking I'd received from Suzanne later that afternoon, and the orgasm she'd finally wrenched from me after keeping me on the verge of coming, had been thoroughly worth it.

Suzanne paid for the socks with a minimum of fuss. I kept quiet, figuring I'd done more than enough to earn whatever punishment she had planned for me. This was all part of the long, delicious game that had begun when we'd walked into the tearoom and would end only when Suzanne decided. We walked out of the store and she hailed a cab. She gave the driver my address and settled back in her seat.

I wondered what she intended to do with those socks all the way home.

The sky had darkened as the taxi nosed its way through the late-afternoon traffic, and by the time we pulled up in front of my tenement building, the rain was falling hard. I hurried to unlock the door, shivering in my flimsy summer dress, while Suzanne paid the driver.

I liked my flat. It might have been up four flights of narrow stairs, and the kitchen was barely big enough to turn around in, but I had a nice view over the nearby park. More importantly, the walls were thick enough that the neighbors couldn't hear what I got up to. That had been a blessing on more than one occasion since I'd first started seeing Suzanne.

Suzanne's heels clicked on the stone steps as she followed behind me. She'd gone very quiet, as she always did before we got into the heart of a scene, giving me time to reflect on what I might have done wrong and where my behavior needed to improve. But I was still mulling over her choice of treat for me. Whatever I'd been hoping for, it wasn't a pair of sports socks.

"Would you like me to put the kettle on?" I asked as I let her into the flat, expecting her to refuse, as she always did. Afterward, she liked to sit with a cup of tea and stroke my hair as I came down from my endorphin high. Never before.

"That would be delightful, Poppy." The response threw me. So she wasn't going to chastise me? I'd prepared myself for a verbal and physical dressing-down and now we were just going to drink tea? If I'd known, I would have reined in my bratty side and been nicer to the woman in the sports shop. Or maybe not. No one should wear fuchsia velour in public.

My disappointment must have shown because Suzanne said, "I thought we'd try something a little different today. Mix things up a bit. I know how well you can take a spanking, but you've been falling down recently when it comes to following orders."

"If you say so, Miss." Surely she knew that I always did as I was told—eventually? I'll admit that sometimes I pretended not to hear her instructions the first time she issued them, but that was to earn a couple of extra smacks. And where was the fun in giving in too easily? It wasn't a failing on my part. At least, I didn't think it was.

"I do. And you can start by making a pot of Earl Grey, which I will have with lemon rather than milk."

"Yes, Miss." I scurried off to the kitchen, thankful that I'd done my grocery shopping the evening before. I fished a lemon out of the fruit bowl and set about slicing it as the kettle boiled.

Suzanne's words had me on edge, but as the butter-flies fluttered in my belly I wondered if maybe that was a good thing. Perhaps we were both guilty of falling into too comfortable a routine. We weren't in a rut, exactly—Suzanne's schedule, which meant that I might not get to be with her for a couple of months while she worked in her company's LA office, didn't allow for that. But I knew what to expect from her when it came to a scene and when to expect it. It couldn't hurt to shake things up every once in a while.

I warmed the pot and spooned tea into it—always loose leaf for Suzanne, never bags. I placed the teapot, a little bowl containing slices of lemon, and a cup and saucer on a tray. After a moment's consideration, I added a second cup for myself, reasoning that Suzanne hadn't told me not to, plus another bowl of lemon slices and the milk jug. Biscuits would be nice, I thought, remembering the packet of chocolate digestives I'd bought on my grocery run, but decided that would be greedy on top of all the cakes and sandwiches we'd had earlier.

"Here we go," I announced, taking the tray through to the living room where Suzanne sat, leafing through the previous night's *Evening Standard*. I poured her tea then offered her the lemon. As I set about pouring my own cup, she raised an eyebrow.

"I don't think you'll have time to drink that, Poppy."

"If you say so." I stopped what I was doing and stood, waiting for her to issue an order. After all, wasn't that what this was about?

"I'd like you to model these for me." She glanced to where the white socks lay on the coffee table.

"Of course." I reached to pick them up. Once I'd snapped the thin plastic tag that connected the two socks, I kicked off my shoes and went to perch on the arm of the sofa so I could put them on more comfortably.

"Not so fast." Suzanne held out a hand, palm facing me. "Before you do that, I want you to remove your dress."

For a moment, I stared at her, mouth a little agape. Something, I couldn't say what, about wearing nothing but those cheap white socks made me hesitate. Suzanne had to know how foolish I would look with them pulled right up to my knees while she sat in her beautiful suit without as much as the top button of her blouse undone. It was humiliating—and that, I realized, was why she'd asked me to do it. Need made my pussy clench and heat flood through me, bringing a flush to my skin.

Without a word, I undid the bow at the back of my dress then pulled it over my head. I let it drop to the floor and stood, allowing Suzanne to take in the sight of my naked body. My nipples were tight points, aching to be sucked. She let her gaze travel down, over the curve of my stomach. In anticipation of our get-together, I'd shaved, leaving only a thin strip of hair on my mound, and my sex lips were slick with desire. All afternoon I had been waiting for this moment, and I ached for her.

When she returned her attention to her teacup, I sat and put on the socks. As I lifted each leg in turn, I was aware that if Suzanne glanced over, she'd get a glimpse of my wet pussy, but she seemed more concerned with reading her horoscope in the newspaper. Her show of indifference only turned me on more, because despite her outward display, it must have been costing her a real effort not to look at me. We'd been apart for too long and I knew her too well to believe she really wasn't interested.

At last, she turned back toward me. I'd been standing for a minute or more, hands behind my back in the position she liked me to adopt when I was naked. The socks were more comfortable than I'd expected. They had padding in the sole, and the elastic at the top didn't grip and pinch as I'd feared it might, even though it was brand new. Still, I didn't think I'd be adopting them as a staple of my wardrobe any time soon.

"Turn around, Poppy."

I did as I was told, presenting Suzanne with my rear view. I hoped it looked good to her. Usually, she preferred it once my asscheeks were blushing red and bearing her handprints.

"Very nice. And now I want you to take the socks off."

But I've only just put them on, I wanted to protest. I knew better than to argue. Before I could begin, though, she held up her hand once more.

"Seduce me with your movements. I want this to be the most erotic thing I've ever seen."

"Of course, Miss."

At first, I had no idea how to obey. These were the most boring pair of socks in Christendom. How could I make anything about their removal erotic?

Then it hit me. I had to pretend I was partway through a striptease. Swaying to music I could only hear in my head, I danced around the living room. I moved my hips in slow, sinuous patterns and ran my hands over my breasts and bottom, teasing my nipples and squeezing soft handfuls of my flesh.

With my back to her, I glanced over my shoulder, trying to gauge the effect I was having. Suzanne sipped her tea, her expression giving nothing away, and not for the first time I decided she'd make a fantastic poker player.

I had to do something to grab her attention. Part of me wanted to sweep all the tea things off the coffee table with my hand and lie on there to remove the socks. But I'd used the only good items of china I possessed, left to me by my grandmother, and as much as I loved Suzanne, I wasn't going to risk breaking anything so precious.

Instead, I propped my foot up on the arm of her chair, right in her line of sight. I caught the scent of my juices, sharp and salty, knowing she'd also be able to smell how excited performing for her had got me. Now I had her.

Like a seasoned burlesque dancer removing a silk stocking, I rolled the sock down to my ankle as slowly as I could then peeled it off over my toes. The second sock followed. Suzanne's gaze never left the movements of my fingers but her face remained neutral. Traces of her coral lipstick stained the rim of her cup, and I wanted to kiss away the rest from her lips, but that would come later. For now, this was all about proving to her I could follow her commands, however difficult that might seem at first.

I laid both socks on the table in front of her and waited for her next instruction.

"You've done well." She smiled at me, just a slight curve of the lips, and I glowed at her praise. "And because you've been a good girl, you get to come."

"Thank you, Miss."

Since the moment I'd begun my bizarre burlesque dance, I'd ached for her fingers on my pussy, stroking and teasing while she slipped her thumb into the tight pucker of my asshole—or even better, her mouth licking and loving me. No one had ever made me come as well as Suzanne did.

"But I told you things would be different today. I am not going to touch you. You are going to touch yourself, while I watch."

Her words pulled me up short. As confident as I was about doing anything she asked of me, something always stopped me in my tracks when she asked me to masturbate for her. I didn't know why it made me so shy. Maybe it was because it was something I did for myself, and I felt uncomfortable about inviting an audience into my private time. Or maybe this way I would have to keep myself right on the edge, when what I craved most was for her to do it.

This was what I got for being a brat. Suzanne, I realized, didn't have to lay a finger on me or use sharp words to punish me. She could make me squirm and beg for her to do anything else simply by telling me to play with myself. But I took pride in being a good submissive, and so I would not refuse her this.

I hoped she'd tell me to go into the bedroom, so I could make myself comfortable on the bed. When she didn't, I took a seat in the armchair across from Suzanne's, hooking my legs over the arms. In this position, I was spread out and open to her gaze. If she wanted a show, I would give her one.

The first skim of my fingertip along the length of my

cleft had me shuddering. Too much sensation, too soon. I needed something to dull the friction. And I had just the thing.

Suzanne quirked an eyebrow when I picked up one of the socks, but she didn't tell me to put it down. I ran it over my sex, rubbing myself the way I sometimes did with the crotch of my underwear. Back and forth, the fluffy material soaking up my nectar as it went. The soft touch was just enough to make me let out a little moan.

Was it my imagination, or did I detect the faintest rattling of the teacup in its saucer? When I looked over again, Suzanne had set her drink on the coffee table, and I smiled to myself at the tiny crack I had created in her controlled façade.

I used the sock to brush my nipples. They peaked, and my core tightened, making me want to press a finger deep inside myself. *Soon, but not right now . . .*

"That's it," I murmured, half to myself but all too aware of Suzanne listening to every gasp, every change in my breathing. She'd know how close I was by those sounds alone, and if she was in the mood to withhold my pleasure, she'd be aware of exactly when to order me to stop. She'd once told me my frustrated pout at being denied was almost enough to cause an orgasm of her own. But today I was allowed to come, and I intended to make the most of it.

I pushed one finger inside the top of the sock, swaddling it. Then I rubbed that finger over my clit, moving in small, tight circles. The light pressure was enough to make me arch my back and push my hips up, seeking to be filled.

Unable to hold back an instant longer, I eased a finger into my hole, then a second. The walls of my pussy clutched on to them.

"You can take more than that," Suzanne commented.

So much for just watching. But I complied, sliding another in and stretching those three fingers wide, reveling in the delicious burn. My eyelids fluttered closed as I fucked myself, still stroking my clit with my sock-covered fingertip.

"Feels so good." I panted between each word, my breathing coming faster and a languid warmth spreading through me. Even though I couldn't see Suzanne watching me any longer, I was sure all her attention would be focused on my busily moving fingers and the frantic jerking of my hips. Every nerve ending cried out for release and the blood roared in my ears. "Please, Mistress, may I?"

"Not yet." Her words were like a slap to my face. I needed this so much. But she was determined to draw this out, for her pleasure as much as mine.

I let the urge to come die away, then built to the peak once more. "Please," I begged, and again she denied me.

How could she be so cruel? I couldn't take any more of this. Yet, somehow, I found the strength to pull back. Suzanne looked on, her face an impassive mask.

I rubbed the sock over my clit once more, sobbing with need. Lost and helpless, I gazed at her with anxious eyes. This time, she didn't tell me to stop.

"Oh god, that's . . . that's . . . I'm—I'm coming."

With that, I came apart, everything around me seeming to fade for an instant before rushing back, the colors more vivid than before. I gasped, letting the sock slip from my limp fingers, and sprawled back in the chair.

It took a while for me to recover from the strength of the orgasm, and when I did, Suzanne was rubbing my shoulders, caressing my sweat-damp skin.

"Let's run you a bath, Poppy," she said, helping me to stand. Her smile was warm, filled with love. "You were amazing. I really liked what you did with the sock. I wasn't expecting that."

"Neither was I," I admitted. "But it felt like the right thing to do."

"Oh, it was. And it got me thinking. There are so many other uses for these we could try." Suzanne bent to pick up the sock and stretched it between her fingers. "For example, I think this would make an excellent gag..."

"If you say so, Miss," I murmured. Already, my mind raced ahead. *Gagged with a sock. Maybe she could even use the pair of them to tie me to the bedposts. I'd be helpless to stop her doing whatever she wanted. Yes, yes, yes...* I placed a soft kiss on Suzanne's cheek and let her lead me to the bathroom.

WHEN
YOU'RE TOLD

Rebecca Croteau

On Sunday, when she was a very good kitten, he put her into chastity. She went willingly enough; that night, everything they did felt good, but nothing they did sent her over the peak. His instructing her not to come was a freedom that let her frustration ease, let him gather her to his chest and pet his good kitten as she tumbled into sleep.

On Monday morning, however, it was clear that chastity was going to be different than she'd thought. He wasn't a tall man, but he was solid; broad at the shoulders and girthy through the waist, made of useful strength and sheer will. He woke her with kisses and fucked her in the shower, but whenever she got close to orgasm, he'd slow down. "Good girls don't come until they have permission," he murmured in her ear.

He came in her ass, and she thought he'd turn her, suck her clit while the shower beat on her tits, but instead, he kissed her mouth and said he'd get her tea ready while she did her makeup. After tea and break-fast, he kissed her on her cheek and pressed her purse into her hands as she went out the door to work. There was a light in his eyes that made her pause; he was hard in his jeans and turned on in his brain, and something was going to happen.

She got to work, and as she turned the key in the ignition, her phone lit up with a text. *Look in the side pocket of your purse.* She did. A thick plug and a packet of lube were tucked there in a pretty purple velvet bag. Her breathing sped up. She texted back: *What do you want me to do with this?*

It was only a moment before there was a response. *Use it, kitten. But remember. No orgasms for you until you have permission.*

It was an hour before he gave her permission to take it out, and she was panting at the sensation of being empty again. When she came home, sure he'd put her on her knees and give her what she was waiting for, he kissed her cheek and told her what a good girl she had been. Every time he said girl, not woman, she glowed with happiness; he'd been the first man to ever listen when she said the word *woman* had never made sense to her, and that *demigirl* was the one that fit around her skin. He was always so careful with her.

He made her dinner and drew her a bath. He fucked her and told her to suck him off, but he never gave her permission to come.

On Tuesday, when she came home from work, he was waiting with the blindfold, his belt looped in his hand. He leaned into her as he trailed the edge of the belt over the curves of her breasts. "You're mine tonight," he said. "You're not going to come tonight. Do you understand? I'm going to fuck you and use you and fill you up and you aren't going to come. Begging doesn't matter. Pleading doesn't matter. When do good girls come, my pretty pet?"

Her voice shook, as aroused by the denial as she was by the sound of the leather over the fabric of her clothes. She fumbled for the words he'd used the day before. "Good girls come when they have permission."

He didn't give her permission.

On Wednesday, she woke to his strong hands pressed into her belly, his body wrapped around her, his morning wood pressed into her ass. "Morning, kitten," he murmured in her ear, and as soon as she whispered, "Good morning," back, his fingers were plunging down into her well-trimmed slit to find her wet and aching. She was absolutely sure it had been years since she'd had an orgasm, and she was on the edge of release within moments of his caress. "When do good girls come?" he asked again, and she had to fight to find the words.

"When—they have permission, fuck—" She fought to find the balance between the sheer delight of his palm slapping into her clit in rhythm as he frigged her, and keeping her breath steady and soft to hold off the orgasm that was now looming over her, demanding and strong.

When he slipped into her cunt from behind, his fingers still dancing over her clit, she had to bite the heel of her hand to keep control. He came in her fast and hard, and she saw stars trying to hold back. He held her so tight and kissed her so soft, and told her over and over again how proud he was of her.

He didn't give her permission.

On Thursday, he told her in the morning that he was taking her out. She grinned; she loved dressing up like his cheap whore and going to seedy bars where they could play like he was a stranger picking her up and taking her home without bothering to ask her name. "Can I come tonight?" she asked.

He shook his head a little ruefully. "I thought you'd learned better by now, kitten," he said, leaning in and pressing a light kiss against her lips. His hand tightened hard in her hair, and he crowded her until she was pressed up against the wall, his thick cock obvious even in his jeans, making her whimper at the thought of being filled by him. He slapped her breast hard, but without any real focus or attention; he caught her nipple in his fingers and twisted hard enough to bring her up on her tiptoes. "When do good girls come?"

"When they have permission," she said, all in a rush, relishing the pain and the fizz and the strange interplay in her brain that turned pain into pleasure.

"And when will I give you permission?"

She stumbled here, managed to hiss out that she didn't know. She thought he might be angry, but he smiled and leaned in and kissed her again. "It's okay to not know. Good girls tell the truth, and when they don't know, they say so. They ask questions. That's how I keep you safe. But the answer to your question?" He twisted harder, making her gasp and curse and beg him to keep going. His voice was as calm and level and soft as it had been just a moment before. "I'll give you permission when I'm ready to give it."

He didn't wait longer; he yanked down her pants, pulled her panties halfway down her legs, and put her over his lap. He spanked her with his bare hand until her ass was bright red with the marks of his fingers, and then he put her on her knees and came down her throat.

After that, he pulled up her panties and told her there was a change of plans: she should do her makeup nice and find a classy outfit. They were going to a sit-down restaurant. And every time she shifted, she was to remember that he still hadn't given her permission.

On Friday morning, she woke up panting from a dream where he'd been sucking her clit while he fucked her with his fingers, twisting deep inside in a rhythm that drove her absolutely out of her mind. She was two quick flicks of her fingers from a screaming, raucous orgasm, a quick press of her thighs from one that probably wouldn't even wake him up where he lay next to her.

But he hadn't given her permission.

She clenched her hands into fists and spread her legs and forced herself to pant out the energy until the sheer need to come faded.

He hadn't given her permission.

On Friday night, when she came home from work, his face was serious, distracted. She went to him, kneeling at his feet and focusing her gaze on the tip of his nose so that she could hold it for longer without the sensory overwhelm digging into her bones. He smiled softly, his hand stroking her hair, wrapping the long ponytail around his fist. "You've been a truly good kitten this week," he said. There was a deep rumble to his voice that resonated all the way down her spine. "Would you like to be my toy tonight?"

"Yes, Sir," she said back, nodding.

"Does the word *no* have any meaning tonight, kitten?"

She took a long, slow breath, running through an internal checklist to feel certain that she could handle the emotional intensity of what he was proposing. "No, Sir," she said.

His soft smile flipped into the intense, impassive expression he wore when he was completely focused on her. "That's the last no that means anything tonight, you understand?"

"Yes."

His hand tightened so hard that she cried out, and he bent her head back to expose her throat. "Try again."

"Yes, Sir."

"Better." He pulled her to her feet and bent her over the arm of the chair he'd been sitting on. He flipped up her skirt, squeezed and pulled at the dark bruises he'd left on her ass, and then spread her lips wide as he worked his zipper. She felt the head of his cock at the opening of her cunt and groaned, shifting her hips. He slapped her ass hard, no warning, right on the bruised and aching handprint. She cried out, burying her face into the cushions. He yanked her head back again, his hand in her hair; if he'd pulled her any farther it would have been hard to breathe. He took her just far enough; he always took her just far enough.

"I want to hear you, toy-girl. I want to hear every

sound you make. Don't hide from me. Don't pretend you're something you're not. Don't pretend you don't want this." He ran his cockhead through the slick wetness of her pussy, and she groaned at the sloppy sound. "This wet, this soft, this hot? You can't tell me this isn't something you want."

"I want it," she managed to whimper. Her cunt was aching, she was painfully empty, she was quite sure she was going to actually die if she didn't get fucked soon. "I want it so much."

He laughed, the sound dry and mirthless. "It's good that you want it, toy-girl," he said. "But I wonder if you realize."

"Realize what?"

His words pierced her at the same time he speared her with his cock. "That it wouldn't matter to me if you didn't."

He drove into her without mercy or preparation, slamming into her cunt, his hips slapping against the sore and aching flesh of her ass. His cock wasn't exceptionally long, but god he was wide, thick and full and getting fuller as he fucked her, spreading her cunt until she ached. Until she wondered if she could actually take him at this speed, without begging him for the bottle of lube she was sure was stashed somewhere nearby. God knew they were stashed all over the house at this point. They'd fucked on nearly every flat or upright surface, and plenty of the slanted or curvy ones as well.

He was groaning into her, as close as she was. He had stamina for days, so she knew without a doubt that he was only this close because he wanted to be. He was looking for a fast fuck, a furious one, something to drive out whatever monsters had taken up residence in his mind while she'd been at work. He tightened his grip on her hair, pulling her up higher, until she had to brace on her hands to keep from actually hurting herself. She could feel herself closing in on orgasm, on coming messy and sloppy all down his cock, and she fought it off as best as she could. But he slammed into her so hard, with no mercy, never slowing down, and Christ it had been so long now, and surely he'd let her—

"You don't have permission," he hissed, his voice tightening as he closed in on his own release. "If you've forgotten that, if you forgot what it means to be a good girl and do as you're told, I will ruin every orgasm you could have in a night. I will make sure you never forget what it means to be a bad girl. When do good girls come, my pet?"

"God—when they have—fucking *permission*, Sir," she managed to choke out, and he broke over her like a wave, her name on his lips as he ground his cock into her, pulsing with his release, his hand tracing a soft path down her spine as he relaxed slowly from the tension of their fucking.

Somehow it was that touch that undid her. She'd been edged for so many days, and she was crammed full of his cock and his come, and that soft touch on her spine when she didn't expect it was a lit match on a fuse that was incredibly short. She cried out and bit her palm and tried to breathe through the wave of sheer pleasure and need, but she couldn't keep from being bowled over by it any more than she could stand against the ocean's strongest tides.

There was one strong ripple of her pussy around his

cock, and then he yanked himself out of her, pushing her thighs wide, giving her nothing to grind against, nothing to fuck, no way to draw out the pleasure and give her the release she so desperately needed. She whimpered and cried at the searing displeasure of her cunt, the sensation of her clit transformed into pain and want.

"I warned you," he said, but there was no heat in his voice, just a soft, sad sort of ruefulness. She felt his breath for just a heartbeat before his mouth latched onto her clit. She squealed in pain and tried to get away, but his arm clamped down on her ass and held her in place. He was gorgeous on her clit, tight and sweet and licking and biting in the ways that would send her over the edge in a glorious heap of whimpering toy-girl if she hadn't just had an orgasm that was days in the making so painfully ruined.

He kept licking and teasing her through the pain, until the heat came back, until she was twisting her hips into him for a completely different reason. Until she was grinding into his face. He rubbed and circled her clit with the thumb of one hand, fucked her with his tongue, and fingered her ass with the other hand. When she started to scream at the pleasure of it, he told her to stuff her fingers into her mouth, make her his own personal gangbang.

He waited until she got close, edging her again, until she was twisting and eager. "Come for me," he whispered, but when she did, his mouth fell away from her, his fingers disappeared, and she was fucking air again, the ruined orgasm turning into agony in her desperate clit. He didn't bother torturing her clit this time; he stood up and pulled her to her feet by her hair, then waited until she went to her knees on her own. "Clean me off," he said, and she did, tears streaming down her cheeks as she leaned forward, licking and sucking until the taste of her cunt had disappeared from his cock. He was shifting against her again by then, his cock wet with precome. When he got close, she redoubled her efforts, ready to take him, to swallow him down, but he pulled back. He came on the floor at her feet while she whimpered at the loss of what she could have had. If only she'd held on just a little longer.

He came twice more that night, and ruined hers until she was sobbing, but she did not get permission.

On Saturday, she thought she would lose her mind.

It had been a full week. Her pussy ached and throbbed with sheer need. She hadn't gone this long without an orgasm since she'd started dating him. She knew all the way through herself that if she told him she couldn't do this anymore and safeworded out, he would respect her, tell her she was a good girl, kiss her, cuddle her, let her come or help her come, whatever she wanted. He was always kind about her limits, always loving and sweet, thanking her for helping him keep her safe.

But she didn't want to stop. She wanted to be the kind of good girl who could hold out until she got permission. If it had actually hurt, if it were turning her brain inside out, she would have stopped. But just wanting to get fucked? She could handle it.

But he spent Saturday in her space. Tiny little touches, sweet little caresses. The kind of contact that, on another day, would have felt like loving and caring. Somehow, it was worse than being edged and having her orgasms ruined. She couldn't put her finger on why.

She didn't even think of asking for permission.

On Sunday, there was something in his eyes as soon as he woke. He was iron hard in the morning, but when she offered to take care of him, he smiled and kissed her and called her a good girl, but said he'd be fine. It didn't taste like rejection, which was good, but she found herself wondering why.

It was a quiet sort of day between them, spent reading and talking and loving each other, and when he took her by her ponytail in the late afternoon, she sighed happily at the tight grip he kept on her. His mouth nuzzled into her neck as he wrapped an arm around her waist. "I want you," he said, his voice soft velvet wrapped around the granite weight of his need. He moved her into the bedroom, and she saw everything laid out there. Soft rope in his favorite shade of blue, a blindfold he'd had dyed to match. Plugs, crops, floggers, vibrators, all of their favorite toys prepared and ready.

She saw all of it and her breath went light and thready. "Please, Sir," she said, and she heard the smile in his voice.

"Good girl," he said. "Good kitten. But I want you to see something first."

She tilted her head and waited while he lifted his shirt, dropped his shorts, and let her see him. His cock was thick and full, the head wet and shimmering with his arousal. She licked her lips and looked up at him.

"I've waited all day for you," he said. "You mean this much to me. You are worth waiting for. Do you understand that?"

Part of her wanted to demure, to shake her head so that he'd keep complimenting her, but being honest was better. "I didn't before," she said. "I do now. Thank you."

"You're welcome," he said, and traced his finger under her jaw. "Do you want to be a good toy for your owner?"

"Yes," she said. "Please, yes."

He stripped her and bound her, rope wrapping around her arms and her ankles, containing her and keeping her safe. She collapsed into the sensation of being held, something deep inside of her freed and released in the space between the knots. He took away her vision and she sagged deeper. He plugged her ass and she shivered, delighted and invaded by the fullness. When the crop fell on her ass, she cried out, whimpering at the pain and eager for the next blow. When the vibrator brushed against her clit she controlled herself with her breathing, feeling the rolling waves of pleasure that she did not allow to peak. She could feel his pleasure, his delight in what a good girl she was, and she savored the approval. She made it hers, luxuriated in it, let it drive her higher; made her control so much more hers. Good girls didn't come without permission, and he hadn't given her permission.

That was when the ropes came away, when the blindfold was gone. He dove between her legs, teasing her clit and fucking her with his fingers while she arched and ground into his face, panting hard. "Close," she told him, "so close," but she didn't beg. She just wanted him to know.

"Good girl," he said, and licked her harder, dragging his teeth over her clit until she thought she'd scream.

When he stepped away, pulling her hips to the edge of the bed so he could fuck her, she was pure, bright sensation; when he filled her to the hilt, she cried out, arching into him, driving him deeper, chanting his words to herself over and over—good girls don't come without permission—like she recited the Lord's Prayer in church.

He slapped her tits, hard, fast enough that the bright points of pain drove her pleasure higher, harder, until she was gasping with every breath at the sheer need for release. He fucked her without mercy, slamming into her, splitting her open. "When do good girls come?"

"Permission," she managed to say, light bursting behind her eyelids at the pleasure that was burning her into cinders.

"Say it."

She wasn't sure how the words came out; talking was hard and not coming was hard and doing both at once felt impossible. She did it because he wanted her to and because she wanted to. "Good girls come when they have permission."

"You have permission."

Her body understood the words before her mind did, and as she processed the words, she was already there, split on his cock as pleasure crested through her, a tidal wave that released days of denial and patience and pulsing, grinding, exquisite need. The orgasm didn't end, roiling through her in ebbs and waves, and he fucked her through all of it, his hands gripping her ass and meeting her throbbing body with his own.

"Good fucking girl," he said, and followed her over the edge. The sensation of him swelling as he came, the feeling of his come filling her, leaking out of her already, sent her into another, smaller wave of pleasure, and she wrapped her legs around his hips, drawing him tight against her as he pulsed into her.

He fell beside her and gathered her up into his chest; it was she who scooted them up to the pillows. They took turns stroking each other, cooing over each other. He kissed the place where he'd tied the ropes too tight and cared for the spots very gently; she thanked him for what he'd done, for how he'd treated her, for his own control. For caring for her so very much. For showing her the value in being a good girl. A good kitten. A good toy.

"Should we try that again, sometime?"

She laughed into his chest, her cheeks bright red and heated. "I bet I could go longer. Eight days. I bet I could."

He held her tight and pulled the weighted blanket up over both of them. "Absolutely you could. My good girl."

BLOW

Val Prozorova

I told you we should have stayed at the cheap place."

"And the cheap place would have had perfect air-conditioning, certainly."

"Older machines are more reliable," Adrian drawled, sprawling beneath Neal on the bed, arms wide, legs wide, underwear and socks light against his dark legs. His shirt had ridden up to his chest, crooked and bunched, sweat already dampening the skin just beneath. "Less bullshit touch screens. Just good old-fashioned temperature control."

There was another series of weak beeps as Neal attempted to coerce the Fujitsu above them into cooper-ating, and Adrian dropped an arm over his eyes with a deliberate deep sigh.

"Next time," he mumbled, "you should listen to me."

"Next time," Neal replied, working his toes beneath his partner's side to find the ticklish spot that made him squirm before setting his foot straight again. "I will not take you with me to a conference. You are a curse upon technology."

"Hardly."

"Hardly," Neal repeated. "What about the car?" he asked, stepping back enough to sink to the bed, kneeling, legs on either side of Adrian's chest where he lay.

"The car was old."

"It was a 2007 hybrid."

"And it's 2017," Adrian countered, setting one hand to Neal's thigh and gently squeezing. The other man huffed a breath, lifting his eyebrow.

"And the stereo?"

"Played awfully," Adrian complained, eyes still closed. "And I had nothing to do with it breaking."

"You were present."

"That's unfair."

A grin that Adrian could not see, but knew was there, spread like warmth from the sun against Neal's lips. Adrian squeezed his partner's leg a little harder in a teasing grip.

"And you can't complain about its replacement."

"The vinyl player?"

"Everything sounds better on vinyl."

Neal snorted. "You sound like a hipster teen."

"I sound like I know what I'm talking about," Adrian pointed out, finally letting his arm slip from his sweaty forehead to rest instead against his hair, messy and bent awkwardly from lying on the pillow.

It was nearing four o'clock in the afternoon local time, and they had gotten into Singapore just three hours before. Neal's conference was scheduled for just before Christmas, as all important business meetings usually were, determined to cancel out people's right-fully earned and government-sanctioned days of lazing. They planned to stay a week after to justify the price of the tickets getting in and enjoy a warm Christmas rather than the sleet and snow of New York.

With recent developments, however, the plans could change.

Or the hotel would, anyway.

"You have to get off me," Adrian sighed, licking his lips and arching up to try and dislodge his partner from him. Neal remained unmoved. "You're too hot."

"You know, that's just what you told me that night you met me at that dive."

"Did I really?" Adrian grinned, plush lips catching against crooked teeth. "I don't remember being that suave five years ago."

"You weren't."

"But the line worked."

"So did mainlining tequila with you for three hours," Neal reminded him. A playful slap from Adrian was met with a grin, and a deliberate maintaining of his position atop Adrian, though sweat gathered where their skin touched.

"True as the words are," his partner continued, "it really is already too hot here without you pressing so close to me."

"And what should I do instead?"

"Something useful," Adrian considered, turning his head to gesture toward the heavy decorative fan hanging over the television with his chin. "You can fan me with that. That would go over wonderfully."

Neal laughed, that warm, wonderful sound that

seemed to vibrate through his bones, and shook his head.

"And if I find myself disinclined to take on the role of pool boy?"

"Then I suppose we will both melt," Adrian mused, reasonably. "I was going to give you the royal treatment right after, but I can't, now, I suppose."

"Why not?"

"You're sitting on me," Adrian pointed out, smile wide and eyes narrowed with it. "I am helpless in my captivity."

Neal deliberately slid back to sit over Adrian's hips instead, and set his hand splayed over his stomach, wet from the heat generated between them. In truth, it was disgustingly hot, and would be genuinely unbearable if the hotel couldn't fix the air-conditioning by the next morning. But the thought of moving, after a ten-hour flight and a sleepless night beforehand, seemed just that little bit worse an option, so Neal held his ground.

He splayed his fingers over Adrian's chest, curling them to leave light marks against his skin, delighting at how different their skin tones were. He could feel Adrian's heart, a quick beat from the heat and the pleasure of being touched this way. He had always been sensitive here—even the slightest tickle and he would be off, laughing and grumbling about it.

Even now, beneath him, Adrian made a fussy sound and dropped both his hands down to Neal's knees in an attempt to slide him off. Adrian was always the first to mope, the first to point out an error or a flaw, and the last to go and fix it. Ironically, it was also inevitably Adrian who managed to find a solution, after Neal fumbled helplessly with whatever it was that displeased his partner at that particular moment in time. He wondered if it wasn't a tactic to have Neal try harder, push from his introverted shell and be more objective in situations.

He would not put it past Adrian to be so devious, or so wonderful.

"That fan is probably attached to the wall."

"It could also *not* be attached to the wall."

"With screws and pressure sensors—"

"That's doubtful."

"—that will go off and howl were I to attempt to remove it."

"A genuinely clever potential precaution, but I can guarantee you that *I* will howl soon, should you not get off me or do something to cool me down," Adrian told him, digging his fingers deftly behind slippery knees to tickle Neal enough to push him forward on all fours. Still close, but not pressing down to him anymore, at least.

Even so, heat pulsed between them.

Neal got a kiss as a compromise. A nuzzle when he sighed.

"What else do you suggest?" Neal asked him, brows up and light eyes seeking between Adrian's own.

"Blow me?" came the coy reply, and Neal snorted. He supposed he should have expected nothing less, from a man whose staple reply—to genuine questions and displeasing situations both—were those two words.

"I think I'll try my luck with the fan," Neal mumbled, dropping his butt back down against Adrian's thighs while he kept his arms against the bed. He stayed that way for a while, a pleasant stretch, before sighing heavily against Adrian's chest, and pushing to move off him, only to find his wrist snared and the other's hooded eyes on him.

"That," Adrian murmured, "was perfect. Do it again."

"I didn't even—"

"Blow again," Adrian told him. "Just there, as you just did. Feels so damn good against wet skin. It's perfect, Neal. Again."

Neal laughed and shook his head, but gathering his breath, obeyed, funneling his lips and exhaling slowly against Adrian's neck.

The other shivered, that distinct motion of pleasure, and one hand slipped from Neal's sweaty skin to rest at the back of his head instead, twined through damp strands of hair. Neal took the cue well enough, licking his lips before taking another breath to blow against Adrian, lower now, over the sweaty expanse of dark skin just beneath his rumpled shirt, over the muscle that pulled taut in stark relief beneath.

"Who needs technology," Adrian sighed, smile contented and eyes barely open, like a cat in the sun, as Neal grinned and drew another cool swath of breath from neck to the edge of the soaked fabric, tugged aside to present his collarbone. Neal kissed the hollow just to feel the hum that grew in Adrian's throat from the delightful pressure of it. The fingers in his hair scraped gently over Neal's scalp in encouragement.

"Up," Neal told him, waiting for Adrian to sigh and arch his back, before he brought his hands to the gathered shirt to pull it off Adrian properly, tossing it to the floor. Neal slipped from his own meager clothes as well, groaning in the relief that that act alone brought. Then he bent to continue the tickling teasing that his breath wrought against the skin he knew so well.

He sighed over the little scar Adrian had gotten while playing hockey in tenth grade, raised and just a little lighter than his skin. He nosed gently above a nipple before taking it between his lips to suck. Neal didn't respond to the demanding moan for him to touch his lover; he kept his hands firmly on the bed for balance, letting Adrian paw at him as he liked. Neal would take his time as he always did, despite Adrian's protests, and would find the man always entirely sated even when his mumbled demands were ignored.

Neal got no greater pleasure than playing devil's advocate with his whims. A gentle bite against his pec, just to feel Adrian jerk beneath him in surprise, before Neal breathed a path across Adrian's chest to suck the other nipple next.

Outside the windows, barely cracked with the safety hinges that kept them from opening no farther than an inch or so, they could hear the traffic from their fifth-floor room. Nothing compared to Queens, where the humming drone was a constant backdrop to their quiet lives, but somehow still strangely comforting. A welcome white noise that lulled them to this gentle caressing, this slow rocking that started with Adrian and translated to Neal above him, first in time then counter to each other. Lips slipped over skin and laughter mingled as Neal nuzzled his lover's chest and breathed against him as he moved lower still.

Down to Adrian's stomach next; sucked in reflexively against Neal's shivering breath, then allowed to relax into its soft curve again as Neal continued to breathe over him, slow and steady. Adrian drew his fingers from Neal's hot scalp down his neck instead, catching the sweat against his fingertips between Neal's shoulder blades. It became a give and take, cool air for a soft massage—Adrian delighting in the shivers he drew from Neal's breath against him, Neal in the goose bumps his sighs brought out on his partner's skin.

"Feeling better?" Neal asked him, eyes up to watch Adrian's, though he knew they would be closed, long enough for the last cool breath to fade and the humidity to cling to him again. Adrian's lips pressed together and parted, the tip of his tongue peeking between them before he swallowed.

"The distraction from the bloody heat is quite welcome," he replied, smiling when Neal laughed against him, just as sweaty, just as hot and miserable in it. Though, if Neal were honest, the misery was easier to forget with Adrian under him this way, entirely relaxed, slick with sweat and pliant for him.

"Good."

Another breath, Neal drawing his nose up Adrian's chest again as he sighed and sat up, shifting back on his knees. He needed time to catch his breath, to bring this blissful dizziness to a manageable level before he continued. He drew a hand through his hair, pushing it off his sweaty forehead, and considered his partner beneath him.

They could take a shower, keep the water barely warm and luxuriate beneath it. They could sit on the floor, backs pressed to the heavy glass and talk, limbs tangled as water fell on them like early spring rain. They could act like children, enjoying their primitive and simple means for getting cool in a tropical climate.

They could take a shower.

Perhaps they should take a shower.

They certainly *would* after this, but for now it was enough to breathe against one body, touch another, and bring genuinely delightful shivers up between them both.

Adrian moaned, a tired and pleased thing, as Neal nuzzled his nose to his navel. He rolled slowly forward to press his forehead to Adrian's stomach and breathed on him this way, the air barely skimming the sparse trail of hair that ran down beneath the waistband of Adrian's underwear.

"Tease," Adrian sighed, and Neal did it again, the breath shaken by a laugh as Adrian whined and tugged his hair in impatience.

Adrian was growing hard beneath the light fabric of his briefs; small darkened patches of sweat and arousal both outlined his cock. It twitched when Neal sat up enough to fold the elastic down to reveal just the head of it, then more and more as Adrian lifted his hips and allowed himself to be divested of his underwear.

It was a tangle of limbs for a moment, Adrian's knees against Neal's arms, as Neal pulled Adrian's socks off too, laughter and snorted curses as they worked themselves to a semblance of comfort again. Adrian drew his knees up, spread, and Neal kissed his way down one knee to the sensitive, sweaty skin of the opposite thigh. With a drawn breath, he left a shivering trail back up to Adrian's knee again, hand hooked beneath it to spread him a little wider.

"*Tease*," Adrian groaned again, and Neal grinned, watching him.

"Is that a demand or a title?"

"God, *both*," Adrian laughed, one hand up to his face, pressing over his eyes before he ran it up into his hair and slicked it back, looking down at Neal between his legs as the other looked back, coy and delighted by his own terrible pun.

"Complete my other demand first," Adrian told him, and Neal found he could hardly deny him that.

Cool breath coiling against Adrian's cock made it twitch again, made it arch from his belly, seeking more sensation. From its base to the tip, Neal moved achingly slow, blowing air against the slick skin and watching, wide-eyed, the response to it. Adrian was already so aroused, from the heat, from the exhaustion, from Neal being so playful and clever and entirely infuriating. Hands settled in Neal's hair again as Adrian coaxed him closer, until not only breath, but soft lips, too, brushed just beneath the head of his cock.

"Blow," Adrian sighed, begging. "Come on."

Neal parted his lips just enough to press them together in a semblance of a kiss, down the length of Adrian's cock and back up it again, relishing the little twitches of muscle, the heady smell of him, before finally opening his mouth to take the head between his lips and gently suck.

He had learned early that Adrian went weak at the knees when he went down on him. He cursed and squirmed, spread himself entirely wanton as Neal worked him with his mouth. There were days when Neal would tease him like this until Adrian would succumb to his own pleasures, weak and delighted to have Neal then turn him over and find the lube in the bedside drawer. Adrian would complain, of course; he would hardly be Adrian if he didn't. But he loved being blown, he always had, and now was no exception.

"God, yes, *finally.*"

Muscles tensed and relaxed in Adrian's stomach, in his thighs that pressed to Neal's cheeks and slipped slick against them. He put his knees up over Neal's shoulders and found they slid down his sweaty arms almost immediately with no friction to keep them hooked there. Adrian snorted, moaning as Neal hummed his own amusement, and cursed. Goose bumps showed up under sweaty skin, pleasure coursing through him, cooling and distracting him from the fact that both of them were drenched in sweat, as though caught in a passing rain shower.

"Please," Adrian sighed, "take me deeper, come on."

Neal did, as addicted to giving head as Adrian was to getting it. His fingers curled where his mouth did not reach, and he stroked in time with how his head bobbed, either up to meet his lips as they sunk down, or following their movement to the very head and then down again to grip the base. Twisting just enough for Adrian's voice to break free again, uncaring for the open windows or anyone beyond the door who might hear.

And in truth, what did it matter if they did?

Adrian was certain the hotel had heard much worse and seen much kinkier. The thought pulled a laugh from him that morphed to a panting moan as Neal slipped the foreskin down and tongued against the slit of his cock. A darker blush poured forth over Adrian's nose to his cheeks, down lower still to his neck. Fumbling hands sought again for Neal's hair, for his shoulders, to draw nail marks over the skin there and soothe them away again with a press of knuckles right after.

Kneading in pleasure, like a cat.

"God, you are so good," Adrian praised, head back and back arched as the unrelenting teasing continued. Neal hummed his thanks and Adrian saw stars behind his eyes from the vibrations that seemed to shake him to his bones. He set a hand against his eyes, teeth bared in a grin, breath panted between them in huffs of warm delight.

"Little more," he pleaded. "A little more, Neal, please—"

A clever tongue drew zigzags over the throbbing vein running down Adrian's cock and he cursed, loud and pleased and drawn out, muscles tensing and trembling beneath Neal's hand that still held his thighs spread.

A little more.

Neal knew this man like a master musician knew his instrument; could play and pluck and draw him any way he wanted. But he held off; a moment longer he held, before peeling his fingers free of Adrian's cock and taking him deep to the back of his throat. He swallowed, over and over, the pressing motion enough to pull Adrian's orgasm from him, pulsing hot down Neal's throat as he pulled back enough to swallow it down.

It was only when Adrian made a sound, high and just a little pained, that Neal pulled off him and ducked his head to catch his breath. He turned his head, just a little, to pool cool, panting breaths over the slick skin of Adrian's thighs, over his balls, heavy and twitching with the aftershocks of his orgasm.

"Fuck me," Adrian sighed, licking his bottom lip into his mouth and releasing it with another groan. He turned his head to rest against a sweaty shoulder as he watched Neal push up on all fours between his legs. He smiled, waiting for Neal to look up, and bit his lip again.

Neal was beautiful, with his pale skin and bright eyes. He was entirely Adrian's own.

"What was I complaining about again?" Adrian asked, his smile widening when Neal snorted, and sat up to arch his back with a groan, hands up behind his neck to stretch his shoulders as well.

"The heat," Neal replied after a while, voice still strained as his muscles were before he relaxed them. He crawled forward to press himself to his partner's sweaty chest again as Adrian's hands settled heavily over Neal's back and drew absent patterns there. "You were complaining about the insufferable, unending heat."

"So I was," Adrian mumbled, content for the moment to just stroke through Neal's hair, over his back, and down to his ass to cup him playfully before letting go. "And it is, in fact, still insufferable and still unending." He could feel Neal's erection press against his thigh as his partner shifted, through the damp fabric of his boxers, and waited until the accidental push became a deliberate nudge.

Adrian set his hands on either side of Neal's face. He kissed him, a long and lingering thing that left them both breathless and sleepy-eyed.

"You hot too, baby?" Adrian asked, smiling when Neal hummed, sarcastic.

"Like Satan's armpit," he replied, droll, and kissed Adrian again just to taste his smile and the laugh beneath it.

"Eloquent boy, is this why I'm fucking you?" Adrian asked.

Neal just lifted his eyes to the ceiling in amused contemplation. "That and my company's exceptional choice in hotels for business trips."

"You know, we'll actually have to give them this one," Adrian replied. "Send flowers. A hotel room so hot it guarantees a blow job."

Neal laughed, shook his head, and only stopped when Adrian held him still again, pressing gently against his cheeks to push his lips out of shape. Sleepy, loving, and silly.

"Turn over," Adrian said, and Neal raised an eyebrow in amusement.

"Why?"

Adrian's nose wrinkled in pleasure from just watching him, eyes narrowed by the sheer delight at being able to touch his partner and make him feel good, to return the favor.

"Because I'm going to blow you, too," he said.

BÖSENDORFER
BLUES

Cecilia Duvalle

The day that *The New York Times* announced Demyan Petrov's final performances at Carnegie Hall, I purchased center of the house seats for each night, booked my flight, and reserved a hotel room across the street. It was months away, but there was no way I'd miss this.

Oddly enough, the newspaper never used anything but Demyan's name, completely avoiding the "he" or "they" article. Demyan's wildly dramatic transition from Darya in the late '90s was simply not discussed. Nor did the *Times* appear to pay any attention to the multitude of interviews where Demyan emphatically denied being either "he" or "she." I chalked this up to something about the classical world's insistence on remaining socially clued in to the Victorian Era, but it could just be discomfiture at using "they" to describe a single person.

As soon as I had my tickets, I wrote them an embarrassing fan-girl email all about how I had been one of the sixteen students in their master class at the Boston

School of Music in the summer of 1995, and how they probably didn't remember my terrible rendition of Rachmaninoff's Prelude in C Minor. It was also unlikely they would remember me from any of their numerous concerts I had attended over the years since, but I didn't bring that part up in my email. It seemed a bit too stalker-like.

It took all my courage to invite them to the Russian Tea Room for dinner or drinks after the concert as it was right next door to the Hall—two majestic structures side by side. I sent the email quickly, before I lost my nerve as I had so many times before. Twenty years of fantasizing about someone was long enough.

As soon as I hit SEND, anxious expectation settled between my legs. I fidgeted for a while, refreshing my email multiple times before giving up. It wasn't like they would read my email instantly.

I warmed my icy hands under hot tap water until they felt like they could move nimbly over the keys before opening my piano. If I didn't have cats, I could leave the lid up and at the ready. As it was, my sweet companions would sleep inside and their hair and dander would wreak havoc on the delicate felts and hammers.

I didn't need any music; it was one of my life-pieces. I'd internalized the prelude so thoroughly it was a part of me as surely as any part of my anatomy. I never performed it publicly. Not since Demyan had taken my hands in theirs, turning them over several times, caressing them, sending shivers through my body. When I close my eyes, I can still smell the musky sandalwood and cedar drifting off them in gentle waves as our fingers touched.

In the end, they had declared the Rachmaninoff a private indulgence for me. *You have amazing dexterity and heart, but no reach with these tiny hands. Play to your strengths.* They were right, of course. I forced myself to love Schubert and Mozart—anything that my hands could reach. But I still loved the heavy chords, the dark and broody nature of Rachmaninoff.

I breathed in deeply and came down as hard as I could, playing the first three chords and letting them ring out in fortississimo. The vibrations from the piano lit through my body, waking up every nerve of my being. As I played, I imagined Demyan's hands dancing across the keyboard. Their fingers, long enough to reach the impossible chords that my stubby ones must roll. It flowed out of me, years of practice making it near perfection. As I played the last and final chord, hushed to the softest of pianissimos, my entire body was alive, pulsing with desire.

I closed the lid and leaned across the curve of the piano. My hand, now warm from the exercise, found the one spot that would bring quiet calmness to my throbbing need. I played a trill with my second and third fingers, my clitoris the only key. It was Demyan's long fingers I imagined at work, their body pressing me firmly from behind into the coolness of the black wood.

I had given up on hearing from Demyan after three months. Either I had been too ridiculously crushy sounding in my email or they got so much fan mail their assistant just deleted mine along with those from other crazies and groupies. I'm not entirely sure classical musicians actually have groupies, but what better word for me? I would go to every concert Demyan played if I could. I would follow them around the world and, if asked, I would do whatever sexual activities they might want. If they had sex.

Their email response the day before my flight surprised me. I stared at the inbox for five minutes before opening it, my hands sweating worse than before any performance, my fingers trembling as I hit OPEN. I told myself their assistant had responded, that it would contain a polite, but firm, declination. I read the email in a state of awed wonder.

My dear Ms. Novak, you do yourself a disservice. I do remember you from the summer of 1995. How could I forget? It was the first master class I ever taught there. You were the only one to attempt that prelude. You and your dear, sweet, short fingers. How I felt for you, agonizing over how hard it must be to reach those thirteenths! I understand you became an expert in Schubert— an admirable composer and one of my favorites. I have no desire to go to the Russian Tea Room... let's just say as a Russian expat, I have my prejudices against it. However, I do believe there is a delightful quartet playing at the Blue Note Saturday after my performance, and I would be very much grateful to not go alone. Perhaps you could buy me a drink there instead. Send me your phone number so we can connect in New York.

Demyan

I reread the email a dozen times. *I understand you became an expert in Schubert.* How would they possibly know that? It's not like I have any CDs out. Or YouTube videos. I'm a successful bit player, happily content to perform with half a dozen smaller symphonies and teach lessons to teens with more talent than I have. A quick Google search would easily bring up my website that shows my repertoire and performance dates. Demyan hadn't followed my career; why would they?

An offer for drinks was more than I had dared hope for. I Googled the Blue Note. Demyan Petrov was into jazz? A few email exchanges later, these within minutes of each other, and I had a date after their final performance in Carnegie Hall, and I had Demyan's cell number memorized.

I arrived in New York Thursday night and spent the night alone in my room, tossing and turning. I gave up sleeping and sat at the window, staring across the street at Carnegie Hall as the sun came up. I spent Friday wandering around Manhattan, daydreaming about the following night and drinks over jazz. At three o'clock, my phone buzzed with an unexpected text from Demyan.

Would you like to watch me warm up? Five o'clock at the musician's entrance. Come dressed for the evening.

There was only one answer to this question. I was only a mile from my hotel, so I jogged back to my hotel to prepare for the evening. I found my way to the right entrance at 4:45. I'd rather wait a few minutes than be late.

A short, swarthy-looking man opened the door a moment later. "Miss Novak?"

I nodded, suddenly unable to speak.

"Demyan asked for me to be putting you in third row for good view and good sound." He waved me in with a smile that made me blush.

As I settled into my seat, not far from where I would sit later with my purchased ticket, I marveled at the grandeur of the hall. I eyed the piano on center stage with envy. Demyan only played on Bösendorfers. Steinways were "too precious" to them. And, well, frankly, the sound is better even if the brand name isn't so well known. They are extremely rare, and Demyan traveled with their own. My Yamaha grand was a toy in comparison.

Demyan appeared onstage wearing jeans and a muscle shirt. I don't know what I had been expecting, but this was not it. I squirmed in my seat and settled to listen. They began with a C-major scale—the simplest of them all. It rippled up and down the hall with a rich clarity. Familiar, almost boring, yet perfectly executed. No stumbles. No fumbles. No breaks.

After a comprehensive warm-up, they played the prelude. It wasn't on the program for the concert either night, so I knew it was meant for me. A private concert. My body responded to each crashing chord with hunger and desire. How I wished for those fingers to touch me with the same precision.

Pushing back the bench as they stood up, they turned to me at last. "I hope you enjoyed this...little rendition of mine?" They beckoned me up to the stage.

I ran a finger along the rim of the piano. So close to the master at last.

"Thank you." What else could I say? There are no words for perfection.

"Sit. Sit. Let me hear you play."

I took a step backward, and Demyan grabbed my hands, examining them closely before their eyes came to mine. Intense, bright, dark, penetrating. "Play something. Anything. Even just a scale. Play."

They pulled my hand to their mouth and kissed my palm. The heat from their lips sent a fresh tremolo of desire through my body. They guided me to the bench and managed to have me seated before I knew what was happening.

"I take it this is yours?" I ran a finger in a silent glissando across the keys.

"I only play my own instrument."

I hadn't warmed up. My hands were stiff with New York heat and air-conditioning. I flexed my fingers, hoping to wake them up. Rubbed my hands together, willing the friction to spread the warmth.

I cleared my thoughts and played a C-major scale, just as they had done. Easy. No mistakes, just as clean and perfect as theirs. At first, I thought the extra blacked out keys of the mighty piano would make it difficult to play, but they quickly disappeared from my consciousness. I switched to C-minor to warm up on the key for the piece I'd decided on. Another life-piece but without any of the gigantic chords Rachmaninoff favored, Beethoven's *Pathétique*. What can I say? I like loud, bombastic chordy music—the stuff my earliest piano teachers told me I wasn't allowed to play because I was a girl.

From the very first chord, my body lightened and

buzzed with the music. The energy from the piano filled my body so that every inch of my flesh rippled with pleasure. I had to keep myself from coming as I played in front of Demyan. I only played the first movement, but it was enough. I was playing the world's greatest piano on the world's most famous stage—as Demyan Petrov watched me with an intensity I'll never forget.

When I was done, Demyan's grin told me they *knew*.

They rounded the piano, their fingers dug into my shoulders, their warm body pressed against my back. The same musky scent wafted over me. "Yes. Yes. I see it. I saw it then; I see it now. You *are* the same as me. The connection to the piano and the music. Do you know how many times I have orgasmed in front of thousands? And none of them have a clue?"

I blushed. "No. It doesn't surprise me at all."

Demyan urged me forward on the bench so that I was perching at the edge. They sat behind me, their legs hugging me close, and chin tucked over my left shoulder. Demyan slipped their arms under mine and reached for the keyboard. New music I'd never heard before hit my already pulsing body with a new passion.

They played a soulful blues piece. The music washed over me as I leaned back into Demyan, who managed to play around me with ease. The music was a story of lust and love and want. I didn't know who the characters were, but I could feel their desire building inside me. I relaxed into the full embrace, my head lolling against their shoulder and baring my neck. I don't know how Demyan could continue playing while kissing my neck, but it wasn't long before the music and the love bites had me close to orgasm.

I stiffened in embarrassment, realizing there must be people in the hall somewhere, working, watching. Wouldn't they know what was happening? I was sprawled against Demyan in a lovers' embrace.

They laughed gently into my ear and tugged at my earlobe with their teeth and brought the song to an end. Demyan wrapped their arms around me, warm and confident. "No, my dove. You will not find fulfillment yet. Not tonight."

The spell broke as Demyan lifted me to my feet.

"I must ready myself for the performance." Demyan tapped my nose with an index finger. "I see I was not wrong in my assumption about you."

"What assumption would that be?"

"You have had a crush on me since 1995. And, you will do anything I ask of you."

"That's one hell of an assumption."

"Am I wrong?"

I looked away.

"I do not allow myself to orgasm before a performance. I need to save myself for the performance. To give it my all."

"Do you always...onstage?" I don't know why, but saying the word *orgasm* in the middle of the stage at Carnegie Hall was just impossible for me.

"Almost. And now, you are one of less than a dozen people who know this about me. Do you like knowing a secret like that?"

"I'll be watching you even more intently during your performance tonight."

"Good. There's something delightful about knowing someone in the audience is watching closely."

* * *

I waited in the lobby with the rest of the audience. I sat patiently, thumbing through my program with everyone else chattering around me. I might not have had anyone I knew sitting next to me, but as soon as Demyan came onto the stage, I did not feel alone.

I kept my eyes fastened on Demyan's face, waiting for the moment, watching for the telltale signs that they were experiencing the ultimate bliss at the keyboard.

Just as Demyan was taking a bow before intermission, they looked directly at me and smiled. Those around me saw I had been singled out by the master. I blushed and hid in my seat during the intermission.

During the last part of the program, Demyan stood up. The audience shifted and people looked at each other.

"I would like to announce a change in the program. I would like to play for you, instead of the Liszt in the program, the entire *Sonata Pathétique*. It is a favorite of mine. I would like to dedicate it to a student and fellow performer who is in the audience. Ms. Emily Novak. Please stand, my dear."

A blinding light hit my face, unexpected and shocking. Demyan had *planned* this. My knees were wobbly bits of flesh. They were looking straight at me. Not just Demyan, but *everyone* in Carnegie Hall. I pushed myself up onto my shaky feet and bowed awkwardly toward the stage.

Demyan blew a kiss at me before throwing their tails back over the bench and plowing into the piece. Why had they chosen to do this? Was it to mock me? But no—it was a signal to me. They wanted me to be prepared. To watch when the moment came for them.

As the third movement began its final circling, chasing, crashing moments, I saw it. The shift in Demyan's hips. Anyone else watching might see it as a natural movement with the change in music. It was the last, light flickering touch of the sweet melody that sent Demyan over the edge.

I squeezed my legs together, trying to gain purchase against my panties and my seat. I needed release. I wanted more. I wanted to fall back on top of the piano with Demyan on top of me. I yearned for their lips against mine, against my breasts, against my aching pussy.

The crowd launched into thunderous standing applause. The *Pathétique* was always a crowd pleaser, and Demyan had rocked it. If only the rest of the audience knew what I knew.

After the concert, I texted them with the measure number where they had come. All I got in return was a smiley emoticon and a note that they would see me after the concert the next evening.

Had I done something wrong? I had expected something more than that after the pre-performance mojo we had going on. Had hoped to be invited back to their dressing room after the performance. They had called me out in front of thousands of people. They had played an entire sonata, twenty-two minutes of music, for me. To me.

I left the hall confused. I wasn't even able to focus long enough to masturbate. I tossed and turned until I finally fell asleep, my hand shoved up against my still-aching and bewildered pussy.

I seriously considered leaving, for a full minute, at least. Maybe two. I wanted to stay angry at Demyan, but I couldn't. They had been toying with me, playing with me. My hunger for them was too much. I meandered through Central Park, stopping at the benches to read the various dedications.

At three o'clock, I got a text.

Demyan: *When was the last time you played Schubert's Fantasia in F Minor?*

My stomach twisted.

Me: *Why?*

Demyan: *I have a yen to play it tonight.*

Me: *Wait. You want me to play with you?*

Demyan: *You can play secundo.*

Me: *Ha.*

Demyan: *Be here in an hour so we can practice.*

Me: *I don't have anything to wear.*

Demyan: *pfft. You are a size twelve? I will have something for you.*

Me: *I can't do this. I'm not up to it.*

Demyan: *I insist. Or, don't come at all tonight.*

I wasn't ready for this. Sure, I'd been performing professionally for years, but never at this level. I was used to being a medium fish in a small pond. I wasn't sure I was ready to land on the stage at Carnegie Hall.

Dread. Fear. Anxiety. Excitement. Happiness? Demyan Petrov had essentially opened the stage to me. It was a dream come true.

As I arrived at the hall, the same man let me in and led me to a dressing room. Demyan spun around, holding up a glittering green dress for me. It matched my eyes. "This will look perfect on you, my dear.

Come. Come put it on. I want a full dress rehearsal. Get it?"

I ignored the lame joke. I glanced around the room for a curtain or something more private, but Demyan gave me a withering look. I shut the door so we'd at least be alone. Underneath my jeans and T-shirt, I had worn a matching pair of underwear and lacy bra, knowing, or at least hoping, that I'd end up like this in front of Demyan. I just hadn't imagined it happening this way.

Demyan held the dress away from me when I reached for it, circling around me and inspecting me instead. "Yes. Perfect."

"Are you going to play games, or are you going to let me get dressed?"

"I'll help you."

Demyan's hands traced my curves as they slid the silky crepe dress over me. The caress sent new shivers through me. After zipping me up, their arms circled my waist and cupped my breasts, long fingers pinching my nipples until they were hard, hungry nubs.

"Will you fuck me tonight, Demyan?"

"Yes. Later. After the Blue Note."

I took my place on the left side of the wide bench and felt an immediate ease as Demyan's hip met mine. I hadn't played the Schubert in at least a year, but I had listened to it while walking from the park to the hall. It came back to me like an old friend. After minutes playing together, we sounded as though we'd been doing it for a dozen years.

"I will invite you onstage after the Chopin. Afterward, you will listen to my final piece and come back out onstage for the curtain. I will take a final bow, alone, and then you and I will disappear to the Blue Note for some jazz. But now, we shall go back to my dressing room and relax until we are called."

We returned to the dressing room. I expected there to be some sort of meal there, but instead, Demyan took off their tuxedo and beckoned me to take off my dress. "We do not want to appear wrinkled." They dropped onto the sofa in their boxers and undershirt.

My fingers itched to explore naked flesh. But Demyan had other plans and pulled me onto the sofa, straddling me from behind.

"I want to fuck you, Demyan."

"I know, my sweet. But I never allow myself such pleasures just before a performance. Instead, I must go on keyed up, ready to burst forth in front of the audience."

It was then I understood Demyan Petrov. The reason there were no tabloid articles about Demyan and rocky relationships. Demyan was so focused on their performance, they got so much pleasure out of being onstage, they didn't really need anyone.

Demyan teased my nipples through my bra with one hand and slid the other into my panties. "I can't wait to bury my face there later tonight."

"Will you let me come now? Before the performance?" I asked, my hips thrusting hungrily against their hand. "I might be too distracted to play."

"No. I will bring you to the edge. It will help you to focus. Prepare you for the performance. I want to feel you squirm next to me."

Demyan's fingers moved with a rapid glissando against my clit, teasing me, daring me to come. I wasn't entirely sure they were right about the focus part.

"Please. I am so close."

"Yes. I want you to feel the first twinges of orgasm…
to bring you to the brink of no return."

Fingers pinched my nipple hard, and I teetered on
the edge. Demyan picked up on it and stopped, with-
drawing their hand from my pussy and holding it up,
glistening wet with my juices before bringing it to their
mouth. "God. You taste delicious."

I collapsed against them. "You're cruel."

"You'll thank me later."

"I need to come. I'm in pain."

"Excellent. You can use that during the Schubert. It
will be an amazing performance."

Demyan brought me to the edge of orgasm three
more times. Each time, I was left feeling raw, on the
verge of physically exploding. I don't know how I got
dressed again. Or how I made it to the soft chair waiting
for me in the wings, my purchased seat left empty. And,
suddenly, there I was, taking my seat next to the most
famous pianist on the planet, playing at Carnegie Hall.

Demyan had been right. I was hyper-focused on
everything. I smelled my own pussy juices wafting from
Demyan's fingers. My swollen, throbbing clit felt every
nuance as I shifted on the bench to move up and down
the keyboard. Demyan and I became one as we delved
deeply into the zone.

Our fingers danced across the keys, our bodies
swaying and shifting as the music demanded. We moved
in perfect synchronicity, part of and yet separate from
reality. As the music swelled into its natural climax, so
did we. Arm to arm, hip to hip, finger to finger—one
shivering, quaking body. We continued to play through

our orgasm, the denouement of the piece paralleling our bodies' gradual calming.

As we leaned over our hands, the final pianissimo chords softening into the great hall, I breathed deeply to gain my composure. Demyan's glazed eyes met mine, and we shared a quiet moment before taking our bows to a standing ovation.

If only they knew.

APHRODITE'S GARDEN

Rebecca Chase

The night started like all weekend events, with the lineup.

Stephanie's heartbeat thundered and her nerves nearly choked her as eyes slowly slid down her form.

It was as if she were back in gym class—eyes inspecting her, opinions being made of her performance. Then, it was a popularity contest she couldn't win. Here it was different. In Aphrodite's Garden, she held queen status. Instead of being ridiculed or ignored, she was regularly the first chosen.

"It has to be her," she heard a soft voice call out. "Athena is the only one I want serving me."

Stephanie, or Athena as she was known in Aphrodite's Garden, felt the familiar weekend thrill electrify her body.

Mondays to Thursdays, Aphrodite's Garden was a normal, expensive Greek restaurant, but during the weekends it became something more decadent. It was still a restaurant but with a sexual tease and unspoken promise.

Casually, she glanced at Electra and Hades, both of them enjoying that their presence alone aroused strangers. They adored their weekends here. They didn't serve for the money but the satisfaction and power that came with being desired.

Fifty pairs of eyes investigated every inch of Stephanie's golden skin, or as much as her short Grecian dress allowed. White chiffon draped across her shoulders before plunging at her breasts, stimulating the clientele and suggesting that for the right price she could be theirs.

At the start of the night, the waiters and waitresses, known as the servers, would line up for those who had booked a table. Each table made their choice of who would serve them and, depending on availability, they'd be allocated that person.

The rest was up to the server. It was their challenge to spend the evening gaining a hefty tip, in whatever way they chose. There were rules, lines that couldn't be crossed, but generally it was known that they had an "anything goes" policy.

The server who earned the largest tip would be taken into the Secret Garden, a room designed for fornication. There they'd be joined by a member or two from the winning table to enjoy an hour doing whatever pleased them. Everyone was a winner.

The restaurant was the brainchild of Stephanie, Dean, and Pam, or rather Athena, Apollo, and Persephone, as they were known in the Garden. It had begun when they were poor and horny at university but over the years had developed into a successful business.

Stephanie surveyed the scene in front of her once

more. Which table would pick, or win, her tonight? She was hot property in Aphrodite's Garden, a goddess who usually got her own way. Need throbbed at her groin, making her subtly roll her pelvis back and forth to enjoy the stimulating touches as her sex rubbed against her panties.

Once a month, a ladies-only night reigned over the restaurant. It pushed her to work every angle to get the biggest tip, including once stripping down to her underwear and offering herself as a sushi plate, a brazen act that had been rewarded by a night with two beautiful actresses in the Secret Garden.

As with a typical ladies' night, there was a heat in the room and all the groups, a mixture of bachelorette parties, birthday celebrations, and work social events, felt it. It was a hunger accompanied by unspoken wants. Could they express their long-held desires safely here?

Athena's eyes skimmed the groups, considering who she'd like to serve that night. There were many beautiful women, respecting the dress code in a variety of colors and styles. She didn't have a type; curves, long legs, tiny waists, or rounded butts turned her on. All women were beautiful to her and she loved showing them how much allure they could have if they learned to harness it.

Staring unashamedly at one group, a work social, she felt the flush of lust that had been absent recently. Standing in the center of the group, her eyes wide, her fingers nervously twisting her long blonde hair, was Megan Stone, who'd been the most popular girl at Athena's old high school.

Megan had never worried about gym class. Her friends would spit out derogatory names at Athena based on her Greek heritage, but Megan herself was never a bitch. Athena had been an odd-looking teenager, with lips too big for her face and dangerously bushy eyebrows, a contrast to Megan's blonde perfection. Megan was the stuff of fantasies and at university, when Athena had started to understand that she was attracted to women as well as men, she fondly recalled her. The rumor was that when the graduating class had moved on to work or university, Megan had headed down the aisle with her boyfriend, her pregnant belly barely showing.

Since then, there had been other rumors, the most recent that Megan's husband had ditched her for a younger model. Athena glanced at Megan's bare ring finger, a white mark visible.

"I have to get that group," Athena whispered in Persephone's ear as she crossed the restaurant, her dark eyes never leaving Megan's face.

"You know you won't win." The pretty, ginger goddess nodded in the direction of a rowdy group of ladies sitting at table six. "They have money to burn."

Athena moistened her lips, wondering how Megan would taste. "Surely you're not doubting me. You know from experience about my skills, honey."

She teased Persephone's neck with her warm breath.

A quiet moan escaped from Persephone's lips. They both knew how acutely aware she was of Athena's abilities. "If you insist. But play fair, okay?"

Athena walked away with a smile; she had every intention of playing tonight, but fair wouldn't come into it.

Unsurprisingly, she had gotten her way. Rolling her hips, which had developed late in life along with her beauty, she wondered whether Megan would remember her. Megan had always been stunning, but something had changed, Athena thought, as she appraised Megan's shape in a tight, cherry-red dress that clung to every curve. She was plumper than Athena remembered, with curves replacing toned limbs and a slight podge at her stomach. Megan was a woman now and Athena had to claim her.

What I wouldn't do to have her between my legs, she considered, eagerly imagining the sight of the blonde waves below her. It was time to earn her tip.

"Ladies," she said. "I am Athena, your server this evening. I will do and be anything you wish. If the food you desire isn't on the menu, I will find it. If my outfit doesn't please you then I will change it. Your pleasure is mine."

The women looked at her with a mixture of curiosity and disbelief, but not with the naughty gazes she was hoping for.

"Have any of you eaten with us on one of our weekend nights before?"

Two of the more confident-looking women raised their hands.

"We're not at school now," Athena replied with a lingering look at Megan. "First I want to thank you for returning to Aphrodite's Garden. Is there anything you'd like us to improve upon based on your previous experience?"

Athena stepped closer to the willowy beauty, whose eyes matched her emerald silk dress.

"You have stunning eyes. What's your name?"

"Carol."

"Well, beautiful Carol," Athena replied, bending in front of her and displaying her cleavage in an attempt to entice her. "What could I do better for you tonight?"

"I would like my salad to have a bit less feta this time," she explained, clearing her throat awkwardly.

Seducing this group wasn't going to be easy, Athena realized, plastering a smile on her face and leaning closer so that her bum brushed Carol's hand as she topped up her wine for her. Encouraging the consumption of alcohol wasn't forbidden, as long as your table didn't cause trouble.

"I shall ensure your salad is perfect. Any other requests?" Maybe tonight wouldn't be her night. She could already see Electra being dragged willingly onto the laps of table six.

"I was wondering," a quiet voice caught the attention of the entire table. Athena felt a tremor in her thighs when she saw the words were coming from Megan's lips.

Athena nodded her encouragement for her to continue, hoping this wasn't another feta-related request.

"If I wanted your hair to be a little different, could you change it for me?" Megan stood. Her hands trembled as she reached out.

"Of course." She fought her craving to close the space between them instantly; seduction was a game, not a demand for gratification.

She slid closer, her eyes meeting Megan's. "Please do whatever you desire with me," she said, slipping herself between Megan and the table, hoping the invitation would be accepted by the end of the night.

The rest of the table was incredulous. Was Megan acting out of character?

Soft fingers stroked the nape of Athena's neck, causing goose bumps to rise on her arms.

"You have a beautiful neck, feminine and yet strong. It would be a shame to hide it," Megan whispered next to her ear, her breath teasing the nape of Athena's neck.

"I need to pin up some of your waves." Megan's fingers stroked through her hair, twisting it slightly. Pleasure traveled all the way up to her scalp, drawing a shiver of longing, her sex pulsating slightly in expectation of more. Deftly, Megan worked, taking tendrils between her fingers, caressing them, inflaming Athena's body. Desire radiated between her legs as if it were the first time she'd been touched by a woman.

"Turn and look at me," Megan requested.

With a dry throat, Athena turned and stared. Her tongue swelled in her throat as they gazed into each other's eyes. Megan's fingertips continued to brush across Athena's skin, her nails gliding across her bare shoulders, her temptation constant.

"You're stunning," she uttered.

Normally, Athena would have used this to her advantage, skill and experience enabling her to maximize her tip, but she was speechless.

To be looked at by Megan with hunger and adoration was unexpected, and the extent of her reaction frightened her. Weekends at Aphrodite's Garden were about lust, the scent of sex hanging in the air, but this was clearly passion and love.

With a dip of her eyes, she offered her thanks before stepping away and explaining the menu to the rest of the table.

Wetness was growing between her legs as she

returned to the kitchen. With a sly look over her shoulder, she glimpsed Megan's flushed appearance and surprised face.

"I'm in trouble."

The first two courses seemed to pass without incident at Athena's table. There was the occasional joke about particular items from the menu that led to blushes and giggles. Satisfyingly, the women at the table were becoming the nice kind of drunk, too, unlike those at Electra's table.

One of the rules about weekend nights was that if your table became too drunk then the server was disqualified from the tips competition and had to pay a forfeit.

"I want to see some vag!" a previously perfectly coiffured businesswoman hollered while dancing on the table. Glasses flew in all directions as she performed an Irish jig on the sturdy rustic furniture.

Persephone rushed over. "Table six, I'm afraid you're out of the running for the top tip competition. Electra's tip will be given to the rest of the servers, so please continue to give generously. As a forfeit, she has to give each of you a kiss."

Any disappointment they may have had at being disqualified disappeared when Electra offered them her lips.

Athena watched as Electra ground her body against each member of the table, licking and sucking the willing women as her "punishment."

The "vag" lady, Sheena, got special treatment. Jealousy rustled Athena's controlled demeanor and touched every other horny lady in the restaurant. They watched as the limber Electra crawled onto her lap. Kisses covered the swell of Sheena's chest before she was ridden cowgirl style. Electra writhed against her, her Grecian dress unable to contain her breasts as she offered herself to Sheena. Athena turned to find Megan staring at the scene, her eyes wide and her hand slipping under the table. Suddenly, her gaze flicked to Athena and for a moment they stared at each other, communicating their longing.

"I said kiss." Persephone's warning was heeded by Electra, who responded with a long, drawn-out kiss with Sheena. Athena watched as a note, probably a phone number, was clumsily slipped between the two. Looking again to an aroused Megan, Athena felt a longing to bed the woman whose hand still moved in her lap.

The hotly contested competition for tips continued, although Hades's table was no longer in the running. A woman celebrating her sixtieth birthday had pulled a muscle in the excitement of having a dirty dance with Hades. The birthday girl had limped out of the restaurant early with a broad smile across her face; she had no complaints about her Greek experience.

Athena returned to her own table ready to take the dessert orders.

Once the laughs over the boob-shaped trifle had subsided, Megan piped up: "What's the Slippery Nipple Surprise? Is it related to the drink?"

Athena blushed unexpectedly. She was the most experienced server, having pleasured customers for years. Nothing, especially not a suggestive pudding name, should get a reaction out of her, but hearing the name of the dessert from between Megan's lips had her burning up.

"It's a special way of eating it. You down a shot of Sambuca then follow it with Irish ice-cream liqueur."

One corner of Megan's mouth lifted in a smile. "I'll have that then."

Athena took the rest of the orders and sashayed back to the kitchen, an idea forming on how she could use the Slippery Nipple Surprise to her advantage. She was going to earn her evening with Megan and she finally knew how.

The hem of Athena's Grecian dress brushed her thighs as she glided back to the table, the silver tray aloft. One by one she'd won over the members of the table. Years of seducing groups had taught her that sex wasn't enough on ladies' nights. Listening to problems, respecting the women, and giving genuine compliments where there were self-esteem issues meant more to some than a nibbled lip and sly caress.

But subtle teases couldn't be ignored either. Through brushes against cheeks, a finger lazily drawn up a bare arm, and a gentle squeeze of a supple thigh, Athena had given every woman a taste of the self-worth they deserved. Hopefully, they'd return home tonight and get the satisfaction they longed for after a night of slow-building desire.

But there was still Megan.

As the rest of the group tucked into their desserts, Athena approached her. Stepping closer, she witnessed with pleasure how Megan's eyes scanned her body, pausing on her breasts before slowly traveling down her legs.

Athena had rarely felt desired so completely.

"Megan," she said, placing the shot glass and marble pudding dish in front of her as she leaned close enough for their naked limbs to touch.

Megan's flesh was as hot as hers, spurring her on.

"You can enjoy this dessert in the boring way," she continued, crouching down next to Megan's chair, giving her the opportunity to inspect her body closer.

"Or . . . ?" Megan whispered, while her eyes stared down the front of Athena's dress, her nipples matching Athena's in turning visibly hard beneath her dress.

"Or there's a different way. How adventurous are you feeling tonight?" Athena resisted the urge to wet her lips and press them together to draw Megan's eyes. She craved a taste.

Megan finally looked up. Eyes that were initially set in challenge dropped slightly to look once more at Athena's bosom.

"I go wherever you want to take me," she replied, her voice dipping to a whisper, forcing Athena to lean closer to hear her, her head nearly in the beauty's lap. "Your breasts are beautiful, Stephanie. I hope you will allow me a taste later."

Athena's heart stopped as time slowed.

She'd called her Stephanie.

Hidden beneath the table, Athena moved her hand slowly, running it in circles above Megan's knee, teasing the soft, naked skin with her fingertips and using the movement to regain her composure. "I'll look forward to it," she replied, noticing how bright Megan's eyes were.

"Tell me, how do I enjoy my dessert in the 'not boring' way?"

"First you have to drink the shot." Athena nestled the glass between her own breasts, pressing it down so that Megan would have to take her time to retrieve the liquid.

Silence had descended over the restaurant as Athena stood in front of Megan, close enough that she could feel the heat radiating from her body.

With a last seductive stare, Megan dipped her head. She opened her mouth wide and wrapped her lips around the rim of the glass.

A collective gasp escaped the mouths of the mesmerized women around them. In one quick move, Megan tipped her head, letting the fiery liquid trickle down her throat.

She's stunning, Athena thought as she watched Megan swallow the searing fluid, her lips glossy and her cheeks flushed red as a new confidence radiated from her.

"And now?" Megan asked breathlessly.

Athena used her finger to scoop up the alcohol-laden creamy pudding. She smeared it across the top of her breasts. Ensuring Megan's attention was entirely on her, she dipped a finger into the crease between her boobs, a place almost hidden by the white chiffon of her Grecian dress.

"And now you have to clean me up."

Gasps transformed into groans of lust. Megan didn't flinch; instead, her mouth creased with a smile as she lowered her head once more.

Her tongue stroked at Athena's skin, causing her to moan. Pressure was growing between her legs, refusing to be ignored. Megan continued to kiss and lap at her, and Athena's head lolled backward as the pleasure over-whelmed her.

Eventually, she raised her head and kissed Megan briefly, the alcoholic cream shared between their mouths.

"You missed a bit," Athena replied, referring to the sticky pudding that remained between her breasts.

Megan whispered in her ear, her hot breath tickling her skin, "I'm saving that for later."

A shout from Persephone broke the tension tempo-rarily.

"We're getting closer to your checks coming out. And you know what that means, ladies. We need your tips because we need a winner tonight. You'll decide which server goes into the Secret Garden tonight. The top two servers will be led blindfolded and nearly naked through the restaurant, but only one server will go to the Secret Garden. As a table, you need to decide which one or two ladies from your table might be joining them. Whichever server wins, be assured that they have gifts in giving pleasure like you've never known before."

Chatter replaced Persephone's voice. There was an energy filling the room, a mixture of excitement and lust. Many would experience intense arousal and delight before the end of the night but for most, it would be in their own homes. Only one or two would be chosen for the Garden.

For now, the servers were banished from the room, the choice of winner no longer in their power.

Athena waited with the remaining five servers. One by one they were dismissed. Soon only she and Calypso lingered. Under instruction, they removed their clothes until all that remained were their white lace bras and panties.

Persephone placed a blindfold over their eyes and paraded them nearly naked around the restaurant. Athena may have been unable to see what was happening but she could still sense the way she was being watched as she was led between the tables. The sexual tension goaded her, causing a natural swing to her hips, surging her confidence as she felt the desires of every woman in the room. Persephone's fingers tickled the palm of her hand. They sought to arouse her, increasing a lust that seemed unable to reach its peak.

Eventually, she was taken through a door and left alone. The same would be happening to Calypso. Athena had experienced it as an unsuccessful server before. The aim was to create excitement and tension, to give the clientele something to remember and encourage them to return another night.

Had she been led to the Secret Garden or the storeroom? It was impossible to know until—

Lips brushed her neck, soft and seeking. Athena had won, but who from her table had joined her? She tried unsuccessfully to distinguish the shape of the lips from the kisses.

Athena fingered her blindfold but a hand stopped her.

"Not yet," a voice said, so quiet she couldn't be sure whose it was. It could have been Megan but it also could have been anyone else, even Carol. Athena had a suspicion that one night Persephone might sneak in when Apollo wasn't watching, or maybe when he was.

The lips continued to caress her flesh, covering every goose bump.

Moments passed, hair brushed across her body, hands gripped her tightly as their bodies pressed against each other. Suddenly a mouth was against hers. The scent of jasmine infused with plum filled her lungs. Longing to be touched at her core made it hard to beckon memories of Megan's perfume.

Fingers threaded through her hair, pulling at the pins, causing a pain that only increased her never peaking pleasure. One by one the pins hit the floor as their kiss deepened, tongues entwining. The mistress behind it continued to remain a mystery. Hunger built with every jerk of her waves and scratch of her scalp. Contact was suddenly broken and she heard gasps for breath.

Athena shook her hair, freeing curls and waves until they rested against her naked shoulders. Her mistress bestowed teasing touches that made her feel sexy and beautiful. This was usually what she gave others but tonight she was receiving all the attention.

A hand grasped hers and led her to what she knew must be the bed.

Cotton sheets comforted her flesh as she was eased down.

Her bra straps were slid down her shoulders, kisses covering where their marks probably still remained.

"Lie down," a whispered voice instructed, emerging from the fog of yearning that led Athena to wherever this woman wanted to take her. Kisses feathered across her body; intermittently a tongue licked at her searing flesh. Moans of delight were dragged from her depths.

The warm mouth sucked at the creamy dessert that remained between her breasts until the laps became ferocious. Even after the dessert was gone, the caresses continued.

"I vaguely remember attending your eighteenth birthday, Stephanie, but I didn't really notice you. I was in love with my boyfriend. I foolishly thought that only guys could turn me on." Athena heard the words between kisses. They settled into the atmosphere above her, mingling with the scent of arousal.

Megan's tongue sucked a nipple, teasing it then biting gently before soothing it with soft licks. She repeated the same painful yet pleasurable action on Athena's other nipple, spreading kisses across her bosom.

Moans of longing came like torrents from Athena's mouth.

"But that boyfriend, later my husband, made me feel ugly and fat. He told me sex wasn't about pleasure: it was an obligation. I tolerated that obligation but unknown to me, he'd found someone else to fuck. I haven't wanted to come in months."

Megan's mouth dipped lower, nearing Athena's sex, making it harder for her to concentrate on the words falling around her, but she fought through the fog to listen and offer understanding. This was important.

"I only came here tonight because my friends told me I had to. I knew I'd hate it. But then I saw you."

As a warm breath blew on her pussy, her juices flowed at the promise of Megan's mouth.

"I haven't been horny for a long time, but all evening I knew I had to fuck you. The cost didn't matter. Now you're mine for the next hour and I can do what I want with you. I want to make you scream."

Suddenly, her pussy was engulfed. Megan sucked at

her clit before nibbling at her, her teeth grazing Athena's sex then sucking it gently once more. She flung her head back against the pillow as her pelvis ground into Megan's face. Her hips bucked as moans left her mouth, chasing each other, barely a gasp of air between them.

"You're not screaming yet," Megan said, as her mouth continued the touches that filled Athena with a delightful agony. The climax was climbing quickly; she was now writhing beneath Megan's hands, which were gripping her hips so tightly she knew they'd leave marks of ownership.

"Yes," Athena screamed, the lips sucking at her clit turning to what felt like a smile.

Without warning, Megan plunged one, then two, fingers inside her. Rapid thrusts gave her no chance to catch her breath; her lungs were bursting. Athena lifted her hips to match each drive of her lover's fingers, forcing them deeper.

The curve of Megan's digits hit her G-spot again and again. Her writhing was becoming more violent. What had started as a simple tease from both of them had become a fucking more powerful than either expected. Sweat covered her body as heat burned her from the inside out.

The combination of her heart and hornyness demanded an intense climax. It might destroy her, but it would be worth it.

Megan bit at her nipples, scratching the delicate skin of each areola in turn. The pain from the sharpness of her teeth somehow served to heighten the sensitivity of Athena's entire body, making the fingers penetrating her body feel more intense. With one last deep push of her fingers, Megan sent Athena over the edge of climax, the darkness behind the blindfold suddenly turning to bright flashes of light and then black.

Athena realized as she regained consciousness that the orgasm had made her pass out. That was rare but not unknown for her.

Soft strokes helped to soothe her thumping heart and trembling body. The blindfold was removed, and in front of her barely opened eyes, she saw the shining, proud face of Megan, the soft lights of the Secret Garden glinting off her golden hair.

"You're okay? Did I do that, make you pass out?"

"Yes and yes," Athena replied with a dreamy smile. Athena pulled Megan closer and they lay down, their arms wrapped around each other's naked bodies, their heartbeats mirroring each other's in speed. "But you know you were the one who was supposed to be the winner tonight."

"I am a winner," Megan replied between kisses. "I don't want this night to end."

"It doesn't have to," Athena replied, drifting off to sleep, certain that this was the beginning of something significant.

ROGERING
NADINE

Richard Bacula

Nadine was wearing a pair of thin purple panties, a sheer black shirt, and sturdy rope. Kerry, her boyfriend for almost a month, had convinced her to do a bit of kinky bondage play. He'd tied her spread-eagle on the bed, each of her four limbs tied by the rope to each of the four bedposts. They'd already been making out for quite a while before he brought up the idea, and Nadine was pretty turned on to begin with. Once she was tied up, Kerry tortured her with soft caresses, whispered dirty promises, and gentle kisses on her exposed flesh. His mouth sought out those special places on her neck, the ones that made her go wild. His hands stroked and squeezed her breasts, pinching her nipples through the almost diaphanous cloth. His thigh rested between her legs, a solid pillar of muscle pressed against her groin. She writhed, moaned, and rubbed her hungry, swollen pussy shamelessly against his leg.

Kerry's hands slipped under her shirt, stroking her bare flesh. He teased one nipple to alert hardness then moved to the other, treating it to soft strokes of his fingertips until it too was fully erect and ready for more.

Kerry wasn't a perfect boyfriend, but he was so good with his hands that Nadine forgave him a lot. Not to mention the things that he could do with his lips, his tongue, and his cock. He even had a trick or two with his feet, although Nadine wasn't entirely certain how she felt about that.

Nadine was so glad that she'd gone to college after graduation. High-school boys had never done much for her, so she'd never done much for them in return. But college men? They were a different story—so mature, so experienced.

Nadine had never exactly been a wallflower in the past, but something about the freedom of living on campus had loosened her up, had even made her run a bit wild for a while. Then she met Kerry, and the two of them fell in love.

Kerry's thigh had left Nadine's pussy, but he replaced it with his hand before her body could feel too lonely. His palm pressed and rubbed against her pubic mound, pushing on all her most pleasant places through the cloth. She could feel herself getting wet, that sweet liquid pleasure building up inside her loins.

He slipped a finger underneath the purple gusset, then another. His touch gave her goose bumps, as he tantalized her intimate flesh with featherlight brushes of his fingertips. Kerry was kissing her on the mouth, their tongues dancing across each other. He was filling her senses, making her desperate with need.

Finally, when her body was aching so much for him that she simply couldn't stand it anymore, Kerry knelt between her outstretched legs. He reached up, grabbed the waistband of her panties, and started to pull them down. Then they heard the front door to the apartment open and close.

Nadine had flashbacks to making out with a high-school boy, and the panic that had assaulted her at the sound of the front door. It always meant that her parents were there and she'd get into trouble. That was another nice thing about college guys like Kerry—he and his roommate had their own place, so Kerry and Nadine didn't have to worry about parents wandering in. They could do whatever they wanted here.

"Shit!" Kerry let her panties snap back into place. "That's Roger! He's going to want the twenty bucks I owe him."

"Tell him to fuck off." Nadine couldn't believe that Kerry was putting their playtime on hold, just because his roommate was home. "We're kind of busy here!"

"He won't take *no* for an answer." Kerry hastily put on his shirt then checked to see if his pants were still zipped. "I've got to get out of here!"

"What the fuck?" Nadine asked. "Fucking untie me!"

"No time." Kerry opened the window. "Shit! He's walking up to the door. Cover for me! Tell him you haven't seen me."

"You piece of shit!" Nadine observed.

Kerry hopped out the window and disappeared into the outside shrubbery, leaving Nadine lying helplessly on the bed. There was a knock at the door.

"Go away!" Nadine said. She had to figure out how to untie herself. This was humiliating.

There was another knock, a little louder this time.

"I haven't seen him all day!" Nadine wondered why she was covering for him after he'd abandoned her like this. She pulled at the ropes, but they were securely tied.

The door opened.

"Hello?" A man entered the room hesitantly. "Where's Kerry?"

Great. Now this guy was calmly staring at her. He looked from Nadine's scantily clad body to the ropes then back to Nadine. He was probably thinking that she was some kind of freak. Thanks for that, Kerry.

"I haven't seen him," she lied again.

"So..." The man was looking her over. "What, you tied yourself up? Or somebody else tied you up in Kerry's bed?"

Nadine groaned, dropped her head onto the pillow, and shut her eyes.

She felt the man sit down on the bed next to her.

"Let's try this again." The man's voice was as smooth as silk. "I'm Roger, Kerry's roommate. He owes me twenty bucks. Have you seen him at all today?"

"Yes." Nadine kept her eyes shut in humiliation. Not only did this stranger probably think that she was a perv now, he knew that she was a liar. Her voice came out low, defeated. "He went out the window just before you knocked."

"He just left you tied up here?" Roger acted incredulous, but he didn't seem genuinely surprised at the news.

Nadine nodded.

"Well, that was pretty shitty of him," Roger observed.

Nadine opened her eyes. "Right?"

She realized that Roger was sitting very close to her. She could feel the heat from his body in the cold room. She was suddenly very aware of his muscular male presence and the fact that she was tied up, completely helpless. She felt a pulse of anticipation between her legs, and she tried to shush it away without much success.

Roger was looking at her. He was checking her out. He wasn't openly ogling her like a complete creep, but he wasn't pretending not to look either. When he looked at her chest, Nadine remembered how thin her shirt was. She wondered how much he could see. Just nipples, or could he make out the dark disks of her areolas? She felt her nipples start to grow hard, pushing at the flimsy fabric.

"You know," Roger said thoughtfully. "Maybe we could work a deal."

"What do you mean?" Nadine didn't like the sound of this.

"Kerry abandoned you here like this," Roger said. "And he owes me some money."

Roger's hand reached out. He patted Nadine's flat stomach a couple of times, the physical contact sending an erotic jolt through her body. She was *so* worked up already, so turned on. Her body was primed for a man's touch, and a man had just touched her. She flinched and tried to jump, but she was tied down thoroughly and ended up just wriggling helplessly in her bonds.

Roger's hand stayed where it was, just resting on her. He was looking a bit lower than his hand, looking at how her panties barely covered her pussy. He could probably see the outline very clearly, could see the contours of her aching cunt. She wanted him to touch it. Her skin was already radiating pleasantly where his hand was resting, and her body was tingling with the thought of what that hand could do just a bit farther south.

"I have a boyfriend." Nadine didn't sound convincing, even to herself.

Roger hadn't actually said what he was proposing, hadn't said that he wanted to fuck her instead of collecting the money that Kerry owed him, but it was clear that's where the conversation was headed.

"You have a boyfriend who left you tied up here," Roger pointed out. He was looking at her again, and a small smile told Nadine that he liked what he saw. He raised his hand off her belly and ran it through the air about an inch over her body, making a slow circle from her breasts to her thighs. Nadine felt her body unconsciously lift up off the bed, trying to meet his hand. "You're all helpless, all turned on. Any man could just walk in here and, well...you can't really *help* yourself, can you? Can't help it if Kerry left before meeting your needs?"

Nadine was firm. "It's not happening."

"Okay," Roger said. "I guess I'll just kind of hang out here for a while. Let me know if you change your mind."

He stood up, unzipped his pants, and pulled out his cock.

Roger was firm.

Nadine licked her lips, feeling her resolve melt a bit. Roger had a beautiful cock. It was big, too, bigger than Kerry's by a wide margin.

"Go ahead," she told him. "I don't care. Just don't touch me."

Roger smiled. He reached down, stroking his cock idly while he looked over Nadine's helpless body. His other hand moved toward her, hovering less than an inch over Nadine's pussy. Her hips moved, pushing herself toward his hand, but he pulled away.

"I'm not touching you," he said, teasing her like one child taunting another.

Nadine almost growled in frustration. She couldn't take her eyes away from his erection, and her body was throbbing with need. She could feel how wet she was, how swollen with desire. Roger could probably feel it too, just from the heat rising off her pussy. She licked her lips again, watching him play with his heavy cock.

"Man, it is hot," Roger said. "In this room, I mean. I guess I'll take off my shirt."

He pulled off his shirt, dropping it to the floor, revealing his washboard stomach and utterly lickable pecs. Nadine gave a little groan of frustration and hunger.

"Huh. Think it's getting a little loose?" Roger was looking at Nadine's pussy when he spoke, but then he turned his head toward the rope on Nadine's left wrist, the one farthest from him. He winked. "The rope, I mean. I'd better check it out."

Roger crawled onto the bed to inspect the knot. His hands were to Nadine's left, supporting his body. His cock was dangling down, inches from her mouth. She caught herself trying to lean forward, to get within licking range.

"No," he said. "I think it's still nice and tight. Guess you're trapped."

His body changed positions, and Nadine found herself lunging, catching the head of Roger's cock in her mouth. She let out a satisfied moan around a mouthful of male flesh.

"Hey, now!" Roger said. "Does that mean you've changed your mind?"

Nadine didn't give him the satisfaction of an answer. She *did* give him the satisfaction of a lick, as he shifted to give her better access. He moved his torso back and up, until he was kneeling next to her head, his penis still in her mouth. She couldn't get much of him into her, just the first inch or so. She found herself making frantic noises of need, sucking hard, trying to get more of him into her mouth. Roger thrust forward, filling her with him.

He was so thick that her jaw opened painfully wide to accommodate him, and he was so long that he was at the back of her throat almost immediately. She choked a bit, and he backed off to a more comfortable depth. She wanted to pull her head away, to tell him to just untie her and let her go, but his hand had found her breast, lightly pinching her nipple. Nadine moaned around Roger's thick cock, feeling an electric jolt of pleasure shoot through her breast.

His hand moved to her pussy, and all thoughts of resistance were lost. This was all Kerry's fault anyway; he should never have run out on her, certainly not after getting her so turned on, not when she was all tied up like this. On any other day, she believed that she could have resisted Roger's advances, but right now she was completely powerless.

Roger rubbed his hand up and down Nadine's panty-covered pussy, and she rocked her hips, pressing herself back against his hand. He pulled her panties aside, sliding his fingers down her slit then back up, teasing her labia, parting her inner lips. He placed two fingers on her clitoris, making small circles, pushing against the most desperate part of her. She could feel her pussy flowering open for him, feel her body's hunger to have him inside of her.

Roger suddenly pulled away from her. His cock left her mouth, and his fingers abandoned her aching pussy.

"Well," he said. "If you're not going to change your mind and let me fuck you, then I guess there's nothing that I can do."

He knew damned well that he could do anything he wanted, that Nadine not only couldn't stop him, but that she'd wantonly welcome it. He was just being cruel, forcing her to say it aloud.

"I . . . " Nadine was reluctant to commit. She didn't want to vocalize her betrayal of Kerry, even though he'd already betrayed her. Fuck it. "I changed my mind. I want you to fuck me."

Roger smiled triumphantly.

"But Kerry doesn't owe you that twenty dollars anymore!" Nadine added. She wasn't sure why that felt like a triumph, when all that it really meant was that she was more of a whore than a slut. It shouldn't have felt better to have the pretense that she was fucking this guy to clear her boyfriend's debt instead of her own stirred-up lust, but somehow it did.

Roger shrugged. Then he pulled up Nadine's shirt, and sucked on her tits. Lightning shot through her nipples as Roger's mouth and tongue worked on her, making her pussy grow all the wetter. If Roger didn't do something about it soon, she was afraid that she'd end up leaking onto the bed. She could already feel moisture leaving her pussy, working its way down to her asshole.

Roger stood up. He watched her helplessly writhe in wanton need for him. He took off his shoes, socks, and pants while she waited in frustrated anticipation. Finally he was naked. He knelt by her head again, and she greedily wrapped her lips over his cock. She could taste the precome leaking out of him.

"Of course," Roger said, "I want to fuck you. I mean, there's nothing I want more right now than to just stick my dick right inside that tight little pussy of yours. But you've got your clothes on, and I don't see how I can get them off of you, what with you being all tied up like that."

Nadine took her mouth away from his hot, hard flesh long enough to say, "Untie me!"

"No, I don't think I can do that." Roger guided her mouth to his balls. She licked them then took one of his testicles into her mouth, sucking on it. "This is Kerry's room, and you're his girlfriend. If he left you tied up, I don't think it'd be right for me to untie you without asking him. That would be just plain *wrong* of me."

Nadine pulled her mouth away again. "Just push them aside. I don't care. Just fuck me."

"What?" Roger feigned shock. "You mean, just push your panties aside, push your little shirt up and fuck you around them? But that would be uncivilized. That's how a slut fucks, and you're not a slut, right?"

Roger's hand went back to her pussy, teasing her cruelly through the thin cloth. She could feel the material getting wet from her body. Nadine whimpered. She wanted Roger to pull her clothes aside, to fuck her like a slut. She wanted that so much, but she didn't want to say it. Then she thought of another way.

"Just rip them off of me," she said. "I don't care."

Roger nodded briefly, then he pounced.

Suddenly his cock was no longer near her mouth. Roger was kneeling between her helplessly outstretched legs, his fingers wrapped in the light fabric of her shirt. He pulled, ripping her shirt right down the center, exposing her chest completely. He looked at her for a moment, as if memorizing the sight of his roommate's girlfriend, bound and topless on the bed. Then he grabbed the crotch of her thin panties with his large, powerful hands and tore the crotch wide open.

A few more powerful rips and the scraps of her purple panties were tossed aside onto the bed next to her. Roger rubbed his cock against Nadine's labia, but he didn't slide in yet. He took his time, playing with her breasts, making her body ache even more for him. She moved her hips, desperately trying to work his cock into her body, but he denied her.

"You know," Roger said. "Those clothes probably cost a lot more than twenty dollars. I'm not sure that Kerry is coming out ahead in this deal after all."

Nadine realized that he was right, that her lust to be taken had destroyed any pretense that she was doing this for money or to help Kerry out in some perverse way. After ripping away Nadine's meager clothing, Roger had ripped away her last remaining illusions, leaving her completely exposed for what she was—a naked, helpless creature controlled only by her own lust.

Nadine's eyes went wide with realized shame, and that was when Roger's massive cock penetrated her with one swift motion. To her further humiliation, that was also when Nadine came the first time.

Her body exploded with embarrassed bliss the moment that he was fully inside of her, his pelvis bumping up against her trembling clit. Nadine cried out, actually screaming, her climax was so sudden and powerful. Her mind was washed away in a surge of overwhelming sensation, lightning exploding through her body, leaving her aware only of Roger's cock, of his chest pressed against her breasts, of her clit grinding helplessly against him, of the unprecedented pleasure that was making her body buck, spasm, and thrash against the ropes that held her down.

Roger kept moving, kept fucking her. His cock was stretching her so wide, filling her so deep, the orgasm didn't seem like it would ever end. When it finally did, another one smashed into her and another one after that. Nadine lost herself completely, crying out, screaming, saying filthy things.

"Fuck my cunt, my cunt, fuck, fuck my cunt!" she said at one point, her words sometimes interrupted mid-syllable, as Roger's cock pushed gasps and moans out of her body. He relentlessly pistoned away inside of her until she lost count of orgasms, until she lost herself completely. She might have passed out.

She came back to herself again when she felt him pulling his cock out of her, leaving her pussy feeling empty, stretched and abandoned. Had he come? Did he come inside her? He hadn't been wearing a condom!

No, he hadn't come. Roger was kneeling over her, stroking himself furiously until he let out a series of grunts. Nadine felt warm splats of semen fall across her torso, hitting her breasts, chest, and stomach. When Roger's cock had fully emptied itself onto her, he climbed off the bed.

"Whew," Roger said. "You're a great piece of ass! Kerry's a lucky guy. He can borrow more money from me any time he likes, as long as he keeps dating you."

Nadine's face was flushed red with lurid shame and afterglow.

Roger gathered up his clothing. He started to put them on.

"Wait!" Nadine cried. "You have to untie me!"

"Nah," Roger said. "Like I said, it'd be rude to untie you without permission from Kerry. It's his room, and you're his girlfriend, after all."

Roger walked out of the room. He shut the door behind him, leaving Nadine as tied up as when he found her, only now she was fucked, covered with come, and lying in shreds of clothing.

Later, Nadine heard the front door close. She knew that Kerry would come back now that Roger was gone. He'd find her here, like this, and he'd be outraged. He'd be furious with her, and she had no defense except that he should have never left her so helpless and horny.

They'd make up somehow, they had to. Nadine would do whatever it took to keep Kerry, even though he'd abandoned her. She'd make it up to him somehow, let him do whatever thing he wanted to her just so long as he didn't leave her, as long as he stayed her boyfriend. She couldn't stand the thought of losing him, not now.

Then, after they were a solid couple again, she'd find a way to make him borrow more money from Roger.

COMING
AND GOING

Tiffany Reisz

Nora didn't want to go.

She sat up in bed to stare at the beauty before her. Outside the window, the world had gone white. Ice encased the bare tree branches and the dozing grape-vines. The hills were hidden under a shroud of silvery snow. The windowpanes had been hand-painted by Jack Frost and Robert Frost was hard at work in heaven, writing poems about them.

But that wasn't the beauty that caught Nora's eye. She ignored the snow, the ice, the glinting winter moonlight.

The view she could not take her eyes from was not outside the window at all. It was in her bed.

Nico.

Nico, only twenty-five, eleven years her junior. Nico, her submissive, her property, her knight, her friend. Nico, who had a life in France that he could not leave. And Nora, who had a life in New Orleans that she would not leave. Except for a month or two here and there and only for Nico.

She glanced at the clock on the bedside table. In two hours they would be leaving for the airport. It was the morning of January 30 and she wouldn't see Nico again until April. She'd kiss him good-bye in winter and when she kissed him again, it would be spring.

She touched his cheek, gently enough not to wake him, and slipped out of bed. Nico lived in an old stone country house in France's wine country. What it lacked in modern conveniences it made up for in beauty and charm—usually. But tell that to her ice-cube toes as she crept downstairs to make tea. In spring, summer, and autumn, she slept naked or in lingerie or in panties and T-shirts designed to look best on the floor by the bed. In winter, she slept in a Victorian housewife's white flannel gown, wool socks, and knitted shawls. She heated up the teakettle and when it was ready, poured the boiling water into a large earthenware mug. Nora didn't really want the tea—she wanted the heat. Cradling the mug in her hands, she climbed up the steep wooden stairs to the bedroom.

Our bedroom, Nora corrected herself. Nico had called it that last night. *"Do you want me to do anything to our bedroom before you come back?"* He'd been asking if she wanted him to paint or move the furniture, buy a larger bed or make room for her things in his closet. But she couldn't answer because the "our" had taken all her words away. She'd merely shaken her head to say no and later told him the bedroom, with its big oak bed and ancient quilts, was *parfait*. Their bedroom. "Our" bedroom. She'd shared her *bed* before. Many, many times. But she'd never shared a bedroom. His bedroom. Her bedroom. Only with Nico had a room in a house ever been "ours."

And so it was with a smile on her face that she stepped back into *their* bedroom, holding the mug of hot tea in her hands. When her palms were sufficiently heated, she set the mug aside and knelt on the floor by the bed like a child saying her bedtime prayers. She put her hot hands on Nico's ice-cold face—one on his forehead, the other on his cheek, and let the warmth and the tender touch wake him gently.

As she waited for his eyes to open, she studied him in the waning moonlight. His skin was brown, his hair was black, and his eyes she called "celadon," though she wasn't sure a word existed to perfectly describe that green glassy color. When Nico woke at last, he scolded her the way a serious child scolds a frivolous adult.

"What are you doing up?" he demanded. "You'll freeze. Get back in bed."

"Yes, sir," she said, a tease since she owned him and not the other way around. He held up the blankets—a flannel sheet, a fleece comforter, a double-wedding-ring quilt as old as the house—and she slid in next to him. He slept naked, of course. On her orders.

He pulled her close and murmured "How long?" into her ear.

"I leave in two hours," she said. All their time was measured backward from the moment she had to leave to the present moment.

"What do we do until then?" he asked though he already knew the answer.

"I want you inside me," she said.

He lifted her nightgown to her hips. Nico loved her nightgowns, the more prim and prissy the better. He loved having something to push up, to lift, to slide a hand under, to unbutton, to untie, to open, to grip with rough fingers, to pull off over her head and toss across the room. He didn't just love to see her, he'd said of her schoolmarm nighttime attire. He loved *unveiling* her. He loved to work for her. He loved the tease.

He parted her legs with his hand and cupped her vulva, pressing his palm into her clitoris as his mouth found her mouth.

Her brat knew how to kiss. All his lovers had been older women—a fetish, but a good one in her opinion. They'd taught him well. He kissed like fire and she pushed her hips into his hand as he pressed his tongue past her lips. She forgot all about the frost on the window and the icy wood floors and the snow on the vines. Outside the house it was January. In the bed it was summer. The blankets were a tropical island. The sheets lay atop the surface of the sun. Nico slid on top of her and pushed his cock against the entrance of her vagina. She lifted her hips, tilting them at the precise angle necessary to take every inch of him all the way into her. He wrapped his arms around her lower back and held her in place, in that precise place, and entered her straight and true, right down the plumb line.

"Ahh..." he breathed, the exact sound she made when she'd wrapped her cold hands around the hot tea mug.

"Don't come," she said, hotly breathing the order into his ear. He laughed softly. "Don't come. Don't come. Don't come."

"I can last longer than ten seconds inside of you." He grinned down at her, a grin that said, *Silly little woman.*

"I mean, don't come at all. Not until I tell you."

"When?" he asked.

"If," she said. "Not when."

The grin was gone. His grin, not hers. Hers remained in place. He didn't argue with her about the "if." Or complain. Points to Nico. Theirs was a new love, less than a year old, and that baby love was still learning how to walk and say its first words. Nico had dated older women before, but she was his first Dominant, his first owner, and learning how to submit to a woman had been a challenge. But he had the one trait all teachers seek in a prize pupil—he loved to learn.

"If," he said and nodded, not in agreement but comprehension.

"Get on with it," she said, waving her hand. "Fuck me. I didn't put your cock in me for my health."

He laughed again and started to move in her. For a few minutes they did nothing but breathe and fuck. Nico could fuck as well as he could kiss. He thrust deep and slow into her, dragging it out, always at the necessary angle so that the shaft of his cock grazed her clitoris going in, grazed it again coming out. He knew how to fuck her long and hard without their bodies ever separating. When he went in, he stayed in.

Nora closed her eyes and clung to his upper arms as she worked herself up and down on his cock. Her heels dug deep into the soft mattress as she pushed up, up, up and against him. Up, up, up, helping him to fuck her deeper, rougher. Up, up, up—she could hear him when he went into her. She heard his cock moving inside her wetness.

"Shit," he said, but in French—"*merde*." He dropped his head onto her shoulder. "I have to stop for a second."

"You can," she said. "But stay inside me."

He stayed embedded in her pussy, but he rolled them onto their sides to ease the pressure. He panted and she stroked his chest with her fingernails. *Poor boy,* she thought but did not say. *Poor mistreated boy.*

"You're so wet," he said, his hand in her hair. "It's killing me. I want to die in you."

Ah, the French. *La petite mort.* The little death. The orgasm.

"And I want you to live in me. And I own you ergo…I win."

"Don't you want my come?" he asked, pouting.

"I always want your come," she said. "I want it on my breasts and rubbed into my skin. I want it on my stomach and on my back. And sometimes I want it in my mouth so I can swallow it. And I want it deep in my pussy. Sometimes in my ass. I always want it. Every drop of it in—"

He groaned and buried his head against her chest. His little gambit had backfired on him. If he'd thought he could cool the moment, he was wrong. She cackled like supervillain, in a cartoon.

"You must hate me," he said.

"Did you know a man's sperm can live inside a uterus for a couple of days?" she asked. "Sometimes when you're out of the house working and I'm alone in here, maybe reading by the fireplace, I think about how your sperm is still inside me hours and hours after we last had sex. And it makes me very happy to know it's inside me."

He groaned again until he laughed. "Did you insult a witch? Is that what happened to you? You insulted a witch and she stole your heart?"

"Two days from now, I'll be all the way across the Atlantic Ocean, lying in my bed in my house in New Orleans, and your sperm will still be inside me."

"If you let me come," he said.

"Right," she said. "If."

"And if I come before you tell me I can?" he asked.

"You wouldn't," she said as she stroked his sweat-dampened hair.

"No, I wouldn't." He met her eyes and she saw the determination in them, the determination to please her or die trying. Ah, her boy was learning.

"Good boy," she said.

He raised his fingers to the buttons at her throat.

"Are you sure that's a good idea?" she asked as he slowly opened the buttons of her prim nightgown.

"If I'm going to be tortured," he said, "I want to be tortured with your nipples in my mouth."

Fair point. She allowed him to undo her buttons, to pull the gown off her shoulders, to bare her breasts to him. He took her left breast in hand, cupped it, and lifted it. Nora sighed with pleasure as he suckled her. She ran her fingers through his thick, wavy hair and pressed her hips into his. On their sides and face-to-face, they slowly fucked each other as Nico kissed her breasts.

"You know why I torture you like this?" she asked. He shook his head but didn't answer. His mouth full of her.

"Because I'm in love with you, brat," she said. He smiled and kept right on suckling. "There's a saying— you always hurt the one you love. It's especially true for sadists. I never grew past the stage where girls kick the boys they have crushes on."

"You have a crush on me?" he asked, pausing between swirling licks of his tongue around her nipple.

"Your cock's inside me. Is that really a surprise?"

"It never hurts to hear," he said and returned to sucking her nipples.

"Yes, I have a crush on you, you twerp."

"What's a twerp?" he asked. They were always stumbling across English words he didn't know.

"You," she said. "You're a twerp."

"I thought I was a brat?" he asked.

"That, too."

"I don't think I'm either," he said, chin up, defiant.

"What are you then?" she asked.

"A gentleman," he said. "Ladies first. Men after."

"Or never," she said, wagging her eyebrows at him. Without warning him first—she was no lady—Nora rolled Nico onto his back and straddled him, hands on his chest to steady herself.

Nico groaned loudly as she moved her hips on his cock.

"Good?" she asked.

"You're evil," he said.

"You're just figuring that out?"

She pulled off the gown and balled it up, tossing it over her head like a basketball player performing a trick shot.

"I'm going to ride your cock for…" She pretended to check her watch. "A long time."

"Can I come?"

"Don't come. Don't come. Oh, and do *not* come."

Nico nodded, then took a shallow breath. He looked like a man being led toward the firing squad.

Nora would have felt sorry for him if she hadn't been so turned on.

She rocked her hips and his cock shifted inside her. Nico's hands lay on her upper thighs but as she pushed against him, his fingers tightened their grip on her. Poor boy. Poor sweet boy.

Nora stroked his chest while she fucked him from on top. Rubbed his chest and scored it with her fingernails. He wasn't much of a masochist—not yet, anyway—but he did love being scratched. Red fingernail marks—claw marks—made him feel wanted, he'd said. If she left red marks on his stomach or sides or back, he'd lift his shirt every time he went to the bathroom to see the marks in the mirror.

She rode his cock hard as his grip on her thighs tightened. Nora gazed at him as she rode him…his fingers digging deep into her skin, his head on the pillow, then head back and eyes closed, those perfect sculpted lips of his slightly parted as he panted, panted like a man in pain. Ah, she'd think of this sight on the plane.

"Why are your eyes closed?" she asked.

"I'm thinking of the last time I had the stomach flu," he said. "It's helping."

"Was it bad?"

"It wasn't as much fun as you riding my cock."

"Well," she said, "what is?"

He opened his eyes and laced his fingers behind the back of his head.

"Nothing," he said, but in French. "*Rien.*"

Nora leaned in and kissed his lovely mouth that said such lovely words in such a lovely language. He wrapped her in his arms and held her close.

Slowly she rolled her hips in a tight spiral, clenching her inner muscles around his cock.

"Don't come," she said. "Don't come. Don't come. Don't come."

"Don't go," he said. "Don't go. Don't go. Don't go."

Nora stopped moving. She pulled back tears in her eyes.

"I have to go," she said.

"I know," he said. He gathered her long black hair in his hands, held it at the nape of her neck, and kissed her throat. "But I had to try."

"You know I can't go unless you let me," she said.

"You think I wouldn't drive you to the airport?"

"You know what I mean."

"So..." He wagged his finger at her. "You're in charge of my coming," he said. "And I'm charge of your going?"

"Only fair, right?"

"I might not let you go," he said.

"Well, I might not let you come, either."

"I want you to stay more than I want to come," he said. "More than I want a lot of things."

Nora took his hands in hers and kissed his work-scarred knuckles. "Me too," she said.

Then Nora slid off of him, separating their bodies.

"What?" he asked, sitting up on his elbows. "What's wrong?"

"Nothing," she said, smiling at him. "Let's take a long hot bath together before we have to leave for the airport."

She ran their bath and they held each other in the steaming water, kissing and touching and scrubbing and laughing. After breakfast, they piled her luggage into his Land Rover and headed to the airport.

He drove. She sat in the passenger seat. He kept his hands on the wheel. She kept her hand on his knee. They didn't speak for the first fifteen minutes. They almost never chatted when he drove her to the airport to leave him. Nonstop talk on the way to his house. Silence on the drive away. If they hadn't said it by the time she left, it wasn't worth saying.

"I didn't mean to kill your boner," Nico finally said as they neared the turnoff to the airport.

"I have got to stop teaching you English phrases and not telling you what they mean," she said, shaking her head.

"I know what it means. I meant, you know, what's it called—lady boner?" he asked.

"I never dreamed 'lady boner' would sound so good in a French accent. But I should have."

Nico turned his head quickly to look at her before putting his eyes back on the road where they belonged.

"I love you," she said. "I shouldn't but I do. You're eleven years younger than I am, and you live across the fucking ocean."

"What were you thinking?" he asked, shaking his head in playful mockery.

"I wanted to play with you this morning because it was either laugh or cry. And then you had to go and be wonderful and sweet." She sighed heavily. "Why would you do such a thing?"

"I told you, I'm a gentleman. Even when we're being tortured, we treat our ladies right."

She squeezed his knee. He lifted her hand off his leg

and raised it to his lips. One kiss. Enough said. They drove the rest of the way to the airport in tender silence, Nora's hand on Nico's knee, Nico's hand on her hand.

One hand on the wheel.

They arrived at the airport and Nico started to park in the closest spot.

"Not here," Nora said. She scanned the parking lot, saw a large paneled van. "Next to that one."

He raised his eyebrow but did as told. The boy was learning.

He parked, turned off the engine.

"Leave it on," Nora said.

Then he knew what was happening. Nora glanced out the window. No one around.

"Do gentlemen fuck their ladies in backseats of Land Rovers in airport parking lots?" Nora asked.

"This gentleman does."

In seconds they were on the bench seat and tearing into each other.

Nora yanked Nico's thick leather jacket off and tossed it into the front seat. He reached under her tight black turtleneck sweater and unhooked her bra. He yanked her skirt up. She hadn't bothered with panties, only stockings and garters since she knew this would happen. Of course it would happen. If she wanted something to happen, it would happen.

Lying on her back in the cramped backseat, she reached for his belt, his jeans button, the zipper. He was so hard his cock popped out when she'd unzipped him. He yanked her skirt up and pushed her thighs wide. She raised her hips in invitation. With one hand he spread her vulva open at the seam. With his other hand he positioned his cock at the hole. With a rough thrust he was in her and after that there was no talking, no kissing, no sweetness, no love.

Only fucking.

He pushed her sweater and bra up to her neck as he rode her hard into the worn leather of the seat. The cock in her was brutal. He was pistoning into her, vicious as a jackhammer. She was barely aware of him kissing her nipples or pinching them or sucking them. There was only the thick organ pounding into her, almost angrily, and the little explosions in her throbbing clitoris, the contractions of her vagina as he speared it.

She slid her hands into his jeans, cupped his perfect twenty-six-year-old ass in her hands and felt as his muscles tightened to iron bands as he rutted on her. She dug her hands into his flesh, goading him on with quiet commands—"Harder, harder . . . " It didn't seem possible he could fuck her any harder, but they found a way. He grabbed her leg, pushed it so wide she had to wrap her knee around the front seat. She was so open he could have fisted her to the wrist if she'd wanted him to. And she did want him to so she told him to...

Nico's chest heaved at the order. He didn't answer, just dug his teeth into the strap of his watchband on his right wrist and wrenched it off.

"That was the sexiest fucking thing I've ever seen in my life," Nora said, panting, now so wet he could have put his arm in her up to his elbow.

He grinned. She might be his Dominant, but in moments like this, he owned her.

"A gentleman removes his watch first," he said as he dragged her by the hips closer to him.

Nico brought his fingers together and pushed the tips into her vagina. The hole widened as he pressed in, and her inner muscles spread as he pushed. Nora writhed on the seat as he opened her, gasping and groaning. She grabbed the headrest of the driver's seat with one hand and the door handle behind her with the other to steady herself as he twisted and turned his fingers...past the knuckles, the palm, finally the wrist.

When it was all in, she looked down and saw his hand splitting her wide open. She felt so filled it was like she would burst. He fucked her with his hand, lifting her hips from the inside. Every knuckle of his hand brushed every nerve in her cunt. She came hard with a quick, vicious spasm that brought her shoulders off the seat. She panted, gulping huge breaths as he worked his hand carefully out of her.

"Can I come?" he asked. Asked and begged, begged and pleaded.

"Yes, you can come," she said.

He turned her onto her hands and knees. He wrapped his arm around her waist and entered her from behind. For about ten seconds there was nothing happening in the whole wide world except his cock slamming into her and his testicles brushing against her still-throbbing clit with each thrust.

He held her breasts in his hands. He squeezed them roughly as he slammed into her hard enough to shake the car down to the chassis. He grunted his breaths, whimpered once, then went silent. When he came, she knew it was happening because he said her name, but he wasn't saying it to her. He was simply saying it.

Nora . . .

When he pulled out of her, she winced, and not just from the thick semen that poured from her vagina. Nico staunched the warm flow with a handkerchief he pulled from his jeans pocket. She took it from him and pressed it between her thighs as she straightened her clothes, hooked her bra, ran her fingers through her hair.

Nico sat back and watched her, silent. She turned and kissed him, but only quickly. If it were a long kiss, she'd never leave.

"Can I go?" she asked.

He grazed her cheek with the back of his knuckles.

"Yes," he said. "You can go."

ABOUT THE AUTHORS

VALERIE ALEXANDER is a freelance writer who lives in Phoenix and LA. Her stories have been published in a number of anthologies from Cleis Press, Samhain Publishing, Running Press, and a variety of sci-fi and speculative magazines.

RICHARD BACULA has spent years studying creative writing at a national university and has spent his entire life studying sex. After receiving his degree, he has decided to combine his two major fields of interest to create fun and fascinating erotica for the world to enjoy.

LN BEY (lnbey.com) is the author of the erotic novel *Blue* and the almost-a-novel collection of erotic stories *Villa*. Bey's short stories have been published in *The Big Book of Submission 2, No Safewords 2, Dancing With Myself: Stories of Self-Love,* and *Love Slave: Sizzle.*

REBECCA CHASE (rebeccahchase.com) is an English rose with a taste for sex and romance. She adores finding story ideas in everyday life and is always looking out for everyone's next book boyfriend. Frequently she can be caught daydreaming in coffee shops or enjoying the spectacle of sportsmen battling with balls.

ELIZABETH COLDWELL lives and writes in London. She is a multi-published author and as an editor has won an International Leather Award for Best Anthology. Her short stories have appeared in a variety of anthologies including the *Best Women's Erotica* series.

GEORGINA COTT lives in England and is a novelist and short-story writer. Recent erotic works have appeared in anthologies for Excite Books (Accent Press) and Constable and Robinson. Georgina also writes under the name of Jeff Cott.

Previously published in Cleis Press and Circlet Press anthologies, **REBECCA CROTEAU** is a full-time free-lance writer by day who explores the dark and the erotic by night. A queer autistic demigirl, she enjoys experimenting with all the ways one can get tied up in yarn. She writes novellas as Caitlyn Frost and can be found at @CFrostWrites.

KENDEL DAVI (kendeldavi.wordpress.com) is a play-wright, fiction writer, and performance artist who lives in Los Angeles, California. Kendel has a passion for jazz music and theater history, which often appears in his fiction writing. Kendel is currently working on his first erotic novel.

Chicago native **ELIZA DAVID** (elizadavidwrites.com) is a contemporary romance author living in Iowa City. She enjoys reading Jackie Collins and indulging in the occasional order of cheese fries. Eliza is also a blogger, serving as a contributing writer for Real Moms of Eastern Iowa and Thirty on Tap.

ELLA DAWSON (elladawson.com) is a twentysomething feminist who counts all of her Facebook likes. Her fiction has appeared in anthologies including *Best Women's Erotica of the Year Volume 2* and *Heart, Body, Soul: Erotica With Character*. Social media editor by day and sex writer by night, you can find her on Twitter as @brosandprose.

CECILIA DUVALLE (ceciliaduvalle.com) lives outside Seattle. Her erotic stories have appeared in numerous anthologies including *Unspeakably Erotic, Owning It, Slave Girls,* and *Cheeky Spanking Stories*. She edits the Blood in the Rain vampire erotica series for Cwtch Press and spends her free time knitting, reading, and cooking.

TAMMYJO ECKHART (tammyjoeckhart.com) writes fiction and nonfiction across several genres but usually with a femdom bent. She lives in Indiana with her poly kinky family. An ancient historian by training, she uses those skills to craft amazing worlds.

JOSIE JORDAN is an Australia-based freelance writer. Her erotic stories appear in *Best Women's Erotica of the Year Volume 2, The Sexy Librarian's Dirty 30 Volume*

2, For the Men, and various Xcite anthologies amongst other places.

T.C. MILL is a freelance editor and writer. Her short stories have appeared in anthologies from Circlet, Mofo Publishing, and Cleis Press as well as on the Nerve and Bright Desire websites. With Alex Freeman, she has coedited two literary erotica anthologies under the New Smut Project.

EVE PENDLE writes smart, snarky, and passionate Victorian-era romance and erotica. She loves dresses, chocolate, equality, liberty, her husband, her dog, and her cat (not necessarily in that order). You can get a free sexy story from her website, evependle.com, and check what she's currently writing via social media.

VAL PROZOROVA (or Velvl Ryder) is a transgender author based in New Zealand. You can find his work in publications by Mugwump Press, Lethe Press, Sexy Little Pages, and Torquere Press. His work was also featured in anthologies for the Seattle Erotic Arts Festival 2017 and Eroticon 2017.

TIFFANY REISZ (TiffanyReisz.com) is the international bestselling author of *The Original Sinners* series from Harlequin/Mira Books. She lives in Lexington, Kentucky, with her husband, author Andrew Shaffer.

LEANDRA VANE (theunlacedlibrarian.blogspot.com) is a sexuality writer and speaker. Her work tackles topics in sexual fantasy, fetish, BDSM, erotic media, disability,

and relationship dynamics. She writes a book review
and sexuality blog entitled The Unlaced Librarian.

ABOUT
THE EDITOR

RACHEL KRAMER BUSSEL (rachelkramerbussel.
com) is a New Jersey–based author, editor, blogger, and
writing instructor. She has edited over sixty books of
erotica, including *Best Women's Erotica of the Year,
Volume 1, 2, 3, and 4; Best Bondage Erotica 2011–
2015; Erotic Teasers; Dirty Dates; On Fire; Come
Again: Sex Toy Erotica; The Big Book of Orgasms;
Begging for It; The Big Book of Submission; Lust in
Latex; Anything for You: Erotica for Kinky Couples;
Baby Got Back: Anal Erotica; Suite Encounters:
Hotel Sex Stories; Going Down: Oral Sex Stories;
Gotta Have It; Women in Lust; Surrender; Orgasmic;
Cheeky Spanking Stories; Bottoms Up; Spanked: Red-
Cheeked Erotica; Fast Girls; Do Not Disturb; Tasting
Him; Tasting Her; Please, Sir; Please, Ma'am; He's on
Top; She's on Top,* and *Crossdressing.* Her anthologies
have won eight IPPY (Independent Publisher) Awards,
and *Surrender* and *Dirty Dates* won the National
Leather Association Samois Anthology Award. Her

work has been published in over one hundred anthologies, including *Best American Erotica 2004* and *2006*. She wrote the popular "Lusty Lady" column for the *Village Voice*.

Rachel has written for *AVN*, *Bust*, Cleansheets.com, CNN.com, *Cosmopolitan*, *Curve*, The Daily Beast, Elle.com, Fortune.com, TheFrisky.com, *Glamour*, Gothamist, *Harper's Bazaar*, Huffington Post, *Inked*, *Marie Claire*, *Newsday*, *New York Post*, *New York Observer*, *The New York Times*, *O: The Oprah Magazine*, *Penthouse*, Refinery29, Rollingstone.com, The Root, Salon, *San Francisco Chronicle*, Slate, Time.com, *Time Out New York*, and *Zink*, among others. She has appeared on *The Gayle King Show*, *The Martha Stewart Show*, "The Berman and Berman Show," NY1, and Showtime's *Family Business*. She hosted the popular In the Flesh Erotic Reading Series, featuring readers from Susie Bright to Zane, speaks at conferences, and does readings and teaches erotic writing workshops across the country and online. She blogs at lustylady.blogspot.com and consults about erotica at eroticawriting101.com. Subscribe to Rachel's monthly newsletter with book giveaways at rachelkramerbussel.com and follow her on Twitter @raquelita.